I0760897

FULL MOON DEMON

BOOK TWO OF AURA HEALERS HALL

THOMAS K. CARPENTER

Full Moon Demon

Book Two of Aura Healers Hall

Hardback Version

by Thomas K. Carpenter

Copyright © 2024 Thomas K. Carpenter
All Rights Reserved

Published by Black Moon Books

Cover design by
G&S Cover Designs

Opening Chapter Image by Grand Failure
Chapter Heading by Angle

Discover other titles by this author on:
www.thomaskcarpenter.com

ISBN-13: 978-1-958498-24-8

This is a novel work of fiction. All characters, places, and incidents described in this publication are used fictitiously, or are entirely fictitional.

No part of this publication may be reproduced or trasmitted, in any form, or by any means, except by an authorized retailer, or with written permission of the publisher. Inquires may be addressed via email to

thomaskcarpenter@gmail.com

The Hundred Halls Universe

Season One

THE HUNDRED HALLS
Trials of Magic
Web of Lies
Alchemy of Souls
Gathering of Shadows
City of Sorcery

THE RELUCTANT ASSASSIN
The Reluctant Assassin
The Sorcerous Spy
The Veiled Diplomat
Agent Unraveled
The Webs That Bind

GAMEMAKERS ONLINE
The Warped Forest
Gladiators of Warsong
Citadel of Broken Dreams
Enter the Daemonpits
Plane of Twilight

ANIMALIANS HALL
Wild Magic
Bane of the Hunter
Mark of the Phoenix
Arcane Mutations
Untamed Destiny

STONE SINGERS HALL
Song of Siren and Blood
House of Snake and Tome
Storm of Dragon and Stone
Sonata of Shadow and Thorn
Well of Demon and Bone

THE ORDER OF MERLIN
The Order of Merlin
Infernal Alliances
Tower of Horn and Blood

The Hundred Halls Universe

Season Two

THE CRYSTAL HALLS
Shadows in Amber
The Emerald Eclipse
The Sapphire Strategem
Chains of Obsidian
The Bloodstone Rebellion

AURA HEALERS HALL
Half-Pint Hex
Full Moon Demon
Blood Witch Curse
Twilight Horn
The Deathless King

Other Works

ALEXANDRIAN SAGA
Fires of Alexandria
Heirs of Alexandria
Legacy of Alexandria
Warmachines of Alexandria
Empire of Alexandria
Voyage of Alexandria
Goddess of Alexandria

KINGMAKERS SAGA
The Stone Tree
The Crystal Bard
The Ghost Tower
The Champion's Prophecy
The Shadow Labyrinth
The Autumn Empire

OTHER SERIES
The Dashkova Memoirs
Gamers
Mirror Shards

FULL MOON DEMON

Arcanium loves books
Coterie adores power
Assassins will kill you
Stone Singers has a stone flower

Animalians is a zoo
Alchemists, you'll devour
Tinkers loves gadgets
Protectors makes you cower

Aura Healers wants to fix you
Blue Flame has a tower
Dramatics loves the spectacle
Oculus has grown sour

One Hundred Halls
Each with their own magic
The Patrons protect
Because faez madness is tragic

In the city of sorcery
Invictus is the Head
His students are many
But the foolish end up dead

- A Children's Rhyme

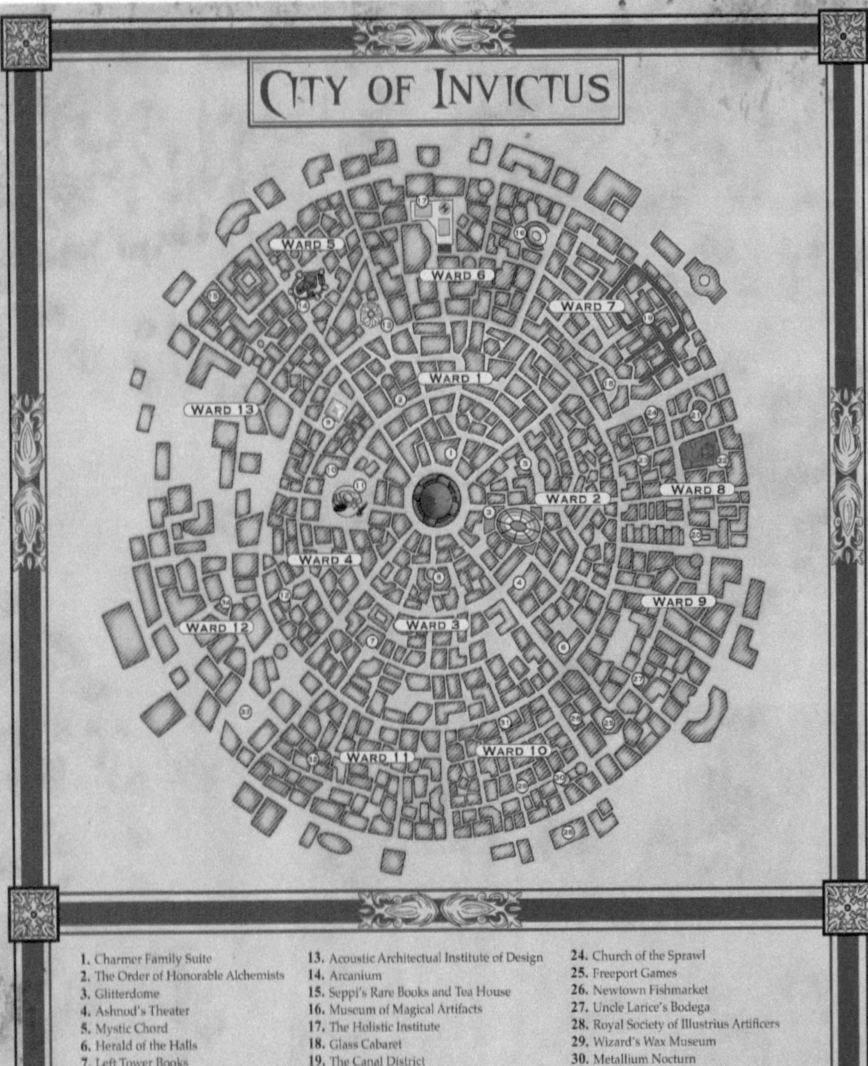

CITY OF INVICTUS
WARD 1
WARD 2
WARD 3
WARD 4
WARD 5
WARD 6
WARD 7
WARD 8
WARD 9
WARD 10
WARD 11
WARD 12
WARD 13
1. Charmer Family Suite
2. The Order of Honorable Alchemists
3. Glitterdome
4. Ashnod's Theater
5. Mystic Chord
6. Herald of the Halls
7. Left Tower Books
8. Protectors
9. Coterie of Mages
10. City Library
11. Statue of Invictus
12. Amber & Smoke
13. Acoustic Architectual Institute of Design
14. Arcanium
15. Seppi's Rare Books and Tea House
16. Museum of Magical Artifacts
17. The Holistic Institute
18. Glass Cabaret
19. The Canal District
20. Oestomancium
21. Animalians
22. Invictus Menagerie and Cryptozoo
23. Goblin's Romp
24. Church of the Sprawl
25. Freeport Games
26. Newtown Fishmarket
27. Uncle Larice's Bodega
28. Royal Society of Illustrius Artificers
29. Wizard's Wax Museum
30. Metallium Nocturn
31. Howling Madwoman's Fortunes and Spells
32. Enoichian District
33. Oba's Autumnal Garden
34. Gamemakers Hall

ONE

The nurses of Golden Willow loved his father. He'd only been in the hospital visiting for a day but they kept telling Damon how sweet and handsome his old man was, even the nurses that treated him like a puppy that had peed on the rug whenever he was in their patient space.

"Your kids are adorable, Miss Bailey. Thank you for showing them to me. You'll have to keep me updated on the whole Casserole Affair. You should write a book about your PTA, it's a hoot," said his father, Arthur.

Nurse Bailey blushed and gave his father a little wave before disappearing down the hallway, dodging a gurney on the way to surgery.

"You have lovely co-workers," said his father.

Arthur was built like a concrete barrel and looked like he could have been a boxer, but that was far from the truth, since his father worked as an accountant for a branch of D'Agastine Industries in Kansas City. But that didn't stop him from charming everyone around him with his blue eyes and soft touch, especially when it came to the ladies.

"The nurses are an integral part of Golden Willow's success," said Damon.

Arthur clapped him on the shoulder. Despite the differences in height—Damon had four inches on him—it always felt like his father was taller.

"This isn't so bad, son. We've been here a day and you haven't been called to an emergency once."

Damon led them towards the student wing for Aura Healers. He wanted his father to meet his classmates and assumed some of them would be in their common area.

"It's been a lot calmer since the spring."

His father winked. "It's okay, son. You don't have to make it sound worse than it is. I know you'd work hard no matter the circumstances."

"It's not that—"

The words on his tongue evaporated when his father froze, putting a hand to his temple and squinting.

"Are you okay?"

Arthur waved him off. "It's fine. Headaches. I've been getting them the last few months."

"That didn't look like just a headache. I should get you checked out while you're here."

"Not necessary, son. We're hearty folk. A little thing like a headache isn't to be worried about. I've only been having one or two a week."

"That's why it's a concern. Normal afflictions don't really bother our kind, but when symptoms start showing up, it's a cause for worry. It's part of the Supernatural Ward's handbook."

"But you haven't started yet," said his father, putting up a forced smile even though Damon could see the twitches in his brow.

"We start tomorrow, but I've been reading all the tomes this summer in preparation. There are so many interesting things I've learned already. I can't wait to get started. Did you know that there are at least three different credible origins of werewolves? I was—"

His father was no longer listening because he'd spotted one of the nurses they'd met the previous evening.

"Miss Jackie!"

The heavyset nurse broke into a grin as his father approached, forcing Damon to follow. He'd been trying to show him what he was doing at Golden Willow, but his father kept flirting with the nurses.

"How are the little ones, Jackie?"

Nurse Jackie's face lit up. "Blythe learned a new word last night."

"What was it? *Dog*, *Dad*, *Mom*?"

"I wish," said the nurse, rolling her eyes. "It was *moon*, which is funny because it's not even a full one yet."

Arthur put a hand on her arm, giving it a squeeze. "I bet Blythe said Mom, but it just sounded like moon."

"I like the way you think, Mr. Wolfhard," said Nurse Jackie with a wink.

"Please, call me Arthur."

"Dad," said Damon. "I'm sorry, Jackie. I can't take him anywhere. In fact, we were headed to the Aura Healers lounge."

Nurse Jackie bunched up her lips. "He's fine. More than fine. You can head out and leave him with me. We'll take care of him." She winked at his father as she licked her lips.

Seeing that his father wasn't going to move in the direction he wanted, Damon said, "Have you called Mom yet this morning? Didn't she want you to check in?"

"Em? No, I did that last night."

Nurse Jackie gave Damon a flat look. "I know your father is married, Damon. We're just flirting is all. No need to get worried." She put a hand on his father's arm. "It's nice to get to visit with a handsome, virile man who isn't lying in a bed from some strange ailment we can't figure out. I get enough of that every day—it's nice to talk with a *very* healthy werewolf."

The compliments had his father puffing out his chest. Damon wanted to throw up. He'd never seen his father outside of the home. He'd had no idea this was what he was like when his mom wasn't around, which left him wondering what else he didn't know.

"Dad..."

At that moment, Arthur froze again, screwing up his face as if he'd eaten a bucket of sour lemons.

"You okay, Arthur?" asked Nurse Jackie, putting her arm around him.

"Dad. Stop screwing around." Damon put his hand on his father's shoulder. "If you want to flirt, fine, but faking sickness isn't the way to do it."

"I'm fine. I'm fine." He held up his hand, but he couldn't open his eyes yet.

When Nurse Jackie shot Damon a look, he knew she was worried too. The nurses had a sixth sense about the seriousness of symptoms from years of experience in the hospital. Dr. Decker told them the best hospital instrument was a long-term nurse.

"How long have you been having these episodes, Arthur?"

"A few times a day."

"Few times a day? You just told me it was only a few times a week," said Damon.

He wanted to say more, but the nurse shot him a look, which reminded him of Dr. Decker's rule about patients always lying. He should have guessed that his father didn't want to be seen as weak in front of his son.

"I wanted him to get tested," said Damon, but the nurse ignored him and focused on his father.

"Have they been getting worse?"

"Slowly. Steadily. But they're nothing to worry about," said Arthur. "As you said, I'm a *very* healthy man."

"When's the last time you changed?" asked the nurse.

He could open his eyes, but his father was affected by the brightness of the hallway.

"Not recently. Maybe a few months ago. I don't find many reasons to, but I needed to move a pallet of dried concrete and it made sense to change. I did, of course, strip down to my boxers so I didn't ruin my clothes."

"I *bet* you did, Arthur," said Nurse Jackie with a wry grin. "But did you have any issues with transformation? Any headaches associated with the change?"

"Really, you two, I'm fine. I swear it's nothing."

"Alright Arthur, but if you have many more, I think your son is right. You should do a scan and some bloodwork. I know you're a healthy older man, but things start to break down when we get older. Even for werewolves."

"Come on, Dad. I want you to meet my classmates. We've been through a lot together." He waved to the nurse. "Thanks, Jackie. I guess I'll be seeing you more starting tomorrow."

She extended a finger in his direction. "Don't think just because I think your father's a cutie, I won't be on your ass if you screw up."

Damon saluted. "I wouldn't have it any other way."

"See ya around, Arthur. Don't forget to say bye before you head back to KC," said Nurse Jackie with a wink.

When they were away down the hall, Damon said, "That's embarrassing, you fawning over her like a horny teenager."

"I have to make up for you, since you treated your high school experience like a very large and boring to-do list."

"I wanted to get into Aura Healers," said Damon, defensively. "I needed to do that, because..."

"I know, son," said Arthur. "I know you're trying to make up for what happened, but you should forgive yourself. The loss of the clan wasn't easy on our family, especially not a young man in the middle of puberty, which is always tricky for our kind. That kind of tragedy leaves deep scars. You shouldn't feel bad losing control during that difficult time, and that young man eventually recovered."

Damon looked away. Even after all this time it was hard to think about. He wanted to look at his hands to make sure they weren't covered in blood.

"Come on, son," said his father, tone softening. "Let's meet your friends. I'd like to hear more about your first year in the Halls."

"I'd like that. Come on."

Damon turned, thinking his father would follow him. He took three strides before he realized that he wasn't by his side. A gurgling moan was followed by the slap of a hand hitting the wall. Damon spun around in time to see his father careening towards the tile like a flank plank, cracking his shoulder and head hard.

"Help!"

The words came out of Damon's mouth before he remembered he was a healer in training. He threw himself to his father's side, checking him for a head wound. Blood leaked from a gash in the back and his eyes were nothing but whites. A quiver started in the arms and traveled up his limbs until his whole body was shaking. Damon was going to shout again when he saw Nurse Jackie running down the hallway.

"What happened?" she asked, sliding athletically to her knees and helping Damon cradle Arthur's head. Foam was building up at the corner of his lips as he shook more violently. Damon tried to remember what that meant, but his mind was blank. He kept picturing his father fall over like an inanimate object, over and over.

"Damon. What happened?"

The sharp tone broke him from his stupor.

"I turned around and he passed out."

Nurse Jackie spoke into her phone. "Code Blue. I've got a Code Blue in the 2D hallway just past the nurses station. Bring a gurney and a shot of wolfsbane."

"Wolfsbane?"

"It'll shock his system and hopefully stop the convulsion."

He knew this, but it felt like everything he'd ever read had been wiped from his mind except the meaning of Code Blue. It meant his father was in serious condition and could die unless he received rapid medical treatment.

The gurney and a team of nurses appeared. He knew he should be helping them lift his father, but they shoved him out of the way. Arthur was loaded onto the gurney as a wolfsbane shot was stuck in his arm. The convulsing reduced but his limbs still shook. The look Nurse Jackie gave him when the shot didn't work left his heart in a blender.

"Let's move! Go, go, go!"

In the blink of an eye, his father was rushed down the hallway towards the trauma center in the Supernatural Ward. Damon couldn't decide if he should follow. Code Blue. It was a Code Blue. That's all he could think about. His father had been standing next to him in the middle of the hallway one second, and then the next he was being rushed off for lifesaving treatment. Code Blue. It was just a phrase, a shortcut for information transfer in the busy hospital, but it took on a whole new meaning when it was his father.

TWO

The needle slid out of the patient's arm like a silk thread. Remi pulled the readied band aid off the back of her hand and stuck it over the tiny pinprick. The patient was a young man a year older than her, admitted to the ER an hour ago after he attempted a levitation spell near the Arcanium moat and fell in, contracting a chest-rattling cough from the water that likely suggested contact with a selkie.

"Now, Miss Wilde, would you put a lung cleansing spell on our aspiring mage, Mr. Nickles," said Dr. Paddock, adjusting his wire-rimmed glasses.

The patient was in town for the trials of magic, which would start in a few weeks. He stared at her with wide eyes and a curl to his lips—the anticipation of witnessing magic.

"Which one?" asked Remi, feeling the warmth of the patient's expectations.

Dr. Paddock didn't look up from the chart, gesturing randomly in her direction.

"Any one will do. You should have at least three memorized by now."

Remi groaned internally. She knew two of the three he was referencing, but hadn't practiced them. Despite the hard work she'd put in over the summer memorizing the tomes, she felt out of her depth when it came to practical application.

"Can I step into the hall and practice a few times? I know the spell but I want to make sure I get the gestures right."

Dr. Paddock's lips turned towards the tile floor. He speared her in his sights.

"If this patient was dying would you have to *step away* to practice?"

A snort from the patient had her cheeks burning. "No. But we have time, I just—"

"No *just this one time*. You either know the spells or you don't, Miss Wilde. If you can't do your job, don't come to the ER."

Remi pushed away the hollowness in her chest and approached the patient. His earlier excitement had turned to curiosity, as if he was wondering how she'd passed the trials. It wasn't her best spell work, but she managed to fumble through the harder part, feeling both their eyes upon her. When she was finished, the patient took a deep breath and broke into a scratchy cough, hunched over while Dr. Paddock stared at her as if she'd stabbed him.

"Miss Wilde!"

Before she could answer, the patient sat back up, laughing. "I'm just fucking around. That worked great. I don't feel like I'm breathing through a sieve anymore."

"Somehow I doubt that," said Dr. Paddock, rolling his eyes. His phone buzzed, which brought a moment's distraction.

"Department meeting?" she asked hopefully.

"A timer," he said with a relieved sigh and continued in a tone that dripped with sarcasm. "Congratulations, Miss Wilde. Your shift is officially over. You have completed your first year in the Golden Willow ER."

"Thank you?"

The withering stare left ashes in her mouth as he tucked his phone back into his pocket.

"Now I can finally get back to work instead of this insipid babysitting they force us to do. Run along, Miss Wilde. You know, you'll make a wonderful phlebotomist at Aura Healers. Good day."

Dr. Paddock left her with the patient, who was laughing behind a cupped hand.

"Wow, that was fucking rich. He roasted you good. I am definitely not putting Aura Healers on my list."

Remi grunted under her breath.

"I hope you get eaten by a manticore," she said, before marching out of his room. "A wonderful phlebotomist. I'm more than that." The pronouncement didn't sound too confident to her own ears in the echoing hallway. She checked her watch. There were a few hours before the start of her next shift, which would officially be in the Supernatural Ward. Time enough to swing by Arthur Wolfhard's room.

As she passed through the emergency room, she halfway expected an acknowledgement of surviving the year, but the nurses and doctors were too busy dealing with patients and no one gave her a second glance.

The Supernatural Ward was the entire third floor of the western wing of the hospital where longer-term residents with conditions or diseases that couldn't be solved in short order stayed. The difference was immediate. No one was shouting. No automatic doors whooshing open and closed every twenty seconds. No crazies were standing on the admittance chairs shouting end of the world proclamations.

Remi almost missed it.

Almost.

She found the right room after checking in at the nurse's station. Damon was sitting by his dad's bed. The steady beeping from the machines suggested that he was stable, but the hunched brow on her friend's face told her otherwise.

"Any change?"

"No convulsions. They're running every test imaginable. Blood work. MRI. They're even bringing in a specialist warlock from a hospital on the west coast to do a full aura cleanse." He rolled his eyes. "They're even checking for parasites."

Remi spotted a pile of ripped-up paper at Damon's feet. The pile looked like it was at least a dozen sheets torn into tiny pieces. She raised an eyebrow.

"Nervous habit."

"He's in good hands. There's no better place that it could have happened, Damon."

"I know that." He bunched up his lips. "But I also know that we don't get sick unless it's something really bad. No one will say it, but the truth is obvious. For him to be affected this terribly means that it's really bad."

A part of her wanted to put an arm around his shoulder, but she still hadn't figured out what their relationship was. It felt halfway between friend and something more, but they were too busy to explore the space. And she didn't want to confuse him when he was focused on his father, so she pulled up a chair and sat with him until it was time for them to return to the Aura Healers building for their second-year orientation.

They were the last to arrive, which meant they were forced to share the crappy, lime-green loveseat in the corner with bad springs in the cushions. Lily high-fived her on the way to the couch as she was curled on a wooden chair dragged from the table. Remi imagined in a normal Hall, they'd be sharing stories of their summer vacations, but in Aura Healers, school was year-round. Everyone was chatting about their final days in the ER when Dr. Decker entered with Dr. Hasan Hunker, the head of the Supernatural Ward.

The room fell silent, which was something of a miracle, but it was unsurprising to Remi. Dr. Hasan Hunker was hot. Mind-blowingly stupid hot. The kind of attractiveness that brought speculations of supernatural blood and made patients and staff alike fall apart around him. The first time Remi had seen Dr. Hunker in the cafeteria she'd thought she was hallucinating, or that he was a visiting movie star embedded in the hospital for a role. His wavy black hair, which was pulled back into a ponytail most days and often had a single curl escaping, left her thrumming with warmth. His black goatee was meticulously groomed, and the arch to his eyebrows gave him a permanent mischievous cast.

"Dr. Hunk in the house," said Boon, whistling suggestively as he preened for the doctor, bringing laughter from the class.

"Alright, children," said Dr. Decker, shaking his head while grinning.

"A lively group, I see," said Dr. Hunker with a silk-over-gravel voice that sent warm tendrils throughout her midsection.

Remi pinched her own leg to silence the obscene thoughts careening through her head.

"Congratulations on making it to your second year," said Dr. Decker. "If you were expecting a party, I'm afraid I'll have to disappoint you. The reward for surviving is more work. While the pace won't be as grueling as the ER, it will be no less taxing. The emergency room was a great place to practice those little things you do over and over." He nodded to Remi. "Like taking blood, repairing stab wounds with a knitting spell, or doing a viral repression reverse-hex. The Supernatural Ward, on the other hand, will never be the same day twice, and the solutions will never be simple. Supernatural beings are notoriously difficult to diagnose, mostly because we lack the detailed knowledge of each species, and because the ailments of the other realms that make their way to the City of Sorcery can be devilishly complex."

"May I step in?" asked Dr. Hunker, receiving a nod from Dr. Decker. "Oren is one hundred percent correct. Solutions in the Supernatural Ward will require research and dedication. The good news is that there aren't as many tomes to learn this year, but the bad news is that you'll get to know the hospital library, and every other library in the city, quite well. Last year, we treated an unresponsive woman who we thought had been possessed by a banshee, but after covering her room in origami cranes with Daniric runes, we figured out that she was a Darkling in disguise and she'd been feeding off our attempts to heal her for two months.

"But don't worry. Not all the patients will be as troublesome as that Darkling. Most are regular supernaturals like therianthropes, fairies, or other common peoples from the surrounding realms. Like your first year, you'll be paired with doctors or healers from my staff on their rounds, performing whatever duties necessary. It's pretty simple on the surface, but much more complex once you get into it. Any questions?"

Boon's arm went up immediately. He looked like he was going to come out of his seat.

"Boon, right?"

The fellow second year fake swooned, before sitting back up. "Is it true that you have supernatural blood?"

Dr. Hunker let out a melodic laugh. "I'm afraid I can neither confirm nor deny such rumors. Next?"

For the next twenty minutes, Dr. Hunker answered questions. What were the doctors like? Which nurses were *really* in charge in his department? Do they have any specific elixirs from Jeb to regularly take? Was he dating anyone? What year did he graduate from the Halls?

"Back, you savages," said Dr. Decker, shooing them away. "I think

Hasan has a staff meeting with Dr. Fairlight in a few. But don't worry, you'll have plenty of time to get to know him during the course of the year." He pointed at Boon. "But not that way."

"Welcome, and good luck," said Dr. Hunker as he left the room.

Remi leaned over to Damon. "Oh, finally. I can think normal thoughts again."

Damon raised an eyebrow, which suggested he wasn't as affected, either due to his supernatural blood, or because he was too busy thinking about his father.

"Now that I have your full attention, I'm going to remind you all that the maintenance closet on the third floor is not for having sex. The head of maintenance is tired of finding his storage area locked when he has to scrub blood from the ceiling."

The entire group broke out in laughter.

"But it has the best acoustics," said Sasha. "And why else would he keep a saddle in there except for sex?"

"The request still stands," said Dr. Decker. "Secondly, just because you're second years now, don't get cocky. You're in an entirely new area with unique problems. Treat it like your first year. Now say it with me."

He held out his hands as if he were conducting a symphony. Everyone shouted along with Dr. Decker.

"We don't know shit!"

The first time Remi had heard that phrase, she'd been angry. Insulted. But after a year, she understood why Dr. Decker drilled it into their heads.

"What new rules do we get this year?" asked Ethan.

"Always the optimist," said Dr. Decker, turning to the wipe board and grabbing a dry erase marker. "And because you deviants can't control yourselves, I'm going to give you all of this year's rules at the beginning."

A couple of whoops and hollers were followed by Dr. Decker shaking his head.

"Rule number four! Listen to your patients."

A bunch of hands went up.

"Yeah, I get it. This one contradicts the rule about not trusting your patients. Which is still true. But you must listen to them. They might not always tell the truth, but they'll tell you what's wrong if you keep your eyes and ears open. This is especially important in a longer-term care ward."

Dr. Decker pulled out a long metal rod from the inside of his coat.

"Rule number five. A divining rod can tell you everything."

No hands went up, but there was ample confusion and shared glances. Remi knew at least two cons involving magical divining rods, so she was nearly certain it was a joke.

"No, it's not a joke," said Dr. Decker with a smirk. "But clearly you're skeptical, so I'll wait until we're on rounds to demonstrate, so we'll move on to the last rule. You can't fix a N.O.C.A.T."

Remi heard the abbreviation in his tone. A few hands tentatively rose.

"NOCAT. Which stands for No One Can Aid Them. You learned about triage in the ER? The Supernatural Ward is no different. You're going to meet all kinds of patients. Some of them you will come to love, others you will hate with a red-hot passion, but most of them will fall in between. But you will really come to love their problems. If the ER is a sprint, then the Supernatural Ward is a delightfully complex puzzle game. You could spend the entire year on a single patient if you wanted. But don't. We always have more patients than people to care for them. You have to use your time wisely. Don't let someone die while you're scratching the itch of your curiosity."

"What does this have to do with NOCATs?" asked Lily.

"They're the worst of the worst. Maddeningly interesting problems with absolutely no hope of fixing them. You can't help them and you can't hurt them. The only thing that can happen is you'll waste your time and lose a patient that actually needed your help. The best thing you can do is turf them to another department."

Damon sat up. "Isn't that defeating the purpose of having them in a hospital?"

"Theoretically yes. But we don't have infinite resources, so we have to deal accordingly. Cynical yes, but if you're not a nihilist by the end of your five years at Golden Willow then I'll think you're either a golden retriever in disguise, or you're a really terrible liar." He checked with the rest of the group. "Any other questions?"

A dozen hands went up.

"Good. No questions. You'll find your assignments and schedules on the board outside my office. Also, when you stop by, grab your divining rod from the pile. One per student. See you on rounds."

Dr. Decker swept out of the room, leaving them staring at each other incredulously.

"NOCATs? Divining rods? And I thought he was fucking with us the first year," said Sasha, heading out of the room after their instructor.

Remi turned to Damon, but he burst from the love seat before she could ask him what he thought about Dr. Decker's second year rules. Damon had his fists at his side as he marched out, heading the opposite way, veins in his forehead standing out.

"What's wrong with him?" asked Boon.

She realized in that moment that except for Lily, no one else knew about his father's illness. Since he hadn't said anything, she shrugged.

"Misses the ER, I guess."

Lily gave her a strange look as she left the room, but Remi wanted to see the new schedule so she could see if her second year was going to be as insane as the first.

THREE

The curious scent of spring flowers caught Lily before she entered the patient's room with Dr. Decker. It was afternoon already, a week into her second year in Aura Healers, and she was happy to be in the Supernatural Ward. She'd come to the conclusion that it was going to be infinitely calmer than her first year, despite the warnings from Dr. Decker.

Lily sensed the problem as soon as she stepped into the room. The patient had brown skin with autumn undertones, dozens of piercings on her face, and a bright red arcing coif with the sides shaved that looked like it'd been borrowed from a punk parakeet. She was adorably cute, the type of girl that did very well on social media if she cared enough to bother. Given the ward Lily was standing in, the patient could be any number of supernatural beings, but she knew the reality even before she saw the chart. A pixie. Probably not full-blooded, but enough to be a serious problem.

"Good morning, Miss...Clover," said Dr. Decker as he checked the chart that was hanging at the end of the bed. "I'm Dr. Decker and this is Healer Lily. How are we today? May I call you Morwen?"

"Certainly," said Morwen with the covers pulled up tight under her chin. Her voice was light and airy with the lilt of the West Coast. Wide brown eyes glittered with specks of gold, belying an innocence that Lily knew was certified bullshite. "And it's, like, my stomach, you know. Can barely keep food down and I have this sharp pain right here."

Morwen poked at a spot that would indicate an appendix on a full-blooded human. Dr. Decker made no indication that he didn't believe her and approached the bed, while Lily found it hard to keep silent. The first rule of pixies was to never trust them. They were some of the worst when it came to tricksters because people tended to think their tricks benign until things went a step too far.

"May I push on your stomach? I'll try to be gentle around the sensitive areas, but I might cause pain."

Morwen nodded. Dr. Decker used two hands to press around her midsection. At a single point near her side, she grimaced and let out a barely believable groan that would have fit better in a porno, which brought a frustrating rage to Lily's chest as she watched how easily the pixie was bamboozling Dr. Decker.

"I see." He stood back and put his hand under his chin. "Lily, what kind of enchantments would you suggest to determine what might be wrong with Morwen?"

The patient stared back with the doe-eyed softness one might expect from a feline hoping for a bowl of milk. Under Dr. Decker's watchful gaze, Lily had to swallow what she wanted to say.

"Perhaps a Dyson's Delineating Diaphragm, or a good ol' fashion Aura Burst."

"Good. Why don't you try both of those."

Lily hesitated, checking back with Dr. Decker.

"Is there a problem?"

She opened her mouth again, before closing her eyes briefly. "Nothing."

"Then get on with it. We have another dozen patients to check in the next two hours."

Lily performed the spells without issue. They were simple enchantments, nothing like the rituals she helped her sisters cast. If Morwen were a different patient, an illuminating elixir would be a better choice, as it would coat any suspect areas in a bluish light that could be seen through flesh, but it took longer to work, which made it the wrong tool.

"Nothing. There's nothing wrong with her," said Lily when she was finished.

"Miss de Meath, I don't think we can conclude that from two simple tests. Is there something you want to tell me?"

"No."

Lily stepped back and clamped her lips shut. Dr. Decker raised an eyebrow in her direction before returning his focus back to Morwen. He picked up the chart and started scribbling notes.

"We'll have to run a few more tests to determine what's wrong with your gut. Do you have a history with stomach issues?"

Morwen sighed and nodded. "Dr. Decker, it's like the worst. I think I get them during my moon time. You know what I mean?"

"Your period."

Lily couldn't help but blurt out, "Pixies don't have menstruation."

A squeak slipped out of Morwen's lips as she pulled the covers up again.

"I'm only half pixie."

Dr. Decker gave her an apprehensive glance. "During menstruation, you say."

"It's worse some months more than others. This is a bad one," said

Morwen with her face scrunched up as if she were in pain. "But you know, Dr. Decker, in the past, I've felt much better with a Black and Blue elixir. It makes the pain go away, really quickly, and keeps it away as long as I have enough for the two weeks it takes them to pass."

"Bullshite," said Lily, crossing her arms.

"Healer Lily," said Dr. Decker. "That's no way to talk to a patient."

"But it's bullshite." Lily gestured at Morwen, whose mouth hung open. "*She's* bullshite. She's a proper trickster, that one. She knew exactly which elixir she wanted! And that ain't no normal one either. Made with essence of black horn and blue-tongued marble lizard. That's serious pain medication, nothing for a stomachache. It's a bloody scam, is what it is."

Lily didn't know how she was expecting Dr. Decker to react, but it wasn't the red-faced anger, followed by a jab of his thumb towards the hallway.

"What in the nine hells has gotten into you?" asked Dr. Decker away from the room.

"She's a bloody pixie!"

"Half pixie."

"Same thing. You can't trust 'em. There were a family of them in Kerry that were always trying to rip regular folk off. Tourists especially, not that I minded when they got their comeuppance, but the point remains. You can't trust a pixie. We had some like her that would come to my sisters, asking for this or that elixir for some common problem. But they either wanted them for drugs, or to sell. Or both."

Dr. Decker's jaw pulsed during her speech. "What's the fourth rule?"

"Listen to the patient. I am. I see right through her ploy. I don't see why you can't."

"Because we err on the side of caution. If I turned down every tweaker that came into the hospital, we'd barely have any patients."

"So you're saying that you know it's a rip-off but you're still giving 'em drugs?"

"Healer Lily. *Second* year Lily. You're missing the point. Our job is to care for them. Unless we have a real and credible reason to believe that they're lying, we must care for the symptoms demonstrated or explained."

"Fuck me, Dr. Decker. I don't know how you don't see it," she pleaded.

"And I don't know how you aren't seeing how disrespectful and unprofessional you're acting. Let me refer back to rule number one. You don't know shit. Bullshite even. I'm overruling whatever it is you think you're doing here and I suggest you get back in line before I have to reprimand you officially. You're a bright, talented healer. With your background, you could be one of the best, but you also have some glaringly obvious blind spots that could make you one of the worst healers. Much like Dr. Paddock."

"You *coabhack*!"

Lily shook her fists at the doctor.

Dr. Decker scowled. "You're lucky I have no idea what that means. But here's what's going to happen now. We're going to go back into that room. You're going to apologize to Miss Morwen and I'm going to write a script for the Black and Blue elixir, which you're going to take down to the alchemy labs and have filled. Then delivered personally to Miss Morwen. Is that understood?"

Lily blinked. She was devastated that he was taking the pixie's side and not hers, but she knew when she was outgunned.

"Understood."

Dr. Decker examined her for a long minute before sighing and leading her back into the room. He gestured for Lily to step forward, which felt like willingly leaping into a fiery oven.

"Miss Morwen, I do deeply apologize for my behavior. You are a patient in this hospital and deserving of my respect."

Morwen offered a sympathetic smile. "Apology accepted. It's totally understandable. I recognize the pixie half of my lineage has quite a reputation."

The admittance and switch in elocution caught Lily off guard, but she didn't have time to ask more questions when Dr. Decker handed her the script. She hurried out of the room, leaving the two of them to converse.

The Black and Blue elixir was common enough that a premixed vat waited for her to draw from. Lily filled twenty vials, placing each one in a plastic container that would keep them from breaking. After signing out the elixir, Lily returned to the room where it was just the patient. She set the box on the table next to the bed where Morwen had the covers up to her chin protectively.

"Here's your medicine," said Lily, looking the other way. "Sorry about earlier."

Morwen's gaze glittered as the corner of her lips quirked.

"You make a fetching courier," said Morwen without the higher cutesy voice from earlier.

Lily wasn't sure if Morwen was screwing with her, but she wanted to catch up to Dr. Decker so she could make up for her bad behavior, so she kept her mouth shut. Lily respected Dr. Decker as much as she did her sisters—having him think ill of her wouldn't be tolerated.

"I hope this helps your stomach. Good day."

Before Lily could leave the room, Morwen swept away the covers, revealing that she'd changed back into her street clothes. The black tank top showed off her sleeve tattoos, and the bottom was short enough to expose her pierced belly button above low-riding black cutup jeans with a thick black belt.

"Thanks for the drugs," said Morwen, shoving the plastic box of vials into an enormous canvas shoulder bag. "It was a pleasure doing business with you."

The half-pixie brushed past Lily, who was so angry she couldn't move as Morwen Clover sauntered out of the room with the skipping cadence of someone who definitely did *not* have a stomachache.

FOUR

The alleyway smelled like old garbage and still water. A haunted light peeked through the clouds, turning the glistening bricks silver for a moment before returning them to their dull reddish-brown. Damon stomped through the puddles with his heart hammering in his ears.

The old wooden door was faded, with gang tags scrawled on the chipped paint. He kicked it open, relishing the way the barrier shattered, exploding fragments across the messy room. Chinese take-out containers sat on the galley kitchen counters surrounded by empty beer cans. A row of dried herbs hung from a coat hanger above the messy sink, half-filled with encrusted dishes.

Damon smelled his prey in the living room. He found him waking from slumber on a dilapidated couch with duct tape covering the armrests. The man had short black hair, ochre skin, and pointed ears. His shouts washed over Damon as if it were a dream, but it was too real to be one.

He checked his left fist to find his claws extended and covered in thick brown hair.

The humanoid surged up from the couch in an attempt to flee, and Damon pushed him back down, but not before being raked across the arm. Damon didn't know why he'd barged into his apartment, but before he could finish contemplating the reason, his right arm rose and then the head came tumbling from the body—

Damon woke in his hospital dorm room, sitting up from his position on the floor. His heart rate was soaring and he could taste blood on his tongue. He peered out the window to see that it was still night and the storm flashed lightning on the horizon.

"A dream," he said, relieved.

Then he saw that he was wearing his hiking boots. A single wet candy wrapper was stuck to the toe along with a light coating of mud. His scrubs were wet, and a splash of blood covered his sleeve.

"It has to be a dream."

Damon checked the time. He'd finished his shift two hours ago and had come back to his room to catch a nap before he started the early morning rotation.

Running his hands through his hair revealed it was damp as if he'd been out in the rain, but the storm had passed the sixth ward around the time he'd come back to his room. Knowing he wouldn't be able to sleep, Damon changed into new scrubs, kicked off his boots for sneakers, and headed to the cafeteria for breakfast and much-needed coffee.

In the hallway with his head in the clouds, Damon ran into the Krak woman, Ash. She was a hair taller than him and was built like a Viking warrior with shoulder-length ashy-gray hair. The orderly clothes barely fit her bulging arms.

"Damon," she said in halting English, grabbing his waist as he tried to pass. "You have time?"

He looked to his watch. "It's a quarter past four, but..."

Ash cupped his chin, let her tongue rest on the bottom of her teeth. "No. Time for firing?"

"Firing?" Warmth rose to his cheeks.

They'd hooked up last year and afterwards she'd made gestures to suggest she was interested in more, but since they didn't share a common language it was hard to imagine anything more than physical.

"Oh, you mean fucking."

"Fucking."

She said it like fooking, which made him smile. Her English had come a long way in the last year.

"I have to."

Damon paused. He didn't know what to say, but his mind was still wrapped up in the dream. He squeezed her arm.

"I have to go."

He left Ash confused in the hallway, and regretted his choice by the time he made the cafeteria. A few hours with Ash might have washed the awful dream from his mind. The cafeteria was half full, which was normal for this time of night. He didn't see any of his classmates. There were a few Aura Healer students in their fourth year, but the classes didn't mix except in emergencies. Damon grabbed three hardboiled eggs and two mugs of coffee, finding a table by himself for breakfast.

The flashing red and blue lights of a police car speeding down the main drag reflected off the cafeteria window while he cracked the hard shell and began picking it off. He didn't hear his classmates until they sat down at his table. Lily's rainbow hair had faded in color, but it still took up a massive halo around her head. Boon had a giant basket of fries and a cup of mustard. He'd shaved his head down to the tight curls last month, but the number of earrings had doubled.

"One of your patients die?" asked Boon, tossing a handful of fries in his mouth.

"No. Why?"

"I saw you staring into the void from the food line."

"Weird dream," replied Damon.

Before Boon could ask a follow-up question, Sasha and Ethan joined their table. The British girl wore Union Jack patterned tights under her scrubs and had an expensive jade brooch in her hair, while Ethan's messy curls looked like he'd just woken up. He put his plastic foot on a chair to adjust the straps.

"Chips for breakfast?" asked Sasha, grabbing a handful from Boon's basket and shoving them in her mouth.

Boon closed his eyes and shook his hands. "They're called fries, Sasha. Not chips. Chips are flat and come in a bag."

"Those are crisps." She glanced to Damon. "What's wrong, mate? You look like you could use a good banging. I heard Ash was asking about you again."

He swallowed. "Yeah, I saw her in the hallway."

"And?"

He took a bite of his egg and spoke around his food. "I'll survive."

"Not on boiled eggs and coffee alone," said Sasha. "If you don't break one loose, you're gonna explode."

"I didn't realize my sex life was being tracked."

"Kinda hard not to when you're the only one not getting any. Well, besides Lily, but I feel like she doesn't count."

The Irish girl extended her middle finger. "Bite my arse."

His first thought was to wonder who Remi was hooking up with. He hadn't seen her with anyone, but then again, their shifts were often during opposite times during the summer, so he'd only seen her sparingly.

"All I know," continued Sasha, "is I'd like to have at least half as much sex as Boon."

The dark-skinned second year fluttered his eyelashes. "It's not *all* sex. I had some really good aggressive cuddling with Ethan the other day."

"Big spoon, little spoon," said Ethan. "I just want to be in the drawer."

The chatter was giving Damon a headache, but he didn't want to leave before he was finished eating, so he started breaking the next shell right when Bryan dragged a chair over and squeezed between him and Sasha.

"Can I have some of those—"

Boon slapped his hand away. "Vultures, all of you."

"Speaking of fries, or chips for Sasha," said Ethan, "the old guy in three-oh-three taught me a little spell that's supposed to add some heat to any food. Like real spice, not the half-assed sauces you get here."

"Taught you a spell?" asked Sasha.

"He claims he's part efreeti, but I think he's just a lonely old guy who misses his dead wife. Can I try the spell on some of your fries?"

"Only if you're eating them," said Boon with a shrug. "I'm done anyway."

Ethan cast the spell on the remainder of Boon's basket. The air sizzled with faez and the fries glistened briefly with an orangish sparkle before returning to light brown.

"Here goes nothing," said Ethan, throwing a handful in his mouth.

While everyone was focused on Ethan, Damon collected his tray, hoping to sneak away before anyone noticed. Nothing seemed to be happening with Ethan, who had a perplexed look on his face.

"Maybe you did the spell wrong," suggested Sasha as she inspected one of the modified fries.

"I don't think—"

Ethan didn't finish the sentence before clamping his hand over his mouth. His eyes bulged and a light sweat broke out across his face.

"You gonna be okay, bud?" asked Boon.

When Ethan pulled away his hand, steam slipped out of his lips, and when he opened his mouth, a burst of flame came rushing out. More flame followed when he tried to speak. Ethan leaned his head back and fire bellowed from his lips as he ran to the water cooler at the end of the cafeteria line and shoved his mouth under the spigot. Water spilled over his mouth and clothes as the entire cafeteria burst into applause.

The table of second years broke into gut-busting laughter, and Sasha, who'd been about to eat some of the enchanted fries, threw them across the table and pulled out a wet nap to clean her fingers. Ethan returned to the table soaking wet, water dripping from his hair and tendrils of steam rising from his mouth.

"I think I'm better now," he said, waving his hand in front of his mouth and looking like he'd run a marathon.

"Until tomorrow," said Boon. "You might want to take a fire extinguisher into the bathroom so you don't burn the hospital down."

"Oh, Damon," said Ethan as he sat back down. "Sorry about your sleeve."

Damon checked down to see his right arm exposed where half the scrubs had been burnt away in the initial conflagration. But it wasn't the tufts of burnt hair that had him frozen.

"Whoa," said Sasha, leaning over. "What'd you do to your arm?"

"I don't..."

Damon didn't finish his sentence because he remembered at the end of the dream that the man had raked his claws across his arm in exactly the same place.

"I need to go change," he finished, hurrying away before anyone could question the wound.

Damon left the cafeteria, heading back to his dorm room to switch scrubs. When he passed through a nurse's station, he saw a cluster of them around the television hanging on the wall. A news reporter was standing in an alley that looked painfully familiar. The camera panned to an opening where a door had once been. A few pieces of faded wood hung from the hinges, but not much else. Damon found himself pulled towards the television in mute horror. The sound was too low for him to hear, but he read the chyron streaming across the bottom of the screen.

ILLEGAL HOBGOBLIN BEHEADED IN THE NINTH WARD — HUNT FOR THE FULL MOON KILLER CONTINUES

FIVE

Remi spent the morning on rounds with Dr. Decker, along with Sasha and Boon. In each room, they'd crowd behind the doctor while he talked with the patients. Sometimes he would ask them questions, or have them perform simple spells. Compared to the emergency room, it felt like they weren't in the same building, and except for the long hours, the work was relatively peaceful. At least until Sasha asked a question.

"When are you going to show us how to use that divining rod, Dr. Decker? Or is that one of your weird jokes?"

He looked up from a chart on the wall outside a patient with a shimmering field over the door. The person inside the room was a fourth-year student from Explorers Hall who had contracted a strange affliction that was turning his flesh to plant material. By the time he'd been rescued, he'd lost the ability to communicate. The disease wasn't contagious, but insects kept spontaneously bursting from his skin and escaping into the hallway, so the barrier had been placed over the entrance.

"Would you rather check on Woody here? Or do you want me to show you how to work a divining rod?"

Boon raised his hand. "I'm partial to Woody. His left leg flowered yesterday and I heard the floral scents are nothing you've ever smelled before."

Sasha rolled her eyes. "Divining rod for me. That whole situation in there gives me the creeps."

"It's down to you, Remi."

"It doesn't have to be. I don't care either way."

"We don't pay you not to have an opinion," said Dr. Decker, putting his hands behind his back. She knew this pose. It meant he wasn't going to take no, or obfuscation for an answer.

"I didn't know I was getting paid."

"Choose, Remi."

She peeked her head around the corner. The guy covered in thick woody material and flowers reminded her too much of last year's craziness.

"Divining rod."

"Yes," said Sasha, pumping her fist.

"Come on, children. I know just the patient for our practice," said Dr. Decker, leading them to a part of the ward she hadn't seen yet.

The lights were dimmer and there were only two on-duty nurses at the station and they were both sitting, drinking coffee, and laughing about something they'd been discussing.

"Can I have the Room 411 chart?" Dr. Decker asked, leaning over the counter.

"Really?" asked the nurse.

He gestured to them and she nodded with an exclamation.

"Have fun," she said after handing over the chart.

They followed Dr. Decker to the room. He hung the chart on the wall.

"Aren't you going to read the chart?" asked Boon.

"No need. There's little information on it. Today you're going to meet your first NOCAT."

"Then why ask for the chart?"

"It makes the nurses feel better," he said, leading them into the room.

Remi had gotten used to strange smells during her time in the hospital, but the stench in the room didn't smell human related. It had more in common with a leaky sewer. The wrinkly older woman in the bed lay with her mouth open and her eyes glazed over. She wasn't connected to a single machine.

"I don't understand," said Sasha. "Why aren't her vitals being monitored? I thought that was hospital policy."

Dr. Decker pulled a silver rod from the inside of his white coat, producing it like a magician on stage.

"For normal patients, yes. But not NOCATs. They're not going to die and you can't fix them, so there's no need to use the monitors."

"That's pretty cynical, even for you, Dr. Decker," said Boon.

"Why are we here then?" asked Remi.

"Because there's no better patient for learning how to use a divining rod than a NOCAT."

Over the next twenty minutes, Dr. Decker poked and prodded the unaware woman who made no indication that she was alive except for the occasional sudden in-breath similar to sleep apnea. Using the rod, he showed them five different tumors, an old necrosis scar on her calf, and the efficiency of her lungs and heart.

Remi was horrified as much as she was impressed by how Dr. Decker could reveal medical truths using the rod and a few common aura spells.

"Why is she even here?" asked Remi towards the end of the demonstration.

Dr. Decker pulled out an antiseptic cloth and cleaned the silver rod while he answered.

"No one knows. I happened to know this woman was dropped off outside the ER two years ago, but it's not the first time I've seen her. The first was nearly a decade ago in Memphis when I did a short rotation to help them out after they had a serious rusalka problem. The best you can do with a NOCAT is turf them to a different department or another hospital entirely."

"She was bitten by a rusalka?"

"No. She was there before I arrived. Nurses said she'd come from another part of the country. Some enterprising doctor had gotten her shipped over on a lie. I tried getting her bounced, but he'd done too good of a job with the paperwork."

"That's fucked up," said Remi, staring at the old woman. She imagined Odette being treated like that and it made her angry.

"Some say NOCATs are a reminder that we can't fix everyone. A little joke from the gods to keep our hubris in check."

"This ain't no cat, it shouldn't have nine lives," said Boon, wrinkling his nose.

"There should be something we can do for her, right?" asked Remi.

Dr. Decker gave her a raised eyebrow. "When did you earn your bleeding heart?"

She gestured randomly. "I don't know. It just seems cruel. What if this was Odette? She has to have a family, somewhere. I can't believe no one's trying to fix her."

"Who isn't?" He shoved the rod back in his coat. "I know this seems heartless, but remember our rule of triage. You can't spend your time on lost causes. It's one of the hard truths of the hospital. We're not gods, even though we feel like them sometimes." He sighed. "Back in Memphis, I was determined to be the one to fix this woman. I ordered tests, did blood workups, spells, charms, whatever I thought might bring her out of this stupor, but nothing worked. Part of the problem is we know so little about how she ended up this way. Or even why she was in the Supernatural Ward, rather than another. The best I could determine was that someone, somewhere along the way, thought she was an oracle. But I think that's just what was put down to get her shipped to Golden Willow."

Remi studied the emaciated old woman, who stared at the ceiling with the blank expression of the dead, her mouth hanging open.

"Come on, ducklings, that's enough instruction on rods and NO-CATs, we've got real patients to help."

The others left, but Remi remained. In the ER, they tried to save everyone as much as they could. It might be a mad scramble filled with rapid diagnosis and quick fixes to get them stabilized, but they were trying. The idea that there were patients they'd completely given up on made her heart ache. Remi couldn't help but see Odette in the bed.

"I'm sorry," she muttered under her breath.

As she turned to leave, the patient gurgled. Remi thought she might be choking and wanted to retrieve Dr. Decker, but realized the others were already down the hall, completely oblivious to her absence. She leaned over the old woman, thinking there might be an obstruction in her throat.

"Are you in there?" asked Remi.

The old woman continued to stare at the ceiling. Remi was about to leave when she heard a wavering exhale.

"Be ware..."

"What? Hello? Do you need help?" she asked at the same time she worried she was hallucinating.

"...the..."

Remi wasn't sure if it were a word, or the sound of her throat getting stuck. She placed her ear above the woman's mouth.

"...egg."

"Egg? Did you say beware the egg?"

A second gurgle was followed by a brief wavering of the eyelids before the wheezing from her throat silenced.

"Beware the egg." Remi shook her head. "Come on, Remi. Don't be ridiculous. Even if those were words, that was nonsense."

She moved to the door, checking back one last time at the unmoving patient before heading after Dr. Decker to continue rounds.

SIX

Dr. Hasan Hunker drew sigils on the patient's chest with a medical-grade marker while Lily watched. The biodegradable paint contained trace amounts of silver and belladonna. The guy in the bed with his shirt off worked in the sixth ward providing seances to those who wanted to speak to the recently dead. Even in the Old Country, such work was demonized, but in the city of sorcery they not only tolerated it, but provided certifications to ensure the medium wasn't a hoax.

Dr. Hunker worked quickly and efficiently while the patient stared at the ceiling. The precise lines and curves were hypnotic. Lily wished her sisters had access to the materials readily available in the hospital. They'd be able to treat so many more people than they normally could. Sigils were usually drawn using goat blood and iodine, which only worked if the goat had been fed plants harvested from the Fae realms.

"Alright, you three," said Dr. Hunker as he finished the sigil. "Why am I using a Di Ka rune as the hook rather than a Ma Ka?"

Bryan and Remi shuffled their feet, trying not to make eye contact. Her classmates acted like idiots around the doctor. Dr. Hunker capped the marker as he stared back.

Remi screwed up her face. "Because you're worried about Veil infection?"

"Are you asking or telling me?"

Remi's expression broke. "Asking."

Dr. Hunker smiled sympathetically. "Why is our patient here?"

Remi averted her eyes as she spoke. "Mr. Lake is a Dead Talker, but he hasn't been able to communicate with anyone across the Veil."

"Then why would you be worried about Veil infection if he's trying to reach across?"

"Right," said Remi. "Sorry. I should have seen that."

"It's okay, Miss Wilde. I bet if you reread the section about Veil-related patients rather than symptoms you'll understand the difference, but I appreciate that you knew that much. Bryan? Lily? Do you have any ideas?"

Bryan rubbed the back of his neck. "It'll work better?"

"Another guess I see," said Dr. Hunker, putting a reassuring hand on Bryan's shoulder. "Lily?"

She'd held her answer back on purpose to give her classmates a chance, but since they'd had their chance she gave her answer.

"Because we don't know if the patient is truly suffering from a Veil break, or that he can no longer hear them. The Di Ka rune will protect him from accidentally causing a Come Over while the Ma Ka would not."

"Excellent answer, Lily," said Dr. Hunker. "You really know your runes and sigils."

Up to that moment, the patient had been smiling and nodding along with the discussion. No one had realized that anything was wrong until

Bryan extended his arm.

"Dr. Hunker!"

The patient's eyes had rolled into the back of his head. He shook, gripping the covers in fists. Soft moans exited his open mouth.

"Is this a séance?" asked Remi.

Dr. Hunker leaned over to examine the runes. "Nothing's wrong with the sigil. This shouldn't be happening. Anyone have an idea?"

"Idea?" asked Bryan. "Are you crazy? Shouldn't you fix him before something gets worse?"

Dr. Hunker raised an eyebrow. "If you don't learn to make decisions, then you'll never become a healer."

"The runes might have given him his ability to reach across the Veil, but not control it," said Lily.

"Good. What do we do next?" asked Dr. Hunker with exceeding calm.

"Should we hold him down or something?" asked Remi.

"The patient, despite his shaking, is quite stable. Look at his vitals, Remi. But leaving him halfway between the living and the dead exposes him to dangers he cannot avoid. We have time, five minutes or so, but we'll need to fix this before something creepy and crawly finds him."

"We need a marker with red poppy infusions to help him control his powers," said Lily.

Dr. Hunker snapped his fingers. "Right on. I don't seem to have one of those on me, so can you run down to the supply closet and grab one?"

Lily jogged to the nearest supply closet on that floor, which she found lacked the correct marker. Sensing she was running out of time, she hurried up one floor to the Supernatural Diseases and Virology Ward, but found it locked when she arrived.

"Dammit," she said, banging her fist on the door.

Lily was about to head to the fourth floor when she heard a muffled moan. She placed her ear to the surface, hearing cries of passion. A nurse walked by shaking her head.

"They've been in there over an hour."

"Who?"

"Some of your idiot classmates," said the nurse before she went around the corner.

Lily banged on the door harder. "Open up! I have a medical emergency."

A faint response reached her. "Give us two more minutes!"

"Is that you, Ethan?" A willowing cry had her adding. "Sasha? My patient doesn't have two minutes. Open now!"

When nothing happened, she pulled out a credit card and shoved it in the gap like Remi had taught her. The lock popped and the door swung wide, revealing her classmates. Lily didn't know what she was seeing at first. They were both naked, covered in runes, and sprawled out on the mixing table with their legs entwined, looking like they'd run a marathon.

The marker board was on the other side of their naked bodies. Neither of them looked like they were trying to hide themselves, which didn't bother Lily, but it told her how enraptured they were. She marched over to grab a marker but their legs were in the way.

"What are you two gobshites doing?"

Ethan appeared almost in pain as he panted. "I was showing Sasha how the Me Phi rune can enhance the sense of touch and well, one thing led to another. Oh Merlin, it's almost too much, but I can't stop."

Lily jammed her arm between their legs, plucking a marker from the container. Her elbow brushed against wetness, which elicited dual moans.

"You fucking twits, you know the Me Phi rune will burn your pleasure receptors out if you use it too long? You don't think some other horny hospital intern hasn't thought of this?"

Ethan nearly fell off the table, grabbing the marker board, which nearly toppled it over until Sasha righted him. The two scrambled off as the door closed.

Lily chuckled to herself, because she'd made up that last part about the Me Phi rune, but if those two cabbages couldn't be bothered to experiment in the safety of their own room, she wasn't going to give them a moment's peace. The line for the elevator was full, so she ran towards the stairs only to stutter to a stop when she saw a familiar coif of hair—bright aqua green now—sitting on the edge of a patient's bed.

Morwen Clover.

The half-pixie met her gaze briefly. Lily thought about stopping to tell the doctor she was a full-blooded liar, but needed to get the marker back to the patient in Dr. Hunker's care.

"I had to go up two floors," said Lily as an explanation for her lateness.

"Would you like to do the honors?" asked Dr. Hunker.

"Aye."

The patient was convulsing slightly, but not enough that she couldn't draw the runes correctly. It took seven runes—one on each limb, another on the chest and back, and the final one placed on the forehead. As she completed the last rune, he stopped shaking and in a matter of seconds, calmed enough to exhale.

"You're a natural," said Dr. Hunker with a wink.

Lily didn't have the heart to tell him she'd probably been making runes as long as he'd been practicing. She nodded instead. After they confirmed the patient was stable with no danger of Veil creatures tearing out his soul, Dr. Hunker led them on more rounds, but Lily asked to be excused for a quick break.

She went right back to the next floor, catching Morwen as she was leaving the room with a box of elixirs. Lily grabbed her arm.

"You're a fucking thief, Pixie."

"Half-pixie, Witch." Morwen yanked her arm away. "You're not supposed to treat me like that. I'm a patient. Hypno-cratic oath, and all that."

"It's Hippocratic oath, but I'm not a doctor. I can do what I want."

"Somehow I doubt that, or why would you be slinging shit here instead of being back in the Old Country with your sisters?"

Lily scowled.

"Yeah, that's right. I know about you and your bitchy little coven."

"And I know your kind, Pixie. Nothing but trouble."

Morwen flipped her hair back. "You don't know me, or what I've been through, Witch. Besides, there's more than enough to go around. Never a shortage, which means they really don't need it after all."

The white-coated doctor who'd been serving Morwen came around the corner. Lily didn't know him, but she'd seen him in the cafeteria.

"Is there a problem?"

"Your intern is hassling me," said Morwen.

"I'm not an intern."

"Whatever, Witch."

The doctor raised an eyebrow. "Shouldn't you be on the floor below?"

Lily wanted to tell him that Morwen had probably bewitched him with her pixie magic, but didn't bother. Dealing with her kind required a defter touch.

"Aye, you're right, Doctor. I'll take myself back where I belong."

Morwen stood on her tippy-toes and placed her lips against the doctor's cheek.

"Thanks, Doc."

He gave her a cutesy wave. "Bye, Morwen. Stay safe and I hope those elixirs help with the pain."

"Oh, they will, Doc. They will. Right, Lily?"

She'd been standing at the corner, but when she was called out, Lily slammed her way through the stairwell.

"Fucking pixies."

SEVEN

The music was too loud, the lights annoying, and Damon didn't want to be there. He eyed the exit, spinning his drink on the standing table while his classmates sang to the song, a catchy number called "Cursed to Lie" that had been all over the city since the beginning of summer.

"Another round of shots!" slurred Dr. Decker at the bartender, a woman with rainbow scales on her head and neck.

The scales could either be modified with magic, or she was from another realm, but it was a supernatural friendly bar, so it made sense either way. He sighed as the shot of glowing purple liquid was shoved in his fist. The rest of his class circled around, lifting their glasses high.

"To blood, sweat, and bandages! And a healer's best friend, whatever the purple elixir is!" called out Dr. Decker.

Before Damon could throw his shot back with the others, he spotted the silvery light coating the street outside the bar. He'd never been worried about the full moon, as it wasn't what made him change, but the dream he'd had during the last one that had matched the death of the hobgoblin changed how he saw the light. It didn't help the news media had been speculating about more murders tonight, which made him leery about coming out with his classmates, but it'd been impossible to say no.

"What are you waiting for?" asked Remi with a delirious grin.

Hair in disarray, face glistening from dancing, and eyes hazy from elixirs, she was a mess, but he liked the way her smile created dimples at the corners of her lips. Especially the little bow of her mouth, pursed as she waited for him to answer.

Damon threw the shot back, grimacing when the heat hit his throat, followed by a tingling sensation that went down to his toes.

"Are you going to let yourself have a good time? Or do I need to forcibly remove that stick from your ass?" said Remi.

He slid the shot glass onto the bar. "You have small hands, it would make it easier."

Remi snorted and elbowed him in the ribs. "You should relax. We don't get a day off very often."

"I know, I know," said Damon.

"Thinking about your dad?"

"Yeah. He's stable, but no one seems to know what's wrong. Tests aren't just inconclusive, they're random and weird. As if they're the results from someone entirely different and not unconscious. They keep finding trace alchemical elements in his blood and nothing what they've been giving him."

"I'm sorry for bringing it up," said Remi. "You can't do anything for him right now. You should take this time to relax. Have a good time. Your patients depend on it."

Most of the class was on the dance floor along with a bachelorette party wearing sashes and tiaras. The writing on the silk bands was an otherworldly language no one recognized. Their instructor was in the center, dancing with the bride-to-be as if it were their last night on Earth.

"I don't know how he does it," said Damon, gesturing to the dance floor.

"Decker? Drugs help. I saw him in the corner with the maid of honor putting something on their eyes."

"That a good idea? We don't even know where they're from or what they are," said Damon.

"Decker does, but he's not saying." Remi took a drink. "I get the feeling whatever made him leave the hospital years ago and go on a multi-realm walkabout was pretty serious."

Damon nodded. "I've heard the same thing, but no one will explain what it was. They did say he was one of the most brilliant, hardworking doctors before whatever it was happened."

"He's still brilliant, he's just, I don't know..."

"Is that what we all turn into eventually?" asked Damon.

"Only if we let it."

"I just don't want to be an asshole like Paddock."

Remi groaned. "I hate that guy. He treats us like idiots, but at least we don't have to work with him this year."

"Anything on Dr. Hunk?"

Remi raised an eyebrow. "If he's a super? Nah. I don't think anyone's going to get it out of him."

Damon narrowed his gaze. "Bullshit, Remi. You've got something up your sleeve, you're just holding it close."

"And what if I do?" she said, smiling sweetly.

"I knew it."

She elbowed him again. "Are you having fun yet? Even just a little?"

"I am."

Remi grabbed his hand. "Good. Let's dance!"

They joined the chaos on the floor next to Lily, who looked like a willow tree in a storm. A little white nose stuck out from the back of her multihued hair. The beat rose and fell like a rollercoaster, driving everyone to abandon. Damon briefly worried that their dancing was a compulsion, but he was having too good of a time to care. For a few hours, he forgot about the hospital, his father's illness, and the full moon.

Sometime later on in the dance party, Dr. Decker left with the bride-to-be and her maid of honor, climbing into a taxi and disappearing. Others left in ones and twos shortly after. Sasha, Boon, and Ethan found another taxi a little while later. Before long, only a few of them were left on the dance floor. Lily was swirling and spinning by herself, and Remi was grinding his leg and scratching his chest during a slow song. He couldn't remember getting that drunk, but at some point, he'd stopped caring and let himself revel in the moment, especially with Remi touching his hip and arm in ways that had him thinking about asking her to go back to his room.

Even sweaty, she smelled like peppermint. He leaned down to whisper in her ear and stumbled into a table.

"Time to go?" she asked with her tongue resting on her bottom teeth.

Damon nodded. "I'm all yours."

"Dangerous. Come on."

As they found a taxi on the street, Lily yelled, "Shotgun!" and leapt into the front seat, much to the dismay of the driver. In the back of the taxi, Remi draped her legs over his lap and leaned her head out the open window. The wind and the music from the taxi stereo had him grinning as he watched the way the silver light cast sharp shadows across the city. He hadn't slept more than a few hours in weeks and the alcohol made him warm and heavy. Damon leaned his head against the door while he kneaded Remi's calves...

—a loud bang had him sitting straight up in the middle of his dorm room floor. The soft light of morning streamed in through the window, forcing him to squint while a throbbing headache played heavy bass on his temples.

"Augh."

His hand shifted into sticky wetness. Blood covered his entire naked chest and pant legs.

"Blood and bone."

A sudden dark concern shot through his mind. Remi. He'd been on his way back to the room with her. The bed was covered in a pile of blankets. He crept to his knees, fearing the worst.

The bed was empty.

Damon sighed heavily, but the relief faded quickly because he hadn't figured out whose blood was all over him. He carefully scraped the thickest material into an old sleeping elixir vial and then wiped himself down and changed into fresh scrubs.

Heading to the testing labs, he ran into Boon coming the other way holding a cup of coffee as if it were precious gold.

"Hey," said Boon, drearily. "I heard you had a good time last night."

"I did?"

"Didn't you take Remi back to your room? I know you two have been dancing around each other forever. Nice to see you finally making a move."

Damon's gut tightened. He felt like a shit that he didn't remember.

"Ah, yeah."

"You okay?"

Damon held up the vial. "Running samples."

He left before Boon could ask more questions. Bob Morehouse was asleep at his desk when Damon arrived. While he waited for results, he checked his phone, finding no texts that would explain what happened after he left the bar. He typed and deleted three separate messages to Remi before deciding that it was too embarrassing not to remember. Switching to his browser, he searched for news of the Full Moon Killer to find that he'd struck again last night on the edge of the seventh ward. Two men had been killed. One was beheaded, while the other bled out from a sword wound to the chest. The article made no mention of their heritage, but the location they'd been killed often went by the name Fairy Town.

Bob Morehead called from the other side of the laboratory. "Results are on the printer!"

Damon's heart was in his throat as he approached the white box at the end of a series of desks. A small stack of papers sat on the exit tray. He pulled the last one out, running his finger down the list of information until he reached the blood type markers.

Fomorian blood.

They'd left their realms a millennia ago, and until recently, had been in Ireland, but having mixed with humans for centuries enough to pass, they'd spread out in enclaves across the world. Damon was aware of them because his old clan had occasional run-ins with Fomorians who had a long-standing grudge against werewolves for reasons he didn't understand.

"Results you were looking for?" asked Bob Morehead. "You've been standing there for a long time."

"Yeah, thanks," said Damon, distracted. "I'd better get back to my ward."

In the hallway, away from the prying eyes of anyone else, Damon put a hand to his forehead. He didn't know for sure, but he felt that it was a high likelihood that the two men killed in the seventh ward were Fomorians. And if that was true, then he might be the Full Moon Killer.

EIGHT

The spell fizzled at the end of Remi's fingertips, sending out a collection of bright pink bubbles that floated to the ceiling and stuck to the tile like bubble gum. The patient stared at her with his head tilted.

"Did it work?"

Remi felt the heat from Dr. Decker's gaze and bowed her head.

"No. I'll have to do it again."

"I need to speak with you in the hall."

She gave the patient a sheepish smile and followed Dr. Decker away.

"What's going on with you? It's like you've reverted to your mistakes from last year. And that was a simple finger flub, nothing that you shouldn't be able to nail every time without fail."

"I don't know, Dr. Decker. I just don't have my head in the game."

"You don't get that luxury, Remi. You should know that. You need to be at peak performance, day in and day out. You're lucky that was a simple wound cleansing spell and that you screwed it up in a way that didn't cause more harm."

"I'll do better next time. I can focus."

He shook his head. "No. I'm going to clean the wound."

"What am I going to do?"

Dr. Decker crossed his arms. "You haven't been yourself since the night out. I hoped to loosen you all up, but that seems to have worked for everyone but you and a certain tall, handsome second year."

Remi swallowed, hating that he was right. "It's nothing."

"Have you and Damon talked since that night?"

"We didn't do anything. He passed out in the taxi and we couldn't wake him. He was like the dead. We had to get Ash to carry him to his room."

"If I were writing a prescription, I'd tell you both you need to get it over with, but I'm afraid you two would only make it worse. Whatever your feelings, you two have to figure things out. You're not the only one making simple mistakes. I want you to go talk to Damon, work out this sexual tension in one way or another."

"Dr. Decker," she exclaimed.

He raised an eyebrow. "You have..."

"Of course, but only a few times. It's not like I've ever lived anywhere for long. Or had friends." Heat burned in her cheeks. "I can't do what you do, leaving with both those women."

"I wouldn't have expected you to be a prude."

"I'm not a prude."

"Then act like it."

"Dr. Decker, I don't think it's appropriate to push me to have sex with a classmate."

"That's not what I'm saying. I'm just telling you an honest conversation will go a long way to resolving whatever is lingering between you.

Because if you don't and keep screwing up, you're not going to last much longer. It's one of the hard things about the hospital. No matter what's going on in your life, you don't get the luxury of bringing it to your job. Your patients deserve better."

"Fine. I'll go talk to him."

He took a step towards the patient's room. "And you really need to get laid."

"Dr. Decker!"

"I'm not saying with Damon. But I assure you that it's a normal part of life, and honestly, it's one of the few free ways of feeling good that counteracts the daily dose of death we deal with on a regular basis."

Remi didn't go straight to Damon's room. She wound through the hallways, formulating a way to initiate the conversation. She'd never felt so embarrassed in her life. It didn't help that her parents had never said word one about sex or relationships. The only thing they'd ever bothered to teach her was how to break into a house, or con a family out of their hard-earned cash. Talking about sex seemed a thousand times more difficult.

She found herself in front of his door before she realized it. The urge to knock was countered by the desire to flee. She raised and lowered her hand a half dozen times and then the door flung open, revealing a confused Damon standing in his scrubs with a pen in his hand.

"How long have you been standing out here?"

Remi lowered her chin.

"Decker sent me here."

"Is there a problem?" he asked, looking down the hall. "Do I need to head to the ward? I was just reading."

"Can I come in?"

Confused, he nodded but let her pass. She plopped on the bed. The tome open on the desk was heavily highlighted.

"What are you reading?"

"A treatise on dream travel and various spells about it."

She screwed up her face. "I don't recall that on our required list."

"It's not," he said, taking the chair. "It's good that you came. I've been meaning to talk to you."

"You have?"

He ran a hand through his messy brown hair. "I don't know how to say this, but on the night of the party, what happened?"

"What do you mean, what happened? You passed out in the taxi and we had to have you carried to your room. By Ash, by the way."

His cheeks flushed. "Ash?"

"It's not like I'm going to carry you."

"So we didn't..."

"No. You really don't remember?"

He leaned back in the chair, rotated it back and forth. "Not only do I not remember leaving the taxi, but there's another problem and I don't know how to bring it up."

"You slept with Ash again?"

The words shot out of her lips before she could corral them. She hadn't realized she'd been worried about it until then.

"No. I don't think so, but no. That's not what I'm worried about."

He chewed on his fingernails and couldn't make eye contact.

"What? Did you sleep with Lily or one of the others? It's no big deal. I know we were dancing that night, but it's not like that had to mean anything. We were just having fun."

"I think we both know I didn't sleep with Lily. She's the only one of us that doesn't seem interested in sex. With anyone."

"Then what?"

Damon massaged the bridge of his nose. He stayed frighteningly still for a long time until he finally exhaled.

"I'm afraid I'm the Full Moon Killer."

"What? That's definitely not what I thought you were going to say." She shrugged. "How? And why wouldn't you know? Or is that what that dream walking is about?"

For the next twenty minutes, Damon explained what had happened during the last two full moons, including the blood analysis and the articles he'd saved from the killings.

"You're not serious, right? There's no way you could have dream walked all the way across the city and killed those people and then come back to your room without being spotted. Especially if you were covered in blood."

"All that is true, but why did I have the exact dream about killing the hobgoblin, and then have Fomorian blood on me for the second?"

"I don't know. Do you think it's some latent werewolf thing?"

"The full moon doesn't mean anything to our kind. But it does have a lot to do with dream walking. The full moon opens up the pathways for travel. Like a dream realm. What if I'm walking through it and killing those people and then making it back to my room before anyone notices?"

"Other than the fact that you've dedicated your life to healing people? Face it, Damon. You're not a killer."

"I appreciate that. But it still doesn't tell me why I keep waking up covered in other people's blood." He screwed up his face. "What did you want to talk about?"

"Seems like it's frivolous now, but Dr. Decker wants us to talk."

"About?"

Heat rose to her cheeks. She looked outside the window. "Stuff, like, you know, the night of the party. After the taxi."

Damon leaned his elbows on his knees and kneaded his hands. "Were you planning on coming back to my room?"

"I was." She paused. "If you wanted me to."

"I did. Honestly, I was afraid I'd killed you when I first woke up."

"That's fucked up."

"Tell me about it." He glanced up, brown eyes twinkling. "But I would have liked if you'd spent the night."

"Even though I'm a selfish thief who nearly ruined your life?"

"Which means you owe me."

"Gross."

"Sorry, that came out wrong. But I would like to try again."

"Now?" she exclaimed.

Damon swallowed. "I have to get to my shift in a few minutes."

She exhaled, relieved. "Good. I mean, my head's not in the game right now. But another time for sure."

"Maybe we could have a meal together?"

"A date?"

"Well, given our schedule, it might be a while."

"I'd be okay with having a sandwich on the roof with you," she said.

He smiled. "I'd like that too."

"I have an idea about your full moon problem."

He brightened.

"Next month, when it's time, I'll stay with you and make sure you don't kill anyone."

"Are you sure that's safe? The full moon falls on Halloween. I worry about that one even more," he said.

She let a grin rise to her lips. "You wouldn't hurt me, right? I can get some stay awake elixirs from Jeb, since the last two times it happened while you're asleep. That should be fine."

"Is this a date?"

"I guess it could be," she said, laughing. "We can have a meal on the roof and watch the Halloween illusions in the second ward."

He stood up. "I'd better get to my shift."

"I have to get back to Dr. Decker."

Damon stepped close as if he wanted to lean down and kiss her. Her face tingled in anticipation and her stomach did backflips. Time slowed down. Remi wanted to grab his shirt and pull him close, but she couldn't move. Before she could get the nerve, he offered his hand.

"See you then?"

His hand was warm and the touch made the back of her knees go soft.

"I'll bring the drinks."

NINE

Say that again, Sammie," said Dr. Hunker with his pen poised over the chart. Lily couldn't believe it either. She placed her hands behind her back as not to make the patient any more nervous than he already was. He'd already twice tried to barricade the door from the inside, and only reminding him that they'd have to bring in the ropes team got him to calm.

"Which part?"

The patient had gray-brown skin, two horn nubs on the crown of his forehead, and furry feet sticking out of the end of the blanket. Despite receiving three bags of blood, which had brought his vitals back to acceptable levels, his cheeks were sunken. Lily was halfway certain he was related to the satyrs, but she'd never seen one outside of the Fae, nor with so many human characteristics.

"The blood part."

Sammie held his arms across his chest. He looked like a rabbit readying to bolt with a hungry dog near.

"I don't know what more to say..."

Dr. Hunker offered a welcoming smile. "We're your doctors. We're here to help. You can tell us anything."

Sammie kept glancing to the doorway. He looked on the verge of hyperventilating. "If word gets out, I won't be safe here."

Dr. Hunker furrowed his brow at Lily.

"Safe from what?" asked Lily.

Sammie scowled. "Aren't you just a student?"

"Aye, but I come from the de Meath family in Ireland. I've spent my life dealing with creatures from the Fae."

"I'm not Fae," he said right away. "Wish I was though. Be a lot easier."

"Mr. Fecit. You came to us delirious and anemic. You were near death from a lack of blood. Did you encounter a creature that tried to take it from you? Vampirism is rare, but there are known vampires in the city of sorcery," said Dr. Hunker.

"To me," said Sammie, leaning forward conspiratorially. "Everyone is a vampire once they find out what my blood can do."

"And that is?"

He sighed painfully, closing his eyes and shaking his head. "Once I tell you, I won't be safe. Please, you can't tell anyone else. On your word."

"Of course," said Dr. Hunker, furrowing his brow. "Confidentiality is part of our job."

"My blood gives great pleasure. Not just great. Drinking it can cause the most mind-melting orgasms known to man. I know it sounds crazy, but it's true."

"And people were taking it from you?" asked Dr. Hunker.

"At first no, I was selling it. But once people became addicted, they couldn't stop and kept coming back to me, demanding more and more and more until I could hardly stand up. I kept moving, but they kept finding me. That's how I ended up in the city of Invictus. I thought someone would be able to help me make it go away. I found this powerful supernatural being on the edge of the city, but once he learned what I was, he tried to keep me. I was only able to get away when he was in the throes of pleasure. Please, you need to make sure no one learns I'm here."

"You have our word," said Dr. Hunker. "We have special protocols for abused spouses that we can place your chart in so it has extra levels of protection."

"How did this come to be?" asked Lily. "It's quite unusual, you know."

"And it'll stay that way," said Sammie. "But if you can fix me somehow, that's all I'm asking. Make the power of my blood go away."

"Could we do a complete blood transfusion?" asked Lily.

"It's a possibility, but I imagine that it would only be temporary. The change might be coming from a part of your body that's creating the blood. We'll have to do some scans and tests to understand this problem."

"Don't take my blood, please. That's how it always starts," pleaded Sammie.

"We'll make sure no one lets it touch them," said Dr. Hunker. "We'll put hazard symbols on the vials. That keeps everyone pretty honest."

"Then you can fix me?"

"Depends on what we find out, but we won't rest until we do," said Dr. Hunker. "You have my word."

Sammie didn't look like he completely believed him, but he nodded tentatively.

Outside the patient's room, Dr. Hunker gave her a script for tests.

"It'll probably be best if you shepherd him through these so he stays calm and doesn't cause more problems."

"Do you have any idea of what kind of shite caused it?" she asked.

"Not a clue." His jaw pulsed. "I assume I can trust you not to get curious with his blood."

"It's not an interest."

He raised an eyebrow. "I heard that."

"You have?"

"It never fails that the incoming students are horny and sex-crazed. You're all stuck with each other for long hours and the pressure builds with nowhere else to take it. It's no surprise that they sleep with those most convenient. So it gets mentioned when one of the students isn't like the others, which isn't rare, but it's usually due to some past trauma. I don't sense that about you, Lily."

"It's not trauma."

"I see you don't want to talk about it, so I'll leave it be."

She grinned. "Unless you want to tell me about your past."

He leaned his head back, laughing. "Trying to win the bet, eh?"

"Thirteen free shifts is a pot of gold around here."

"That it is," he said, handing over the paper. "I'll take care of the upgraded protocols. You take care of our Sammie."

Normally, Lily would have called the phlebotomist, but she didn't want to involve anyone else and the cabinets had been removed from the room after his barricade, so she headed to the supply closet at the end of the hallway. She passed the room where Damon's father was located. To her surprise, he was sitting up in his bed, fiddling with his monitor.

"Mr. Wolfhard, you're awake!"

TEN

Damon had been with Dr. Morrison in the ER during his off-shift time when word came of his father's improving condition. He arrived in time to find Remi and Lily standing by the bed laughing.

"...and that's when we found him sleeping in a ditch in the middle of the forest, sound asleep with a dead deer lying at his feet." His father looked up, blue eyes glittering. "There he is. My boy."

Relief and confusion blasted through Damon, leaving him speechless. He swallowed and approached the bed.

"How did this happen?"

His father raised an eyebrow. "Not happy to see me? Of course, you'd want to know the medical reasons first."

"No, I just—"

"It's fine, Damon," said his father, smiling. Exhaustion haunted his gaze. "It's nice to meet some of your friends. Your witch-friend was the one to find me."

"You shouldn't—"

"That's okay, Damon," said Lily with a smirk. "He's not wrong."

Damon reached for the chart. He read through the recent entries. Dr. Hunker had given his father a new round of alchemical infusions.

"Are you experiencing any trembling or spotty vision? Any feelings of uncontrollable rage?" asked Damon.

Remi gently wedged the chart out of his hands and pushed him next to the bed.

"You can be a healer later."

"I'm feeling much better," said his father.

"Then why are your hands balled into fists in the covers?" said Damon. "I should call Mom. She'll want to talk to you."

His father held up a hand that was curved with rictus into a claw.

"I've been unconscious for months, son, I wouldn't expect to be normal right away. And I've already talked to your mom. She's already headed to the airport."

"You can't leave yet, we don't know what's wrong."

"I'm not leaving. But she wanted to see me while I'm awake. The twins would come but they have a game this weekend."

Damon said nothing. He'd never seen his father looking so weak, gray. While he shouldn't be surprised, given the months of lying in bed, Arthur was a hearty werewolf, which should have protected him from the worst of being bedridden. He was about to ask Remi when Dr. Hunker was coming down, but he noticed the dirt under his father's thick fingernails.

"How did you get that?" he asked, touching his fist lying on the blanket.

"Oh, this? It's something different, an old unrelated problem," said Arthur, holding his fist to his chest.

"You need to tell me."

"Son, it's—"

"No, it's important. What is it?"

Remi caught his desperation and made a nod of understanding. She touched Arthur on the arm.

"Your son's right. You can't count anything out. You'd be surprised how things are connected when it comes to medicine."

"Are you sure?" asked Arthur, bushy eyebrows rising. "It's about the clan and its end."

A shot of adrenaline ran through Damon. "It could be important."

"Help me into a better position," said Arthur. "And something to drink. My throat's already dry from talking so much."

After they adjusted his bed and got him a glass of water, his father began speaking. He started off in a low hoarse voice, but grew stronger as he spoke.

"To understand the clan and its demise, you have to know our history. Our origin. In the olden times, our people were led by King Nuada. He was a just, honorable king who cared deeply about his people. But as things went in those times, other tribes were jealous of King Nuada's empire. They're called the Fomorians, but that's just a name for beings from the land of nightmares, who warred with the Fae realms and were prone to chaos. Many of them made their home in the isles and they were jealous of King Nuada's wealth, and many disparate tribes banded together to assault his people.

"In time, King Nuada realized he was losing. The Fomorians had too many tricks from their home in Mara, their numbers were too great, and they were ruthless, without regard for their own people. He knew his kingdom would be lost if he did not find allies, but there was no one who could help him. So he did the only thing he could to save his people. He went to the Summer King.

"Entering the Fae was easier in those days. As modern portal magic has taught us, the Fae realms were nearer this one in those centuries, which is when many of their kind came over. King Nuada brought with him the required gifts, performed the right rituals, and because he'd been respectful of the Fae, was granted an audience with King Oberon.

"Now, a meeting with the Fae is always fraught with peril. Doubly so in their realm, and the king himself? Just speaking to a being like that could drive one mad. But King Nuada was a hearty soul and had always followed the Old Ways. He managed to persuade King Oberon of his need. The King of Summer granted his request and had his smiths forge him a sword that would drive the Fomorians from his lands. It was called the Shining Sword. Claíomh Ag Lonrú. When drawn, the blade sent fear into the hearts of the Fomorians and banished the shadows in which they hid."

"What did he give in return?" asked Lily. "No Fae, and especially not the King of the Fae, gives a prize like that lightly."

Arthur winked.

"Of course you would know that. I wouldn't be surprised if you could tell me more about my history than I could."

Lily kept a tight-lipped grimace. He hadn't been paying attention, but now that he was aware, he could see she had thoughts lurking behind her green eyes.

"It's not my place to tell your story, Mr. Wolfhard."

"Then I shall continue." He took a long drink of water. "In return for the sword, King Nuada agreed to return to the Fae realm once every month during the full moon to sit at Oberon's side and join the Great Hunt. But not as a man, but as a huge wolf.

"When King Nuada returned with the Shining Sword, he led his people against the Fomorians, routing them from his lands and providing peace and prosperity for his people. And he did as instructed by Oberon, returning to the Fae as a wolf and joining the Great Hunt. This bargain lasted for decades, well into King Nuada's old age. And during this time, the Fomorians plotted to return, but every time he beat them back with his Fae-forged blade.

"Then towards the end of his life, he was tricked by an old man that some claim was a traveling trickster, but I believe was a Fomorian in disguise. He managed to hide the full moon from King Nuada so he missed his appointment with Oberon. Now, had this happened in the first few years, the punishment might have been much worse, but since he'd been a faithful companion to King Oberon on hearth and hunt, leniency was given. King Nuada was banished from Fae and cursed to turn into a wolf when he raged. There are also those that say it wasn't really a curse, but a gift for King Nuada to pass down to his descendants to protect them from the Fomorians."

Remi had been enraptured by Arthur's story, nodding and grinning, but Damon wasn't so excited. He'd heard this tale many times in his youth, though usually with more detail on the battles and embellishment on King Nuada's bravery.

"What does this have to do with the clan?"

"I'm getting to that, son." Arthur turned to Remi. "He was an impatient child, always wanting me to rush to the big, flashy parts, but that's not where the real tale lies. The part that even Damon doesn't know. It would have been his right to learn about it, and the twins later when they came of age, but by the time they grew up, there was no more clan and I didn't want them to long for something that could never exist again."

Damon put his hands on the bed. "What are you talking about?"

"Besides being a tight-knit family of werewolves, some might even call us the original werewolves, we were also the keeper of the Shining Sword. The Claíomh Ag Lonrú. The Greatest of the Four Treasures."

"I can't believe you've never told me this," said Damon, angrily.

He felt his fingernails ache and his teeth loosen in his mouth. Damon pushed the urge to change back down.

"I'd always planned to tell you, but you were so busy with the hospital, and after everything that happened in high school, it seemed like an additional complication. The clan's demise had a big effect on your ability to transform. Those early years were difficult.

"And the sword's existence was a well-kept secret. This was an ancient artifact of immense power and while the world doesn't turn on the existence of magical swords anymore, it could be used for great evil, so it was closely guarded. Every generation, one of our clan was named Keeper. That honor and responsibility fell to my half-brother, Connor Black." Arthur gripped the blanket and glanced out the window, close to tears. "At least until he and everyone else was slaughtered."

"I'm very sorry," said Lily. "But who killed them? And how did you survive?"

"No one knows for certain. If I had to bet, I'd say it was the descendants of those Fomorians, exacting their revenge. But in this day and age, there are more powerful beings than those ancient warriors, and the Shining Sword would be quite the prize. While my heart tells me it was revenge, I think it was probably just simple greed that felled our clan. As for our survival, a falling out between my half-brother and I made me leave the clan compound and move my family to Kansas City."

"Why is that?" asked Lily. "And how does this relate to the dirt under your fingernails?"

"Because my mother, Damon's grandmother, came from another clan of werewolves. A smallish clan known for their oracle abilities. It was why we moved. I won't repeat the entire tale, because I'm tired and my throat is sore, but there was a vision about what came to be and Connor wouldn't listen to the warnings." He held up his hand. "This dirt? It's a product of the visions."

"You've had visions?"

He shrugged. "I don't recall, but I've been unconscious." Arthur took a drink. "I'm tired."

"You should rest," said Damon.

He left with his classmates, taking them to a little alcove away from the nurse's station. They both had questions brimming in their eyes. Secrets revealed brought more questions.

"The Claíomh Ag Lonrú," said Lily, great need in her gaze as she paced. "I can't believe your clan kept that ancient weapon hidden. I knew the story of King Nuada, a slightly different version, but the balls of it were the same."

She was so worked up about her own thoughts that it took her a moment to notice the way Remi was staring at Damon. She glanced between them.

"What? What secrets are you two gobshites hiding now?"

Damon gave her the shortened version of the last two full moons when he'd woken up covered in dirt and blood.

"You have powers of the oracle. Not a surprise, given your lineage," said Lily.

"No, that's not what I'm saying. I don't think those are visions. I tested the blood last time. It matched the type of the people killed. Fomorians. I'm afraid I'm the Full Moon Killer."

"Bloody hell, Damon, that's a lot to spring on a girl. You're serious too. The next one is in a week. Do you have a plan?"

Remi explained that she was going to stay with him and keep him awake with elixirs from Jeb. They'd both had their shifts switched to earlier in the day in the ER, since that night was one of the busier ones of the year.

"As good a plan as any. I'd help, but I'm on rounds with Dr. Hunker that evening."

"It's okay. We should be able to handle it," said Remi.

"But what about the sword?" asked Lily.

"What about it?"

Lily screwed up her face. "You mentioned they were killed with a sharp blade. Why use a sword unless it's sending a message about your history?"

"Oh shit," said Damon, putting both hands on top of his head. "I didn't see that. But why kill fellow Fomorians? That part doesn't make sense."

"No, it doesn't," said Lily. "Like anything to do with the realms, there are always more questions than answers."

A buzz in Damon's pocket had him looking down at the same time as his friends. They checked their phones to find a group message to the class from Dr. Decker. It appeared a patient had arrived who was coughing feathers from a harpy curse. They headed to the other side of the ward, promising to continue the discussion about the killer and Damon's history later.

ELEVEN

The woman in the ER bed wore a soft pink frilly dress and carried a long wand with a star on the end. The metal glowed with silver and gold, occasionally spitting off harmless sparks. She was probably only a few years different than Remi, but she looked frightened and weary, making her appear even younger. Her pupils were so large there was barely an iris.

"Are you sure you didn't drink any strange elixirs?" asked Dr. Decker. "No judgement. It's a night for revelry."

Remi found it hard to look at Dr. Decker. He was wearing a cheap "sexy nurse" outfit found at local costume shops, including a blonde wig and a stuffed bra. The bright rouge on his cheeks made him look like a prostitute after a long night.

"He's a doctor, right?" asked Tooth Fairy.

"A very good one. You have nothing to worry about," said Remi, who'd chosen a pair of cat ears and a tail to wear as her costume along with bright crimson scrubs. A couple of layered enchantments made them move and sway like the real thing, matching her stride and mood.

"Ester said it would make the party more fun, but I keep seeing dead people or sometimes there are people I know, but they have wounds or bruises and look sick."

"Do you have supernatural blood?" asked Dr. Decker.

"My mum always said we had the gift of oracle, but it's never been confirmed."

"Remi. What kind of common party elixirs might have adverse effects with an oracle?"

She closed her eyes and imagined the section of reading related to those who could see glimpses of the future.

"Bay laurel?"

"Is that your final answer?"

"Yeah. Bay laurel. Used by the Oracle of Delphi to help induce visions, but also a common ingredient for hallucinogenic party drugs. Miss Jefferson, did your elixir have a menthol or eucalyptus flavor?"

The girl's eyes brightened. "Yeah. It was sharp, like eating a cough drop. How did you know?"

"I think we've confirmed that you do have oracle blood," said Dr. Decker. "I can give you a simple antidote which should get you back to normal."

The girl exhaled. "Oh, thank Merlin. And thank you, both of you. I don't think I could survive if I had to see any more dead people."

After Dr. Decker sent for the antidote, they returned to the hallway.

"Nice job, Remi. You're starting to come along with all the reading."

Remi stared over Dr. Decker's shoulder. "Thanks, but you know it's really hard to look at you right now."

He chuckled. "I think your shift officially ended forty minutes ago. Feel free to take off. I'm sure you'd like a night of revelry just like our

Tooth Fairy."

"Thanks, Dr. Decker."

"That's Nurse Decker to you."

Remi rolled her eyes and headed towards the Aura Healers dormitory. She had a wicker basket filled with charcuterie waiting in her room. The plan was to hang with Damon for the evening on the roof, then join the rest of the class for a party in the common area when everyone finished their shifts. They'd both sworn off alcohol or drugs of any kind to stay alert.

She passed Boon and Dr. Hunker on the way. Her classmate had painted his face like a lion and wore a fluffy mane while the head of the Supernatural Ward was wearing a bright orangish-red bodysuit beneath his scrubs with illusionary flames coming off his shoulders and the crown of his head. Boon looked like he wanted to lick the doctor.

"What are you, Dr. Hunker?" she asked while sliding by.

"An Efreeti, of course," he said, holding a grin between his teeth.

"Does that mean…?"

He shrugged as he backed away. "It's just a costume. Doesn't have to mean anything. Unless it does!"

A comfortable warmth filled her chest as she made it to her room. Lily was on her way out, dressed in gauzy silks the color of the deep forest. Her hair was covered in sticks and bits of antlers, and a black bar of make-up crossed her eyes.

"You look absolutely frightening."

Lily curled her shoulders forward and hunched her back. "I'll put a curse on you, my pretties!" Then she relaxed. "It's not too much, is it?"

"Dr. Decker will love it."

"I'm in the ER with Dr. Paddock," said Lily with a crazed look.

"Even better!"

"Have a good time tonight," said Lily as she hurried down the hall.

Remi was going to change out of her scrubs, but if she put on the skintight black bodysuit that went with her cat costume Damon might get the wrong idea about the night. It wouldn't be good to get distracted given the stakes.

The night air was chilly enough to create frost at the exhale, forcing Remi to apply a weather enchantment. When a comfortable warmth trickled down her body, she shivered, relieved to be a mage with such abilities. She would have loved to have been able to use magic when she was younger, holed up in a shitty apartment with windows so warped that a cold breeze would leave her buried under blankets with three sets of clothes on.

The Spire was in full Halloween mode. The enormous tower reflected images of ghostly apparitions climbing the glass. The illusions had turned the building into a giant TV screen for the whole city. The second ward was in full swing too. An illusionary black horse with bright red eyes was hauling a carriage made of a rotten pumpkin to the Glitterdome, where the Garbage Kings were putting on their yearly Halloween show.

Remi inhaled, relishing the cool air, and went in search of Damon who should be waiting for her at the picnic table. Halfway across the roof, she heard a wicked crunch from the area around her destination.

"Hello?"

The night tightened around her as she edged forward with the wicker basket hanging on her left forearm, keeping her hands up for the five elements.

"Is that you, Damon?"

A second crunch followed by an agonized moan had her hurrying forward. The picnic table and Adirondack chairs were empty. She peered around the HVAC building, looking for signs of Damon or whoever was making the noise.

"I swear to Merlin, if you're going to jump out and scare me I'm not going to feel bad when I roast your ass with fire."

The hair on the back of her neck went straight up. She spun around, finding no one. The whirl of a helicopter descending onto the landing pad on the opposite side of the roof made hearing difficult. She watched the flashing lights and ER team rush to the side door to remove the patient. The aerial craft would be busy all night.

As the helicopter rose into the air, she heard a crash from the HVAC structure. Remi hurried to the side in time to see a hairy shape leap from the building. She spotted a four-legged beast sprinting across the parking lot.

"Merlin's balls."

Remi threw the basket away from her, spilling cheese across the roof as she ran to the emergency scaffolding, throwing herself down the stairs in hopes of keeping up with Damon in werewolf form. She dodged around an incoming ambulance and ran past a confused family headed into the ER.

Legs pumping, she got winded by the time she hit the far edge of the parking lot. Leaning on her knees, she tried to figure out where Damon had gone, but there was no sign of him on the streets. The only thing she saw was two groups of older kids trick-or-treating.

"Where did you go, Damon?"

The answer came as a high-pitched scream from a block over. Remi ran in that direction, knowing there was a park on the opposite side. She reached the darkened open area as a woman pushing a stroller hurried away while glancing over her shoulder.

"Damon!"

The night absorbed her voice, leaving her suddenly cold despite the enchantment. She crept across the grass under the flickering light of a lamp post going out. Movement in a cluster of trees drew her forward.

"Damon?"

She reached the tall oak, keeping her fire elements at the ready, wishing she was from a Hall that had more defensive magics. A faint scratching came from the other side. She crept around the trunk.

Leaping movement had her blasting flame.

A sputtering gout of fire charred the bark as a squirrel scampered into the night with a singed tail.

Remi broke into laughter at the jump-scare, leaning on her knees and wishing Damon was there to chuckle with her.

"I'm going to kill you when I finally track you down."

The crunch of a leaf had her spinning around in time to see bright fangs leaping from the darkness.

TWELVE

Damon woke in the bushes to the taste of copper in his mouth. He lay naked in the dirt, covered in leaves and a sticky liquid he assumed was blood. A rumble in his stomach brought bile and rage, despite having changed back to human form. He didn't know what time it was, but the air felt colder as if it were well past midnight.

"Where am I?"

As he crawled from the bushes, he realized he was in a park. The architecture of the three-story brownstones suggested he was in the sixth ward, probably near the hospital. He knew of two parks within walking distance.

Using the back of his hand, he wiped the blood from his mouth. It tasted different than the previous times. For one, he never had it in his mouth, and two, he could feel flesh in his teeth. For werewolves, hunting was a personal thing. Many never did, but when he was a youth, his father had taken him into the forests near Kansas City so he could hunt deer. He did every hunting season until he attacked the kid in high school, then his appetite for killing dropped precipitously.

He stomach rumbled again. He felt sick. It'd been so long since he'd tasted flesh and he wasn't used to it. The idea that something had died by his claws made him ill. Especially because he didn't remember. The hunts of his youth were burned into his brain, but this one happened in the throes of vision, which twisted the memory to an unrecognizable lump of regret.

"What's happening to me?" he asked, putting a hand to his forehead.

Getting back to the hospital without being spotted naked and covered in blood was going to be difficult. But that wasn't his biggest concern. He needed to know what he'd killed. He prayed it wasn't someone's pet. He'd never forgive himself.

A foot sticking out of the bushes had his heart in his throat. He'd assumed he'd killed an animal. But a human? He'd never be the same.

Damon rushed to the bushes, pushing through the sharp branches despite his nakedness to find Remi's entire scrubs covered in blood.

"No!"

He threw himself by her side, feeling for the wounds to realize that they weren't as severe as he thought because she was wearing crimson scrubs. But she was bleeding. He found a gash on her left shoulder and another on her side, then checked for a pulse.

At first he couldn't find one, but realized he couldn't hear it above his own beating heart, which was thumping like a drum. Profound relief overcame him when he realized he hadn't killed Remi. Naked and kneeling in the dirt, he cast three successive spells to stabilize her and then two more to close the wounds which clearly he'd caused. The claw marks were unmistakable.

"Remi?"

Her eyes fluttered, which made the enchanted ears bend and move as if they were alive.

"Damon?"

She stared at him through hazy eyes.

"It's me."

"What happened?"

"I think I nearly killed you."

He helped her sit up. She glanced at his naked body, her cheeks flushing.

"You're naked."

"You're observant."

"I'm also an idiot, chasing a werewolf into the dark on a full moon on Halloween."

"We don't change based on the moon."

Remi rubbed her neck, which had been repaired but would need more care at the hospital.

"Says the werewolf who ran off when we were supposed to be having dinner on the roof. What happened?"

He crossed his legs and put his arms over his crotch. "The last thing I remember was staring at the reflection of the moon on the Spire." He squeezed his eyes closed. "I almost killed you."

Remi inspected her shoulder where the scrubs had been torn away.

"I'm going to have a good scar."

"A spell can erase it."

She cocked a smile. "Maybe I want it as a reminder."

"Remi..."

She looked up, realization on her face. "Not about you. My stupidity."

"I appreciate you came after me. What if I had killed someone? I don't know if I can be trusted anymore." His stomach twisted. "I think

I have to leave the school. How can I be a healer if I tried to kill you?"

She put a hand on his calf. The touch was more than reassuring.

"I won't leave your side next full moon, and we'll find a way to counteract the change, or keep you from running away."

He focused on the problem to keep himself from reacting to her soft touch.

"How? I nearly tore your head off."

"Ropes and chains?"

The idea of being tied up by Remi had him warming despite the chilly air. He stood up suddenly and marched away, afraid that she'd see him aroused.

"Did I say something wrong?" she asked.

He stood on the other side of the tree. "No. The exact opposite in fact. I liked what you had to say too much."

"Too much? Oh..."

"We should get back, but I don't want to waltz into the hospital naked."

The sound of rustling was followed by a pair of crimson scrub bottoms being handed around the trunk.

"I don't think they'll fit."

"Wrap them around your midsection like a skirt."

He tried, but he kept sticking through the fabric, making the makeshift clothing useless.

"Let me help."

Damon faced away while she took the scrub bottoms. She whipped the fabric around his front, grabbed the other side, and deftly tied it at his waist.

"Shall we head back?"

He took a long look at her standing in the park, the hem of her crimson top barely covering the top of her pink panties. Damon looked away and took a deep breath.

"Problems?"

Damon squeezed his eyes closed. "Nope. Nothing."

They strolled out of the park together. At least it was later in the night when the streets were empty.

"Did you have any visions?" she asked, keeping her attention faced forward.

He massaged the center of his forehead as if that might free them from the depths of his fear. A few flashes surfaced, but they were fuzzy and vague, nothing like the previous full moons.

"I don't remember." He shook his head as they stepped onto the mostly empty hospital parking lot. "What a shit show. I'm sorry. Worst date ever."

Remi glanced up with a faint smile. "Worst? Nah. Certainly memorable. Besides, now we know something extremely important."

"We do?"

"If someone dies in the city tonight, we know it wasn't you. You might have almost killed me, but we know you were in the park, and not somewhere else in the city."

He contemplated her words as they entered through the ER automatic doors right behind two howlers. Three sets of stretchers produced kids around their age covered in glitter and laughing hysterically. No one gave them a second look as they passed through the busy ER center on their way to the Aura Healers dormitory. When they reached the split in the hallway, Damon didn't know what to do. The awkward pause continued until he held out his hand.

"Thanks for saving my ass tonight."

Remi grasped his hand, held it. "It's a nice ass."

There was a moment he thought she was going to ask to come back to his room. Then she smiled wistfully.

"Try not to kill me on our next date."

THIRTEEN

The patient's room was empty. Lily approached the bed, noticing that the wires went underneath.

"Sammie. It's just me. You can come out."

The brown-haired patient stuck his head over the bed. "I heard two doctors talking about unusual blood. I think they're onto me."

Lily blinked. "It's a hospital. We talk about blood all the time. And this is the Supernatural Ward. Unusual blood is more common than a raven at a burial cairn."

"Are you sure?"

"Positive. Please, Sammie, get back in bed. I have something I want to try."

"It'll fix my blood?"

"Possibly," she said as she closed the door. "It might be painful."

He narrowed his gaze. "I thought you were just a student healer?"

Lily dumped her carryall on the stainless steel tray. Clumps of plant material tumbled out along with markers and a set of electric candles.

"I am, Sammie. But before I came here I treated folks in the Old Country. My family has a long history of helping people. I think I could help you."

He glanced over her shoulder. "Then why isn't Dr. Hunker here?"

Lily sighed. "Because he wouldn't approve of this solution. Drawing from the Veil is not allowed in the hospital, nor is it easy to do because of the wards, but I think we might be able to find a solution. But you have to give me your permission and trust me."

His jaw wavered and his eyes darted around the room. "I don't know."

"You want to be cured?"

"I do."

"Then let me try. I promise you I won't let anything bad happen."

He screwed up his face before nodding. "But you have to tell me what you're doing."

"Are you sure?" she asked as she grabbed the paint markers, locked the door, and pulled down the shades. "Sometimes it's better not to know."

"Just tell me."

Lily knelt on the hard tile and began drawing rune lines in a circle in the center of the floor.

"You know what the Veil is, right?"

"The place where the dead live?"

"Not exactly," she said, carefully marking the runes that would protect Sammie during the ritual. "It's the place between the living and the dead. When someone or something dies, they're dead. Forever. But on the way to eternity, they pass through the Veil. Occasionally folks get stuck, especially if they have something that ties them to this world."

"Ghosts and apparitions."

"Like that," said Lily, nodding. "But *everyone* who heads to eternity leaves traces of themselves, memories, thoughts, sometimes whole parts of their being. I like to think of the Veil as a junkyard for souls. That's not entirely a good metaphor, but it serves my purpose."

"How is this junkyard going to help me?"

"That'll be in the devil's handbook. We'll see if anyone who passed through left anything of value."

Sammie crossed his arms. "You're right. I shouldn't have asked. I don't know if I want to do this now."

Lily finished her rune and looked up at him. "Is there someone or something that you're afraid of?"

He hesitated before answering. "No."

"Then you'll be fine."

She was certain he was lying, but that was part of her purpose in the Veil ritual. Rule number four: listen to your patients. Despite her regular questioning, he'd never admitted to how he ended up with blood that gave pleasure. Testing had proved he wasn't Fae related, despite looking like a satyr.

"Come, Sammie. Sit in the center of the circle. Once this starts, you can't move, or you'll break the protections and things will go pear-shaped quick. No matter what you see or hear. Stay put, you got it?"

He nodded tightly.

Lily pulled out a jar of salt from her pocket and carefully sprinkled it over the outer ring of marker. Then she took the wrapped dried plants, a special mix from her sisters, and placed them in three bowls. She couldn't burn them or the fire alarms would go off, so their existence would have to be enough to bypass the wards that protected the hospital from the Veil. Then she placed the electronic candles on the outside of the circle.

The moment she started speaking, Sammie flinched, but remained in the center, watching her with wide, fearful eyes. Lily quickly lost herself to the ritual, letting the words tumble over her tongue as she applied faez to the incantation.

When the electronic lights dimmed briefly, Sammie let out a squeak. Wind rose outside the circle, tussling her hair around her face, but she didn't let it distract her.

"In the gray lands, where the dead sleep

Lies become truth when the mind weeps

Forge the Veil where souls ache

Bind the past or eternal you will forsake!"

A greenish glow filled the room outside the circle. Lily felt invisible hands tug at her scrubs and hair, but she continued infusing the ritual with her power.

A crimson thread appeared from Sammie's chest. He jumped, but stayed in the circle. The thread snaked away, circling upward and out of sight.

"What is that?"

Lily ignored him as she was navigating them through the trickiest part. Immense pressure collapsed around her as if she were being squeezed, but she persisted. When the temperature dropped and breath turned to mist, she knew she'd caught her prey. A shadowy figure lurked outside of the circle, opposite her. When Sammie turned his head, he cried out and started to scramble from the circle. Lily feared he would break the barrier, but he stopped short, sitting with his back against the edge.

"Not him."

Lily spoke to the apparition. "Who are you?"

The figure pointed his arm towards Sammie, who was trying to shrink inside himself. A painful keening blasted her ears, making her wish she'd put wax in them before the ritual.

"Who are you to Sammie? What answers do you have for him?"

A hiss came out that sounded like words.

"Heeee keeeel meee..."

"I'm sorry, but I had to."

The shadow battered the outside of the circle with electricity. Lily sensed great power in the apparition, which was unusual. She was about to dismiss the Veil being but it turned towards her, eyes like gashes drilling into her.

"Hag!"

The blast knocked her across the room, and she slammed into the nurse cabinet. The air left her lungs and stars filled her vision. She staggered to her knees as the shadowy figure approached, wispy edges of its being drifting through her knees. Images exploded in her mind. Visions of an old house in the countryside, surrounded by vast forest with a single gravel track. A cage in the basement held Sammie as he banged on the bars. Another vision revealed him bound to a table with lines running from his arms.

Lily didn't realize she was choking until she heard Sammie shouting at the apparition. A dense fist of air clogged her throat as she tried to push the figure away, but her corporeal being couldn't affect the shadow. She reached into a pocket, pulling out a silver coin that had been minted in the Roman Empire and owned by a sorcerer of the time. With no words available, she threw the coin through the apparition. It recoiled, giving her a chance to inhale. As soon as cold air filled her lungs, she barked out a dismissal.

"Begone, Daemhan!"

It wasn't the correct counter, but she infused it with enough power to break the apparition's hold on her world, sending it back to the Veil. Lily collapsed onto the floor, catching her breath while Sammie watched from the circle. He had his knees pulled to his chest.

"Are you okay?"

With her face on the floor, she gave him a thumbs-up. Eventually she made it back to her knees, but hesitated to stand, worried she'd pass out.

"How did you make it go away?"

"A coin from Simon Magus, a sorcerer from ancient Rome. It was his lucky coin. He kept it with him for a few centuries, which imbued it with his power. It's somewhere in the Veil now."

The loss of the item was painful, but better than death. She'd traded with the Witch of Mongan Bog to acquire it. Lily dusted herself off.

"Who was that mage? I saw how he kept you in his basement, experimenting on you. Taking your blood."

"Can I come out of the circle? The tile is cold."

She nodded and he climbed back onto the bed, pulling the covers to his chin like a child waiting for a bedtime story.

"He made me. Not like that. I was born human, but he paid my parents for me when I was six. Infused me with a being from another realm, which one I have no idea, and then experimented on me for years. Spells, enchantments, cutting. Taking my blood. It was endless."

"You killed him."

He screwed up his face. "Does that make me bad?"

"No, Sammie. No. He was an awful man, using his power in awful ways. Don't worry. I won't tell anyone. Secret's safe with me."

"Thank you."

"Remember his name?"

Sammie looked away. "No. I don't even know where it was he kept me. After I killed him, the guardians of the house tried to end me. I escaped in the night, ran for a day through the woods, and eventually found a train idling on the tracks. I climbed aboard and spent the next few months traveling around the Midwest, learning about the world from hobos, until I realized the only place that might be able to fix me was the Hundred Halls."

"He was a shite person, Sammie. You don't have to feel bad."

"Can you fix me?"

"I rightly don't know. But I'll try. I promise you that."

"Thank you, Lily." His face was broken with indecision. "If you wanted to sample my blood, I would let you."

"It's okay, Sammie. You don't have to offer that."

He exhaled deeply. She spent the next ten minutes cleaning up the runed circle, including using isopropyl to scrub the marker from the tile. The work gave her time to consider what she'd learned. If Sammie hadn't killed the old mage, she'd probably track him down and do it herself. The gall of some people. She never understood it.

When Lily left his room, she was hot from cleaning and thoughts of magicide. She was marching through the hallways, headed to the cafeteria, when she spotted Morwen headed the opposite way. Still hot from thoughts about the mage that had experimented on Sammie, Lily quickly caught up to Morwen, grabbing the half-pixie's arm and spinning her around.

"You leech. You fooking thief. You're a cancer on this hospital."

Morwen recoiled, clutching a box of vials to her chest.

"Get away from me, Witch."

Two nurses stuck their heads out of patient rooms with concern on their faces, but Lily didn't care.

"You have no business being here. You're not sick, you're a lazy pixie, bottom-feeding on the good will of the nurses and doctors at Golden Willow."

Lily grabbed for the box of vials, but Morwen batted her away. She tried again, knocking it out of her hands. When it hit the tile, glass broke inside. Pinkish liquid leaked from the cracks.

"Look what you did, you bat-crazy Witch!"

Before Lily could say or do anything, she heard a booming voice from behind.

"Lilith de Meath!"

She turned to find Dr. Decker bearing down on her, red-faced and blustery.

"What are you thinking? Have you gone mad?"

"But she's—"

"But nothing. Morwen is a patient. *You* are a healer. Or supposed to be one. Right now you're just a bully. And not a very good one."

"Dr. Decker—"

"Don't Dr. Decker me." He stepped to the side. "Miss Clover, are you okay?"

She was kneeling on the tile with the case open. Two of the twelve vials had cracked, spilling their elixirs.

"It's not too bad."

"I can get you more elixirs if you need them replaced."

"It's okay. This will do for now. I'll be back next week, of course."

Dr. Decker gave her a soft smile, which only enraged Lily.

"You do that. We'll see you next week. And don't worry about cleaning that up. Lily will do that for you."

As Morwen headed the opposite way, Lily threw out her arms. "Am I the only one who sees what's going on?"

"I don't care what you think you see," said Dr. Decker. "Rule number one. Your job isn't to freelance and make decisions about people and situations you don't understand. You're letting your prejudice blind you."

"Prejudice? Me? She's a gobshite half-pixie. You can't trust them!"

Dr. Decker crossed his arms. "This is the last time you will ever utter those words. You'll either listen to my direction, or you'll march out of this hospital and take yourself back to Ireland. Are we clear?"

Lily bit back her words and gave the smallest nod despite her insides being a raging ball of fire.

"Good. Now that we've established the hierarchy here, I'm going to give you more direction. The first is that you are forbidden to ever talk to or interact with Morwen Clover. I don't care if she's about to burn down the hospital. You ignore her. Second, you will find the nearest janitorial closet and grab the appropriate tools to clean up this mess. And third, you will volunteer for ten extra shifts in the alchemy lab for the next month to make up for the valuable elixirs you broke."

"Ten shifts? I barely sleep as it is!"

"Maybe you should have thought of that before you assaulted a patient."

A vast emptiness filled her chest. The lure of her homeland was strong. She stared back at Dr. Decker, while he waited for an answer. Back in Ireland, she could reunite with her sisters, who understood her for who she was.

Maybe she could reconnect with Medb.

But that was the problem.

Medb. Her sisters. Her family. They were relying on her to figure out what was wrong with their Patron. If she left now, they'd never find a cure and wither away to skin and bone. She'd be sentencing them to death. Lily let her chin dip to her chest.

"Yes, Dr. Decker. I accept your punishment."

He narrowed his gaze as if he was detecting obfuscation, but eventually he nodded.

"Good. I hate to lose one of the most promising students in decades."

The anger in his gaze had turned to sympathy. The corners of his eyes rounded before he turned and went the other way. Lily stood in the middle of the hallway with the ashes of her decisions clogging her throat.

FOURTEEN

The elixir Remi drank hours ago was wearing off. She wanted to swing by Jeb's lab for another, but then she'd never be able to sleep when her shift was over in two hours. Remi tried to remember what feeling rested was like. It seemed like forever ago. She wondered what her parents would think if they could see her now. They'd call her a fool, say she was being conned into free labor by the hospital, for very little in return.

But that's where they'd be wrong.

Her year and a half at Golden Willow had taught her that not everything had to be transactional.

Remi checked her list. Dr. Hunker had her checking on patients with acute conditions. She'd just gotten done with Mr. Blackwood in Room 318 who'd been bitten by an unknown spider that they suspected had an infernal origin. His skin was hot and flaking off near the wound. She had to change the packing and reapply the spell every hour.

Her next stop was an older woman named Mrs. Angel. Someone had dropped her off at the ER two days ago with a note that she wasn't welcome anymore. Whatever that meant. Her blood signaled that she was a supernatural being of unknown origins, and every few hours, her skin started turning luminous until it would eject a flash of bright light that destroyed the electronics in the room. They'd removed all the equipment, but Remi would need to use an enchanted silver spigot to drain the light from her flesh. The leftover material was quite remarkable, and Jeb was experimenting with it for new potions.

Remi was halfway to the room when she heard a crash from the opposite direction. She had the inclination to ignore it and get on with the rest of her rounds, but the idea that whatever had happened would only get worse the longer she didn't take care of it was like a geas on her mind.

The door to the small alchemy lab on their floor was open, but no lights were on. It was normally locked to keep the curious and untrained out. Not that it had the same levels of materials as the main laboratory. This one was for quick mixtures and poultices that required relatively normal reagents. No mystdrakon embryos in here.

"Hello?"

The darkness in the room seemed to absorb her voice. She didn't see anyone right away. The light switch didn't work when she clicked it and a simple light spell sputtered upon completion. Remi thought about going to get help, but that would delay her even more and she needed to get back to rounds.

"Anyone? Hello? You're not supposed to be in here."

She toggled the switch a few more times and tried the spell again. Nothing. She knew there were light or magic dampeners used for certain classes of supernaturals like Mrs. Angel, but she couldn't figure out why one of them would be operating in the alchemy lab.

Leaving the door open for maximum illumination, Remi crept into the room. Three steps in the back of her neck bristled with the idea that she was being watched. As she edged around the mixing table, her sneaker crunched glass. A titration flute had been shattered.

She knelt down, finding wetness, but didn't dare stick her finger into the liquid. One of the early rules of the alchemy lab was to treat every material as if it were poison.

A faint click had her spinning around.

Nothing.

The room wasn't big enough to hide anything large. Maybe twenty by twenty with eight marble-topped tables along the walls or in the center. A critter could have snuck in, drawn by a particular material. Jeb had told a story of finding a nest of domovoys in a cabinet, eating the plastic box that had once held a manticore heart. She tried to remember what he said about how he got rid of them, but that had been last year. Besides, it was extremely doubtful that she was having the same issue, and manticore hearts were kept in a chilled freezer in enchanted stasis boxes in the basement.

A whispered voice from behind shocked her into immobility. The fright of realizing she wasn't alone and that it could speak had her slowly turning with her hands up, ready to launch a wind spear.

Before she could turn all the way around, something large and human-shaped disgorged itself from the corner of the ceiling and leapt past her, skittering down the hallway. Remi hurried after, but slipped on the spilled liquid, crashing into a table and slamming her knee on the tile. Bright pain lit up her vision before she managed to scramble into the hallway.

Empty.

"What the…?"

The hallway was a long stretch. She didn't think there was any way something could have gotten down to the corner on either end before she made it out.

"Where did you go?"

Checking the tile, Remi spotted blotches of liquid, the same stuff she'd slipped in. She followed the trail towards the nurses station and past the maintenance closet. It ended at a door four down from the laboratory. When she looked up at the number, she was wrought with confusion.

It was the NOCAT's room.

Remi checked the liquid splotches on the tile. There were faint imprints of toes. Not that she was an expert in tracking. She debated for a while before daring to open the door.

The old woman was lying in her bed. Since she was a NOCAT, no wires were hooked to her. Remi checked the tracks, but they ended one step into the room. She approached the bed, expecting the old woman to spring at her at any moment.

"Hey," said Remi, even though she knew the woman was a NOCAT. She wished she knew her name, but that had been lost years ago in the constant transfers from hospital to hospital.

She pulled back the covers and checked the woman's feet, finding no wetness. Then Remi peeked under the bed. Nothing. None of the cabinets contained anything other than the supplies listed on the front, and the window was locked in the closed position.

"I don't understand," said Remi, pacing before the unconscious woman.

Remi recalled the voice she'd heard in the alchemy lab. The words had been lost to darkness and fear. She couldn't quite remember except that it'd been two short words. *He comes* was the best she could do, but she was certain that wasn't right.

After finishing her investigation of the room, Remi decided that whatever had gotten into the alchemy lab had used the NOCAT's room as a diversion and it'd really headed down the hallway while she was searching.

Remi closed the door behind her. Something had happened that she couldn't quite understand, but it was entirely too late and she was too tired to worry about it anymore. Besides, she had a half dozen patients to check on before she could crawl into her covers for the night.

FIFTEEN

Damon helped his father pull the mask off his mouth since the trembles had returned to his hands. The interior was covered in condensation, which dripped out as it came away from his face.

"Hey, Dad."

Bloodshot eyes stared back. There'd been a good week, back when his mom came to visit, but then he'd gone downhill. The elixirs had stopped working and he spent most of the day asleep. At least he wasn't comatose, but that seemed like thin relief.

"Damon.

The name came out as a wheeze.

"Don't tax yourself. I just wanted to come by and check on you."

It was hard to look at his frail father, but Damon made himself meet his gaze. Patients had to struggle not only with their disease or injury but also with the loss of self, feeling as though something vital had been taken from them. He didn't want to do that to his father. Or any patient. No matter how sick or scared they looked, he had to be their rock. Let them know that they would be okay. Even if they might not.

Arthur put a trembling hand to his forehead. A tuft of graying hair came away. His father was an accountant and rarely showed off his physical prowess, but Damon had watched him lift up an SUV when one of the twins lost a lacrosse ball beneath it.

"We're gonna find a solution," said Damon. "I promise."

His father spoke slowly. "I don't think there's a medical answer."

"What does that mean?"

He broke into a lung-rattling cough. "I don't know. But this isn't just sickness. I can feel it in my bones."

Damon wrapped his hands around his father's forearm. "I'll find a solution. Whatever it takes."

Bloodshot eyes regarded him. "Don't do anything stupid, son. Sometimes life just fails."

"Not here," said Damon. "Not in the hospital. You have to keep fighting."

"I am, but it's a losing battle." He closed his eyes momentarily. "When I dream, I'm trapped in thick, rotting vines, unable to escape. They're choking me. I can't breathe. Even when I'm awake."

The mention of vines had Damon thinking back to his first year with the White Worm, but once he'd been felled, there'd been no more attacks of crazed people. And his father lived in Kansas City, where none of that had happened in the first place. The dream vines had to be pure imagination, a mental image of a physical problem.

A thickset nurse pushed a cart into the room. "It's time for your father's checkup and bath."

"Thanks, Sandra."

The nurse caught him as he left. "He's a sweet old man. We'll take care of him."

Outside the room, Damon leaned against the wall as an emptiness swirled inside. He wanted to become a healer to help people, but he couldn't help his own father. Damon wiped his eyes with the back of his hand and marched back to the dormitory, finding Lily in the common area lying on the ratty couch reading a book while Neko lay on her belly.

"Did something happen?" she asked, sitting up.

"It's my father. He's getting worse."

"They're doing everything they can for him."

"It's not enough."

Lily's forehead knotted. "What are you asking?"

"Are there other ways to heal him?"

"Always, but they often require bargains with beings that don't take credit cards. Are you willing to hurt someone else to save your father?"

He put both hands on his head. "Aren't there artifacts that can heal him? Or other things like that? I'm not suggesting we do something bad, but I at least want to know what my options are."

Lily stroked Neko's white fur while she stared into the distance.

"I know of a healer. She might be able to help us, or point us in the right direction."

Hope bloomed in his chest. "When can we talk to her?"

Lily's lips squeezed flat. "I promise nothing but an introduction. She's of the Old Country. They are fickle beings."

"I'll take my chances. When can we go?"

Lily pulled out her phone, thumbed through it for a moment. "Looks like we're both free in a few days. Remi too. We can head into the city."

"Thank you, Lily."

He was about to leave when he saw a newspaper article stuck to the whiteboard.

"You probably don't want to read that."

Damon ignored her and marched to the board. It was the *Herald of the Halls*, the biggest newspaper in the city. The headline read: Where Wolves? He skimmed the article, which talked about concerns of the Full Moon Killer. An alumnus from Justicars Hall claimed it was a werewolf and he was hunting it down. The second part of the article mentioned a family of werewolves in the Enochian District getting evicted because of concerns.

"Blood and bone."

"People do terrible things when they're afraid."

Damon nodded. He was well aware. After he'd attacked a kid in high school, they'd tried to kick him out. For weeks after it happened, strange vehicles sat near their house, or would follow him to school. His father said to ignore them and they'd go away, which they did eventually, but Damon never forgot the way people looked at him afterwards as if he might change and kill them if they did something wrong.

SIXTEEN

Remi spotted Damon standing by the Golden Willow sign in the parking lot. He was staring into the distance, not paying attention, so she snuck up behind.

"Surprise attack!"

She grabbed him by the hips and he spun around with a fist up.

"Whoa," she said, holding her hands back.

"No. My bad. Sorry."

He rubbed the back of his neck while his jaw pulsed. Lily joined them before she could inquire into his mental state, not that it was difficult. He looked ready to break in half.

The tenth ward was on the opposite side of the city. Lily gave them iron bracelets carved with ancient runes to wear, explaining that once they found their destination, they would need to take them off or insult their host.

"Do you know this person?" asked Remi while they rode on the train.

Lily pursed her lips. "I've met her once."

"Should we be worried?"

"Only if you have ill-intentions."

The November evening was cold. They'd worn heavier coats as not to give away their magical abilities, looking like everyone else with their hands shoved into pockets. Lily led them across several blocks in a searching pattern and ignored any questions about their destination.

When they found themselves in a foggy alleyway and the air was no longer chilly, Lily bade them to remove their iron bands and coats and leave them on the sidewalk. Old-timey gas lamps appeared out of the fog. Lily spoke unintelligible words and the mist parted, revealing an old building with glass bulbs buzzing with the name of the establishment: The Mists.

"Did we go back in time?" Remi asked.

A pale androgynous being with dark spots like a leopard, a Mohawk, and barely any clothes leaned on a balcony, whistling softly.

"Come on up, sweetheart, Tumble will show you the greatest night of your life."

"You're taking us to a brothel?"

The searing look she received from Lily had her shrugging. Both her friends seemed extra on edge.

The red double door opened upon approach. A heavyset woman wrapped in a pink feather boa greeted them inside.

"The Lady will see you in the parlor."

Words like *parlor* had Remi thinking she was in a wealthy home, but it also wasn't like that. She couldn't help but catalog the things she might steal if she were there on other pretenses. It was hard to turn that part of her brain off when she was outside the hospital. She stood by the player piano, plinking on keys until Lily shook her off.

The woman that entered after the doors swung wide made a breath catch in Remi's throat. It wasn't that she was beautiful—she was—but there was something raw and powerful about her that made Remi check the exits. She wore an aquamarine dress covered in shimmering scales that hugged her body as if it were painted on.

"Lady Nimueh," said Lily. "Thank you for allowing me to return."

The woman sniffed. "You left your beast at home."

"I did not want to offend."

"What a strange pair you bring instead." She approached Damon, running her fingernail across his chest. "One of the last of his clan." Lady Nimueh turned towards Remi, which made her stiffen inside. "And you. You stink of mixed loyalties. I've seen your kind. You might be human but you have trickster blood if I've ever seen it."

"Are you a healer?" asked Damon, surging forward. "My father is sick and I don't know how to fix him."

Lady Nimueh ignored him and approached the small bar in the corner. She poured four glasses of amber liquid.

"Come. Let us share a drink before we discuss heavier matters."

Remi snatched her drink away from the bar, stepping as far away from Lady Nimueh as she could without insulting her. Based on Lily's preparations and the strangeness of the building's appearance in the fog, Remi knew she was dealing with a supernatural being. But it was different than the White Worm last year. Her power was more acute. Deeper. Remi imagined that if the Lady soured on their presence, they'd find themselves undone with the snap of a finger.

"It's whiskey, a fine batch from last century," said Lady Nimueh when Damon sniffed the glass. "You need not fear me."

"What is this place?" asked Damon.

Lily rolled her eyes behind him, but Remi wasn't surprised. He was used to charging through every problem.

"A brothel. After we're finished with our discussion, you're welcome to entertain yourself. My treat." Her smile was sour as her gaze flickered towards Remi. "But I see you are already entangled. What troubles you, Damon Wolfhard of the Zev Clan?"

"Something strange ails my father. He shouldn't be sick. Werewolves don't really get ill. But he's dying. I can smell it on him. It's like something is eating him from the inside."

Lady Nimueh sauntered past him, letting her fingers slide across his chest seductively. Remi squeezed her hands into fists. She didn't like the way the woman was messing with Damon, who was clearly hurting. It felt like a cat toying with an injured mouse.

"You don't think it might have to do with the failure of your clan to protect its charge?"

Damon spun on his heel. "What do you know of that?"

"I come from a line of guardians myself. I know the stink of failure," she sneered.

"Leave him alone!"

Remi stepped forward, eliciting a sharp laugh from Lady Nimueh. The smirk on her lips suggested that the comment had been intended to invoke her reaction.

"Don't worry," said Lady Nimueh. "I don't know what it is you couldn't protect, but I know that it's a piece of your father's illness."

"Is it the kalkatai?" asked Lily.

Lady Nimueh stared at nothing for a moment. "A component of the Great Corruption, but not the root cause. No, this issue is more personal. Familial."

"Does it have something to do with who killed my clan? Or the sword?"

"You know something of it, don't you?" said Lady Nimueh.

Damon glanced in her direction. "No."

"Don't lie to me in my own house."

"I'm not lying."

"Then you're not being truthful with yourself."

Remi stepped forward. "Can you help him or not?"

"Him or his father?"

"Same thing."

Lady Nimueh smirked. "Not always." She stood behind Damon and put a hand on his shoulder. "If you want an answer you're going to have to give me access."

"Access to what?"

"Everything. And it will hurt."

Damon lifted his chin. "I'm not afraid of pain."

"Everyone has their limits."

Damon looked to Lily. "Will I be safe?"

The Irish witch lifted her shoulders. "There's no such thing as safe when it comes to the Old Magics."

"Fine," said Damon. "I'll give you access."

Lady Nimueh circled around Damon until she was facing him from only a few inches away. She was nearly as tall as him, reaching out and curling her hand around his neck, pulling him towards her until she pressed her mouth against his.

Remi almost said something but Lily shook her off, which brought heat to her cheeks. She wanted to look away, but also, not. Damon opened his eyes and briefly glanced in her direction, but then shut them. She watched as he kissed Lady Nimueh. The initial resistance disappeared and he leaned into her embrace. Remi sensed Lady Nimueh was performing as she ground her hips into Damon's. Remi kept watching for signs of pain, but she saw nothing that was hurting him. In fact, he looked like he was enjoying himself entirely too much, which made her inexplicably angry.

"That's enough!" said Remi. "There was no pain. This is a farce."

Lady Nimueh pulled away, wiping her mouth with the back of her hand while serving a mischievous grin.

"I didn't say he'd be the one hurt."

Damon swallowed and avoided her gaze. "Did you learn anything?"

Lady Nimueh returned to her glass of whiskey and downed the remainder of the amber liquid. She exhaled with pleasure and let her tongue circle around her lips and teeth.

"He's a magnificent kisser."

"About the family curse."

Lady Nimueh raised an eyebrow. "Whoever said it was a curse?"

"Whatever."

She turned towards Damon. "Your father hasn't been completely honest with you. And the fate of your clan isn't over. In fact, there may be an opportunity for redemption. Or the final end."

"What do you mean?"

Lady Nimueh shrugged as she poured herself a second glass and threw it back. "I'd forgotten how heady one of King Nuada's brood was. What was I saying?"

"You were telling him what's wrong," said Remi.

"Oh yes. I see threads leading from you into the city. One of them is to your father, and others lead to the rest of your family, but there are even more in the city. This is your crucible. This is the test that decides your clan's fate."

"More in the city? What are you saying?"

"No one's fate is theirs alone."

"Is this why I'm having visions? Waking up with dirt under my fingernails and blood on my chest?"

Lady Nimueh arched an eyebrow. "Finally, he utters the truth. As for those visions, I cannot say the reason for their existence, but they're another sign of the tangled web in which you're ensnared."

"You've said a lot but nothing about a cure," said Remi.

The ancient being let her mouth shift to the side. "What ails him and his family is beyond a simple cure. While there are artifacts that might fix him, most of them are lost to time, or held by those who would never let you even know they had them. Nor would you have the power to take them. For now."

Her gaze flickered to Remi, spiking fear in her heart, but then the Lady looked back to Damon.

Rage built in Remi's chest until she couldn't hold back. "So you can't help. You're as useless as Dr. Paddock."

Lady Nimueh held out her hand and suddenly Remi felt like she couldn't breathe. It was like an iron fist had grabbed her heart.

"A trickster with a loose tongue is a liability. I should end her now and save you both the trouble of her friendship."

"No!" said Damon and Lily at the same time.

Spots formed in Remi's vision as she fought against the invisible force.

"She's our friend," said Lily. "She's the one that ended the White Worm last year."

Lady Nimueh checked to the side and then let her hand unclench. Remi fell to the ground, dizzy and breathing heavily. Damon helped her to her feet, holding her steady. She clutched his side, even as she was feeling better.

"A trickster always betrays," said Lady Nimueh.

"She's not a trickster," said Lily.

"Very well then. If you vouch for her." Lady Nimueh plucked a hair from her head, then pulled a needle from her pocket and wrapped the strand around it. "This should help you with your father's illness. For now. It will keep him from getting much worse, but its power will only last so long."

"How long?"

Lady Nimueh frowned. "Weeks. No longer than a few months. If you want a longer-lasting salve, then you should seek out a Caladrius. The snow-white bird's down can be mixed with a changeling's blood for a potent elixir." She paused. "Do not dawdle. Time is of the essence."

Damon accepted the gift, putting it in his wallet. "Thank you."

Remi reached for the whiskey on the table to clear her head, but as her fingertips brushed the glass, she found herself standing in the middle of the street, surrounded by mist.

"What the…?"

"It's her way," said Lily, gesturing towards the coats and iron bands lying against the dirty brick wall.

"Who was that?" asked Remi, turning on her friend.

Lily looked away. "A maid of the mist."

"I don't know what that is," said Remi.

Damon spoke behind her. "From Merlin's time. Or that's what the myths say."

Remi shook her head. Magic she could understand, but when people talked about old stories as if they were real it made her head swim. They headed towards the train station a few blocks away.

"I didn't like her."

"She did try to kill you," said Damon.

Lily scoffed. "If she'd wanted to kill you, you'd be dead. That was something else."

"What?"

Lily shrugged. "The Old Ones like to play games. When they've been alive long enough, they get bored. It makes them dangerous, but also a great source of help because they have nothing better to do."

"What's a Caladrius?" asked Damon.

"A bird that has great healing powers," said Lily. "But that's made them extremely valuable, and those that keep them, they don't like to share."

Remi suspected Lily had more experience with the bird than she was letting on. The alleyway led them to a darkened street with a few flickering light posts scattering shadows.

"Which way was the station?" asked Damon. "I'm all turned around."

Remi lifted her arm, but the hairs on the back of her neck rose before she could finish the gesture. She glanced in all directions.

"You okay?" asked Lily.

Remi put a hand over the pendant under her shirt. "Something's wrong. Do you think the Lady changed her mind and is coming to kill me?"

"I doubt it," said Lily, cocking her mouth to the side. "But anything's possible."

"Hey—"

The sharpness of Damon's word had Remi checking back to him to see him staring at the top of a four-story apartment building on the opposite side of the street. A hulking dark figure was outlined by the city lights.

"I don't think it's the Lady," said Remi.

Before anyone could say another word, the figure leapt from the building. The height would have killed a normal person, but the shadowy figure landed in a crouch and revealed a sword from beneath its cloak.

SEVENTEEN

The night had been weird even before the shadowy figure showed up. Damon's thoughts were bouncing between the kiss from Lady Nimueh, the way Remi had looked at him while he was being kissed, and the comments about his clan. It was too much to think about already. The appearance of the Full Moon Killer—it had to be him with a sword, right?—had his brain short-circuiting.

"Run!"

There were three of them and only one of him, but Damon knew instinctively they were outclassed. His friends didn't argue, running with him down the city sidewalk as the figure with the sword pursued.

"Which way is the station?"

"The other way," said Remi.

"We'll have to circle around somehow," said Damon.

"I think the road is keen on him. We're not gonna make it that far," said Lily.

Sure enough, the Full Moon Killer closed half the distance in a short span. Damon tried to access his rage, but he was too confused from earlier to completely let it change him. He managed to extend his fingernails into talons.

"This way," said Lily, surging ahead with her rainbow hair streaming behind. She led them down an alleyway and stopped halfway.

Damon slowed but she said, "Keep going."

He continued running with Remi as their Irish friend spoke in low tones. When she was finished, a glistening web of electricity filled the alley, blocking the path behind them. She caught up to them.

"If that doesn't hold 'em we're deep in a bog without a rope," said Lily.

The shadowy figure reached the barrier of crackling electricity, took one look at it, and pulled out his sword. The moment he swiped through the warding, the sparks exploded into light and disappeared, leaving the way open.

"Not good," said Lily.

Damon spied a heavy blue door and slammed his shoulder through it, leading them into a big space covered in swirling carpet. The moment they stepped away from the door, automatic lights popped on. But not just any illumination. Black lights revealed an arcade filled with booths and machines glowing with neon intensity.

An apparition appeared before them. A woman with pigtails and a cut-off half-shirt. Damon swiped through her before he realized it was benign.

"Welcome to the Arcade Parade! Tokens can be purchased at any kiosk, but remember you must be able to access faez to initiate the games. Have fun!"

"You've got to be bloody kidding me," muttered Lily.

The black light revealed large paw prints across her clothes. Damon checked behind them when they heard a heavy thump.

"Go on," said Damon. "He's my family's problem. I'll deal with it so you can get away."

"You're an idiot, Damon. He'll cut you in two," said Remi. "Let's find our way out of here."

The door exploded behind them. The hulking figure stepped through the shards of wood. Damon couldn't see his pursuer's face beneath the contours of a black beard, but he sensed the menacing hatred. Was this the person who'd killed his clan? And now he was tying up loose ends?

"I'm the one you want," said Damon, trying to fill himself with rage. "Let my friends go."

"Damon, look," said Remi by his side.

The sword in his hand was glowing from within. It pulsed with eldritch energy. The Shining Sword. Claíomh Ag Lonrú. Seeing his family's heirloom in the hands of the killer brought his rage to the surface.

"You bastard!"

Remi pulled on his arm. "Come on!"

Damon's muscles rippled, but he couldn't get them to change. He needed his werewolf strength. How could this be happening now when he most needed it?

"Over here," said Lily.

She was standing before an arcade machine handing out fist-sized balls.

"Imbue them with faez before you throw them."

Damon was still reeling from his body being mid-change as his friends lobbed the balls at the Full Moon Killer. The arcade devices rippled with colors, but their pursuer sliced them in half out of the air. Their destruction caused crackles of multihued energy, but otherwise barely slowed him.

"Where's the damn exit?" said Remi, glancing around. "Shit, it's over there."

Damon saw where she was pointing. It was on the far side of the Full Moon Killer. He approached with his arms wide as if he were going to swallow the three of them whole.

"What the hell," said Remi, beside him, but he was too focused on the Killer to see what she was referencing.

"I'm sorry—"

Damon leapt forward, hoping to catch their pursuer off guard. But as he flew through the air, claws extended, he realized he was going to be too slow. The Killer lifted his sword at a strange angle, but even the awkward pose would be enough to cut him in half. Damon hoped his friends would make it away because of his sacrifice.

A shoulder knocked Damon off his feet. He tumbled into a big arcade machine called Five Element Duel, which triggered an announcement.

"Step right up, little mage! Are you quick enough to defeat Black Byron and his devilish minions!"

Damon climbed to his feet as the arcade flashed with multicolored lights. He thought he was seeing double as he saw two similarly sized figures standing in the middle of the arcade. Each held an enormous sword. Weapons clashed, sending a spray of sparks across the swirling carpet. The only way Damon could identify the original attacker was the glow of his sword, which was increasing in brightness.

"Come on," said Remi, dragging him away.

He hesitated, wanting to see the fight, but Remi tugged harder. As the two figures battled in the middle of the blacklighted arcade with multicolored flashes briefly illuminating their forms, Damon ducked through the open door and onto the street.

Lily waved down a taxi that was heading past. It slowed, and they threw themselves into the back.

"Go, go!" said Lily.

"Where to?" asked the taxi driver, checking over his shoulder.

"Just go. Golden Willow. Hurry."

The driver shrugged. He hadn't put the vehicle in motion yet. "Someone pregnant back there?"

The door exploded onto the street, sending glass across the sidewalk. The original attacker with the glowing sword landed not far from the taxi. The driver slammed down the gas pedal as they spun into the street, tires squealing and sending up smoke.

Damon checked behind to see the Full Moon Killer take one last look at them before sprinting the opposite way in a loping gait. Moments later, the second sword-wielder appeared on the sidewalk, but the taxi turned before he could see where he went.

The taxi continued speeding down the street. Lily put a privacy enchantment on the back seat.

"Branch and bough, what is going on?" asked Lily. "I didn't think there were two Full Moon Killers."

Damon's heart pounded triple time. "Neither did I."

"That was the sword, right?" asked Remi, looking at something in her hand.

"Yeah. I think," said Damon. "What's that?"

"A piece of cloth that came from the second guy. It flew off when the sword cut it."

"Hold onto that." He looked out the window at the passing lights. "The Full Moon Killer must be who murdered my clan."

"Then who was the second one?"

"I don't have the foggiest idea," said Damon, even as his heart told him something about them was familiar. "But now I know that's who I'm seeing through my visions."

EIGHTEEN

A knock startled Remi as she stared out the window at the silvery moon hanging over the Spire at the center of the city. Damon entered when she called. He was still wearing his green scrubs and his dark hair was messy. He glanced to the eyebolts embedded in the concrete wall.

"How'd you manage that?"

"A small bribe to the head of maintenance," said Remi, shrugging.

"Whose room is this anyway?"

Remi gestured for Damon to sit on the bed with his back against the wall.

"A first year who scrubbed out after two months and his roommate moved in with someone else. No one was using the space, so I appropriated it."

Damon cocked his mouth to the side. "And this is going to hold me?"

She lifted the chain links, rattling them. "I had Lily put some runes on them. Should be strong enough, even if you decide to change."

He settled on the bed, edging backwards until his head was against the wall.

"I can't believe I'm letting you do this."

"You're welcome to run naked through the park again if you choose."

Damon blushed and glanced away.

She'd never noticed before but he had a boyish quality beneath his square jaw and piercing gaze. She'd always felt like she'd had to grow up at an early age. Damon hadn't yet completed that transition. Or maybe he had and she wasn't giving him enough credit.

"Hold out your wrist."

While he watched patiently, she hooked the manacle to his arm.

"The lining is a nice touch."

"The first version hurt. Lily suggested the fur."

He snorted softly. "I shudder to think why she knows about softening manacles. It certainly ain't sex."

Remi furrowed her forehead. "You suggesting she's sacrificing people?"

"No, no. That's not what I mean." He screwed up his face. "I actually don't know what I mean. But I know after a year and a half I still don't really understand her. She knows more magic than half the staff and keeps a supernatural creature in her hair."

"Which is why it's good she's on our side, even if I don't have the slightest clue who Medb is."

"And what side are we?" asked Damon with a smirk as she crawled over his thighs and hooked the second manacle to his other wrist.

Remi paused. "I don't know. The side of Golden Willow? You know, sometimes I feel like we're in the wrong place." She tightened the chain. "That's not too tight, is it?"

"Depends on what you're planning tonight," he said, letting his tongue rest on his bottom teeth.

Remi yanked the chain, eliminating the slack and making his arm retract to the wall. She settled cross-legged next to him. Close enough she could feel the heat of his body and smell the peppermint on his breath.

"I was thinking how we did more good last year eliminating the White Worm than we did in the ER."

"What are you talking about? We did tons of good." A grin rose to his lips. "I think Gerald Lyons had a very positive experience from his time in the hospital."

"Ha," she said, feeling warmth rise to her cheeks. She'd forgotten about the lead singer from the Krakens, even if the nurses occasionally called her Half-Pint.

"You know he put you in a song?"

"What? Really?" She punched him lightly in the ribs. "Are you messing with me?"

"No." He tilted his head. "I thought you knew. It came out last month."

She recoiled, thinking about the increased use of her nickname recently. "Is it good? Or do I need to wear a bag over my head in shame?"

"And deprive the world of your wit and good looks?"

"I can still talk through a bag." She punched him again. "What are the lyrics?"

He rolled his eyes back in thought. "I think it goes like...she got me going halfway, heartache, all day. Charms and whips, love and hips, with a spell I dance, that half-pint hex made me blow my chance."

"Wow."

Remi rubbed her temples. "I'm not sure what to think. What's the song called?"

"'Give a Load of This.'"

"Don't you mean, Get a Load?"

His grin split his face wide. "Nope."

Remi pulled out her phone. "Do I want to hear it?"

When she looked up, his expression had lost the playful quality. She didn't see it at first until she realized he was jealous. Remi tossed the phone away.

"I'll listen to it later." Sensing his discomfort, she asked, "Any more thoughts about the other night? Any ideas who the second swordsman was?"

He looked out the window and sighed. "No idea, but I feel like I should know. There was something familiar about the first one, but I can't put my finger on it."

"No more visions?"

"Not yet." He tugged on the chains. "I think I'd like to have one now. Maybe I could figure out what's going on without worry that it's me doing the killing."

"It's good that your father's doing better."

He nodded. "I wish we could find a Caladrius bird, but when I asked Dr. Decker about them, he just laughed and walked away. I guess they're hard to come by. Even a tuft of down is worth a fortune."

"At least the hair from Lady Nimueh stabilized your father for the time being. I wish it was a solution, but maybe it'll give us enough time to find one. If you want, I could check with an old friend."

Mention of the owner of the Mists had Damon blushing.

"That would be great." He smiled but she sensed his apprehension. "About that night. I wouldn't have, you know, if it weren't for needing her help."

"Kissed her?"

His chin dipped towards his chest. "Yeah."

"Why is that?" she asked, already knowing the answer.

"Remi..."

"Isn't this all rather backwards?"

He hunched his forehead.

"I've got you tied up and I've seen you naked already but we haven't kissed."

His eyes grew wide. "Is that something you want to do?"

"I don't know," she said as she brushed his thigh with her hand. "Do you?"

"Remi..."

"You keep saying my name, but not what you want."

"You know you're infuriating," he said.

She moved her hand to rest on his thigh, which made him breathe deeper. "I've been told that before."

"I bet you have."

"When I was in Utica, the guards took bets on how many times I'd get beat up for my mouth."

"And what was the result?"

"Only once. At the end. And it was to keep my friends safe."

"Remi."

"Yeah?"

"Could you scratch my neck?" he asked, lifting his chin. "Right above the shirt."

She leaned forward, using her short nails to scratch his flesh. He made cooing noises with his eyes closed. Leaning forward, she could smell his heady scent. It reminded her of the forest. She could imagine him loping through the trees on the hunt, naked and on all fours.

"Ouch."

He recoiled away. She checked her nails to see she'd drawn blood.

"Sorry."

"Why are you breathing heavy?"

"I am?"

Remi could feel her heart pounding in her chest. Her thighs were resting against his and she was only a few inches from his face. Using her thumb, Remi wiped the crimson bead from his neck. Before she could lose her nerve, Remi jammed her mouth against his. Lips mashed together as she climbed atop him, straddling his legs and cupping her hands around his neck. She pulled away briefly, relishing the taste of his lips on her tongue.

"This is fun."

He nodded, eyes wide and breathing heavily. "Do you think it'd be safe to unchain me?"

Using both palms, she pushed him against the wall. "Nope. I learned my lesson at our last date when you tried to kill me."

Remi kissed him again. She ground her hips into his crotch, which had become quite aroused. Before long, the grinding became rocking as she ran her hands across his muscled chest.

"You know, I really want to—"

He nodded enthusiastically. "I do too."

"It's a good thing I didn't bind your legs."

"Yeah, but one problem..."

Remi cursed under her breath. "Right. I didn't think about that either."

"So this wasn't planned?"

She chuckled. "Not consciously." Remi climbed off. "Do you have any condoms in your room?"

"Bottom left drawer."

As she started leaving the room, he said, "My key is in my pocket."

"Why would I need that?"

Remi jogged to the stairwell and ran up to their floor, thinking about how much she'd wanted this night to happen. She had her picks out, but the door was unlocked. Remi didn't think it was unusual until she stepped into his room.

A stuffed wolf hung from a noose suspended by the ceiling fan. The belly of the furry animal had been cut open and red paint splashed around the stuffing. She examined it to find a tag from the gift shop still hanging from a paw.

Remi thought long and hard about hiding the evidence and returning to Damon with plans of telling him afterwards, but it wasn't the first sign of a rising anger towards therianthropes. There'd been attacks in the city. Nothing fatal, but enough to let Damon know that people could be uneasy around him.

She carried the rope and stuffed wolf down to the other room where she'd left him tied up. His grin died the moment she stepped into the room.

"I'm sorry."

"So am I."

"Does this mean…?"

She exhaled. "Not forever."

"Right."

Remi crawled onto the bed and lay in the crook of his arm with her hand resting on his thigh.

"It's gonna be a long night," she sighed.

"Better than being on call."

She glanced up at his smile. "True."

They sat in quiet contemplation for a long time. Remi wished she could rekindle their earlier interactions, but the way the silver light of the moon was shining through the window and rhythm of his breathing had her feeling more relaxed than she'd been in years.

But eventually his nearness reawakened her desire.

"Hey Damon, I forgot to mention..."

She reached into her back pocket and tossed the packet of condoms on the bed. Remi glanced up, expecting to see his wide-eyed stare, but was met with a snort, followed by a snoring exhale.

Damon was fast asleep. She poked him twice, but he didn't move. They'd both been on double shifts for weeks. It was unsurprising that he'd fallen asleep.

"Oh well."

Remi cuddled against his side and let her eyes drift closed.

She slept like a rock, but woke when the pink light of morning peeked into the room. Damon was still asleep, his head lolling to the side, no sign of change or vision on him. She carefully unhooked the chains from the wall and left the key for the manacle on the bed for when he awoke.

Remi checked the time. Her shift started in a half hour. Enough time for a shower and breakfast before another fourteen hours in the Supernatural Ward. She kissed him on the forehead and crept out of the room without waking him.

NINETEEN

Half the second-year class was crowded around the table in the corner of the cafeteria. The energy was palpable. Lily saw them like an overeager pack of puppies, falling over each other in all ways. It was the opposite of her earlier life with her sisters. The Elders claimed that because they were linked to Medb, knowledge of the past was carried through them unbroken. They'd always called her an old soul, and while she'd felt like she knew the answer even when she had no reason, she never felt as wise or ancient as they liked to joke with her. But their reverence was the only reason that they'd allowed her to leave the family and come to the Halls. They'd thought she was a Wise Old One in the body of a youngster, making a sacrifice that no one else could. While really she was as scared and confused as the rest of them. She'd known there were others as talented to find a fix for Medb's illness, but they were too old and wouldn't survive the change of patrons. She'd been young and strong enough to manage both.

"You'll have to loosen your throat and shove it down without swallowing," said Boon with his hand on the platter cover at the center of the table.

"You have an advantage on us then," said Sasha.

Remi flicked her nail against the stainless steel with a sour expression on her lips.

"You really eat these things?"

"They're a delicacy in Krakatow. Ash gave them as a thank you to our class for being of great help to her."

"Is that a euphemism?" asked Damon.

"You should know," said Ethan, grinning.

Damon blushed and glanced at Remi, who was pretending like she hadn't heard.

"Bets on who finishes theirs first?" asked Sasha.

"It's gotta be Boon, right," said Ethan.

"I think it's Lily," said Sasha.

Lily hadn't really been paying attention, but checked back to the others.

"Me?"

Sasha cocked a grin. "Because you more than anyone else here can stomach the weird and gross things we do on a regular basis. I saw you put your forearm completely up that changeling's ass to unclog his mucus gland."

"I have small hands."

"No more chatter. We don't want to keep the glow grubs waiting," said Boon. "Everyone throw your money in. Winner takes all."

Crumpled bills piled on the nearby table. The rest of the cafeteria was looking on with faint amusement.

"One, two, three!"

When the lid came off, Lily snatched a glow grub from the platter.

The little wiggly creature was the size of a finger with spots along the back that shone like a lightning bug in summer. She threw the grub into her mouth, ignoring the way it tried to escape past her teeth, and used her tongue to jam it into her throat, forcing a swallow. Leaning her neck back let the grub slide down until it passed her esophagus.

"Done."

The others were struggling with their meals. But Lily barely noticed as a heat rose from her belly, not unlike eating spicy food. The warmth was pleasant and brought a tingle to her face and lips.

The others finished long after. Damon was second, which she assumed came from his ability to hunt as a wolf and consume the flesh of his kills.

"That was delicious," she said, offering a belch as everyone patted her on the back.

"Ah crap, I have to get back to Dr. Hunk," said Boon as he handed the wad of cash to Lily.

She shoved it in her carryall and headed to her room, as she had a few hours before her next shift. The warmth of the glow grub made her feel content, which helped stiffen her mood when she spotted Morwen leaving the elevator towards the side exit.

Rest would have been the more sensible next step, but she found herself following Morwen out of the building. The half-pixie had aqua-blue hair and a set of white headphones, which made her easy to pick out as she crossed the parking lot, headed towards the train station.

Lily hesitated before following, keeping the larger vehicles between them. While she knew where Morwen was headed, she had to arrive in time to get on the same train if she wanted to know what she was up to. Morwen's head bobbed with the music, making her easy to follow.

Swiping her card at the entrance, Lily followed Morwen to the station as the train pulled in. She got into the car behind Morwen, sitting by the door so she could see when she left.

The train was headed counterclockwise around the city, which was built like a wheel with the Spire at the center like a hub. They passed through the fifth ward. Lily grew distracted by the huge building shaped like a stone flower, currently opening at a glacial pace. The Acoustic Architectural Institute of Design's building was one of the most interesting in the city. The only one Lily found more fascinating was Coterie of Mages, which was a giant obsidian obelisk.

The thirteenth was after the fifth. Most of the ward had been reclaimed by wild parks, the remaining buildings falling into disrepair. Lily suspected there was more to the ward than appeared, because otherwise developers would have moved in long ago.

The twelfth was old industrial complexes that were no longer in use with occasional pockets of housing. Lily kept checking on Morwen to make sure she hadn't left. The half-pixie climbed to her feet as they entered the Enochian District in the eleventh ward, which had become highly gentrified after the Event.

Lily waited until Morwen was off and the train was about to close its doors before slipping out. She followed her through the streets, passing high-end restaurants with valet parking and then old rotted-out buildings until Morwen headed into a club called the Hollow Nine. Bright crimson neon signs glowed onto the street.

A little suspicious in her hospital scrubs, Lily put a Look Away enchantment on herself. It wouldn't work on Morwen but would keep normal folk from noticing her. Despite the early afternoon, the club was relatively packed. In the back, men and women danced half-naked on stages, revolving around poles and rubbing themselves on customers for money. Lily spotted a woman with leopard spots and a tail bending over for a group of businessmen on the nearest stage.

"Twenty dollars for entry," said the bouncer. "Remember, no touching the trogs unless they touch you."

Lily shoved a bill in his hand and hurried to a corner where she had a good view of the place. The bouncer's slur confirmed this was a place where regular humans could interact with non-humans for money.

It took a moment to spot Morwen, who had joined a group at the end of the bar. They were patting her on the back as they took the case of elixirs. Lily spotted the person in charge as the others gave him space. He was tall and handsome. Surprisingly youthful. Dirty blond hair fell into his face as he spoke to Morwen quietly. After the half-pixie finished talking to their leader, she sat in a nearby booth next to a girl who had the same nut-brown skin. A younger sister probably.

That it was a strip club for non-humans was clear, but how Morwen and her sister fit into the equation was a mystery. One thing Lily was sure of—her visits to the hospital had criminal intent.

Morwen and her sister headed into the back, disappearing behind a door protected by a bouncer. The case of elixirs was taken to a separate door that led to a basement. Lily thought about trying to follow, but checked the time. With a sigh, she headed out of the Hollow Nine and back to the train station. Her beef with the half-pixie would have to wait.

TWENTY

Damon tapped on the door with his knuckles. After a muffled answer, he opened it to find Remi cross-legged on the bed reading a tome with headphones on. She was nodding along to the silent beat.

"Hey."

"Hey," she responded, pulling the headphones down around her neck.

"Is that the Kraken song?"

Remi quickly switched off her phone as she glanced away. "I haven't gotten around to listening to it yet."

Damon was certain of what he'd heard, but he wasn't going to press her because he needed her help.

"You don't have another shift until late tonight?"

"That's right."

She tilted her head.

"The other night. On the full moon. You mentioned you could check with an old friend about the Caladrius bird."

Remi rubbed the back of her neck. "Yeah. A long shot, but I could."

"Can we go ask your friend now?"

She checked her tome and drummed her fingers on the pages.

"Please, Remi. I know it's unlikely, but my father is sliding back into unconsciousness. I just left him. He barely acknowledged I was even in the room."

The tome slammed with emphasis. "Alright. Let me grab my things."

The ride to the eleventh ward was made in relative silence. Not that Damon didn't want to talk to Remi, but the crowded trains for the busy holiday season left them crammed against the door until it was time to leave.

"That was insane," said Damon as they strolled into the district. "I bet the pickpockets are out in force."

When she glanced away, he stopped and crossed his arms. "Remi."

"I didn't keep anything. I just took a few watches and rings and then slipped them back in their coat pockets. They'll be confused but still in possession of their things and hopefully more aware next time."

Damon wasn't sure he believed her but wasn't going to press things when he needed her help.

She led him to the edge of the district, away from the high-end restaurants where the seedier clientele visited. They passed a bar called the Hollow Nine before finally reaching the Charm & Hammer.

The music inside instantly gave him a headache. When the bartender saw Remi, he started shaking his head, but she flipped him off and kept walking.

"What was that about?"

"He's an asshole."

"I take it that wasn't Warnock?"

Remi led them into a dim hallway. After rattling a locked door, she opened it, revealing an empty desk.

"Must be downstairs."

"Basement?"

The smirk told him that it was going to be more interesting than that. She walked to the end of the hallway. A series of taps on a hidden compartment had the door sliding wide.

"Wild."

She led through a darkened stairway. The thump of music had him curious, which lasted until the door swung wide, revealing an office space with a one-way mirror looking out at the colorful lights cascading across a packed dance floor. A few feet from the mirror, a customer was snorting pink powders. When he coughed, smoke in the shape of a dragon burst from his lips, roared fire, and dissipated into the air.

"I never should have showed you that entrance."

Damon startled.

The man behind the ebony desk had a presence, even before he gained his feet. Damon found himself face-to-face with a towering figure of muscle. Ice-blue eyes shot out from his dark umber skin beneath a head of graying dreadlocks.

"I'm Damon."

The handshake was like grasping a piece of iron. "Warnock."

He softened as he turned to Remi, leaning down to give her a warm embrace.

"One of your classmates?"

Remi nodded.

"How could you tell?" asked Damon, checking to see if he was wearing scrubs, but he'd changed into street clothes.

"You smell like bleach and sterilized tools." Warnock gestured towards a pair of leather couches. "Care for a drink?"

Damon started to say no, but Remi answered for both of them.

"We'd love one. Sorry to spring this visit on you."

"You wouldn't be Greta and Archer's kid if you didn't show up out of nowhere looking for favors." He glanced over his shoulder as he poured three glasses of bright blue liquid. "Anyone else I'd probably shoot for barging into my space."

The announcement sounded like a joke until Warnock turned and Damon got to see his flat gaze.

"They must have done something really good for you," said Damon, accepting the glass and giving it a sniff. It smelled like sage and liquid smoke.

Warnock settled on the couch across from them. He circled the ice in his glass before taking a drink.

"We go way back. Some debts you can never really repay."

"How's business?" asked Remi.

Warnock leaned back with his arm over the back of the couch as he checked to the dance floor. A couple dressed in manticore onesies with plushie spike tails and manes around their heads gyrated against each other, their eyes hazy and unfocused. Illusionary birds flitted around them like satellites.

"It's the holiday season. Business is always good."

Damon took a sip of his drink. The alcohol burned as it went down his throat.

"People getting a chance to see their families?" asked Damon.

Warnock snorted.

Remi put a hand on his knee. "This is my friend, the werewolf."

A soft whistle exited Warnock's lips as he inclined his head. "Zev Clan. My condolences."

"Thanks," said Damon, surprised that he knew about it. "That's kinda—"

"Why is business good?" asked Remi, cutting him off.

"Ever since the Event, people are a little freer with their money. They want to escape, get away from the illusion of safety that they project onto their lives and was stripped away when a horde of murderous demons came charging up from the Undercity. It's not like the city has gotten that much better in the aftermath. I mean, the city has always been crazy. You don't get a name like the city of sorcery without some weird shit going on, but it seems extra fucked these days."

"We see a lot of it at the hospital," said Remi.

Warnock set his glass down, shaking his head. "I still can't get my head around that. You couldn't take her to the park to play with other kids without her leaving with half a dozen wallets and billfolds in her pockets. She has a gift."

"I've heard."

"You certainly won't see it. Fingers like silk. She could steal a horn from a unicorn."

"I didn't come to reminisce," said Remi.

Warnock snorted under his breath. "Not even twenty years and already old before her time. Is that the hospital or growing up with your parents?"

"A little of both."

Warnock narrowed his gaze. "What's the ask? I've got a meeting in twenty with some hard folks. Rather not have them see you with me and think I've gone soft with a couple of pink-cheeked doctors in my company."

"Do you know what a Caladrius bird is?" asked Remi.

"Know? I'd pay a large fortune to get my hands on one. Do you know the kinds of drugs you can make with those feathers? That's the high-end stuff you find at society parties or at Coterie of Mages."

"You can get some down?" asked Remi.

"I don't think you can steal enough reagents from the hospital to pay for that."

"I'm not doing that anymore."

"Then what are you offering?"

"My services," said Remi, holding out her hands.

Damon stiffened. "Remi..."

She shook him off. His gut hardened as he thought about her getting into trouble for him.

Warnock smiled, but glanced to him. "The job I have in mind would actually be much easier for your friend. After all, this is *his* request."

"It is, but he's not in the business."

Damon turned to Remi. "I helped you get the Cyclone data."

She tilted her head back. "You were the distraction. You were never in danger. I wouldn't be able to forgive myself if you got thrown in jail and kicked out of Aura Healers."

"I told you, Remi. This isn't your kind of job."

"A rough up?"

Warnock nodded.

"What's a rough up?"

"I got a business associate that hasn't been paying his bills. His name is Varn Hassam. He lives in the ninth ward in the apartments next to the Newtown Fishmarket. I need someone to send a message and not a polite one. This kind of message should get me my money right away and leave my associate with some long-term pain to remind him why he shouldn't miss his payments."

"Warnock..."

"You came to me, Remi. And he clearly needs this Caladrius tuft badly. I can see it on his face."

She leaned forward. "Tell me where the bird is. I'll steal a feather."

"No way, no how. The owner would know that information came from me and that would be very bad. And I need his help with my associate. He's extremely paranoid and has avoided my attempts to collect my debts, but your friend here, he doesn't smell like danger, wouldn't be suspicious, and has the requisite physical ability to handle my former associate."

"You want me to beat someone up and ask for your money?" asked Damon.

"If by beat up, you mean leave within an inch of their life, then yes. And get my money." Warnock leaned his elbows on his knees. "Do we have a deal?"

The urge to say yes was strong. He wanted the feather for his father, but he couldn't hurt someone, even someone deserving of it. It was against his oaths as a healer.

"I'm afraid I can't, Mr. Warnock. As badly as I need the feather."

"It's just Warnock, but I understand."

"You're an asshole, you know," said Remi, standing up, lips curled with fury.

Warnock chuckled. "You're just now seeing that? And I think you're an asshole too based on past performances." He checked back to Damon. "It seems that working in the hospital has helped her grow a conscience."

"He needs help," said Remi. "His dad will die without the feather."

"And I need my money. I can't go to my friend and ask for the feather without something in trade and since you don't have anything else to offer, that fiery job is my payment." Warnock lifted his eyebrows towards the bar. "This all looks nice and sweet, but it's built on shaky ground. I don't have spare capital to give away, as much as I'm sure your father needs it."

Before Remi could yell at him, Damon stood and put a hand on her arm.

"Remi. It's okay. I understand. It's not like we work for free at the hospital either. Everything costs money."

"Damon..."

"It's okay." He held out his hand. "I appreciate you meeting with us.

I'm sorry it didn't work out, but it was nice to know someone who knew her before the Halls."

Warnock accepted his handshake, but this time it wasn't a contest, but a genuine parting. The older man winked.

"It was a pleasure as well. I'm sorry about your father. I hope you can find another solution to your problem."

Remi had fists at her side as she stared at Warnock. He opened his arms and shook his head.

"You ain't gonna be mad at me."

"I want to be," she pouted.

She leaned into his embrace, resting her head on his chest. When they were finished, he held her at arm's length.

"If your parents ever show up, I'm going to teach them a lesson for abandoning you."

"I don't think we have anything to worry about," said Remi.

Leaving the Charm & Hammer made Damon feel empty inside. He had the urge to rush back and tell Warnock he'd do what he asked, but he couldn't convince himself that it was the right thing to do.

"I'm sorry, Damon."

"No. Don't be sorry. It was my choice. I appreciate you bringing me here. It meant a lot, even if it wasn't the right solution."

He wasn't sure when it happened, but halfway to the train station, he noticed they were holding hands. Damon gave hers a squeeze as he tried to think of another solution to fix his father, but he worried that there were some illnesses even the famed Golden Willow couldn't heal.

TWENTY-ONE

A light snow left a blanket across the city. If Remi had been at the hospital, it would have been serene, but padding across the concrete on her way to do a job was the worst time for the white stuff. If it were heavier, tracks could be buried beneath the new snow, but it was falling slow enough to leave her exposed to being followed.

The wind shifted, making the snow swirl around her feet, bringing with it the scent of fish from the nearby market. The place was closed since it was after midnight, but it still stank. Remi slipped into the alleyway, orienting herself until she identified Varn Hassam's apartment on the third floor.

The face-obscuring charm made her face tingle, which was the only way she would know that it worked. It was better than a mask, which was obvious to passersby.

Climbing wasn't her strong suit. Remi preferred up-close sleight of hand, or a carefully constructed con, but sometimes a little window work was the answer. She downed the elixir she'd gotten from Jeb at the hospital. It was meant for the ropes team to help them deal with trolls, but it would give her extra strength to make the climb easier.

A downspout provided a creaky, but solid way to ascend, especially with her light weight. She reached the third floor, and using a bungee cord to hold herself to the metal, freed her hands to pull the glass-dissolving vial from her pocket. The spotted dark green solution was another potion taken from the hospital. This one was used for removing glass stuck in wounds by melting it into smoke, rather than trying to remove it directly, which often resulted in additional damage to the flesh. Remi dumped the liquid into a plastic sprayer and squeezed the trigger two dozen times in a careful pattern.

By the time she was finished the glass slumped away and turned to brown smoke that drifted the opposite direction, leaving an opening into the apartment. Remi pulled herself into the room, hoping the sudden cold breeze wouldn't alert the owner of her arrival. The temperature inside brought beads of sweat to her forehead, making her glad the window was open.

She pulled out a shock baton that she'd taken from the ropes team. They rarely used them since it might hurt the patient, but sometimes the risk was required. She hoped it wouldn't be necessary.

The apartment was messy with numerous overflowing ashtrays, empty bottles of beer, and a collection of hot sauces that took up the entire island in the kitchen. She saw two doors and a third that led to the hallway. The mixture of old cigarettes, stale beer, and fish from the market was repulsive.

"Where would you keep your money?" she whispered to herself.

She checked the freezer, but it had been turned off and was empty. Not a single ice cube remained. The refrigerator was filled with beer and hot sauce, but no food. She'd met some pretty strange characters over the years, so the contents weren't completely off-putting.

The cabinets proved disappointing, being entirely empty. No bowls, glasses, anything. Nowhere to stuff a wad of bills. She methodically checked the vents, another popular place to hide ill-gotten gains. Nothing. She'd hoped she could find the money outside his room, but it was clear that Varn had stashed it somewhere more private.

Remi peeked under the first door, determining it was a bathroom. She crept inside and performed the same thorough search which produced nothing but a single prescription for heartburn.

"Should be industrial grade based on the kitchen," she muttered to herself.

Remi approached the bedroom door with apprehension. She pulled out a small spray bottle full of a knockout gas—another prize from the ropes team. A few spritzes and Varn would be put out, if he wasn't asleep already, giving her a precious few minutes to scour the remainder of his apartment.

Standing to the side of the door as a precaution, with one hand holding the spray bottle, she touched the door handle finding it extremely warm. Hot even. Remi pulled her hand away, examining it for contact poisons, when the door exploded outward.

Her positioning saved her from the worst of the detonation. The flaming door scattered across the apartment. She had a radiation burn across her face, but it would have been much worse had she been in the way of the door. Fatal, probably.

"I hear you, you sneak thief."

Remi peeked around the corner to see Varn in the middle of his bedroom, hair aflame. His dark brown skin glowed with inner fire like a tiger's eye lit from within, burning away his clothes until he was completely naked.

An efreeti. Not good.

She cursed herself for not inquiring about Varn's history before breaking into his apartment, but she'd had a free shift and thought it'd be a good opportunity to help Damon with his father's illness.

"Warnock's not happy with you. I'm here to collect your debts," she yelled from around the corner.

"I'll collect your charred corpse first."

Varn hadn't come out yet, which meant he was as concerned about her as she was about him, but that was only because he didn't know who she was. If he figured out she wasn't as powerful, then she was in real trouble.

"Why would you collect my charred corpse? You're not a cannibal, are you?"

"What? That's not what I meant. I'm not a cannibal."

"Okay, I'll give you that, but you're a welch. You should have known Warnock would send someone to collect. You and I can have a much better night if you just hand over what you owe him."

"I don't have the money."

Remi leaned her head against the wall. "Bullshit. Unless those hot sauces cost a grand each, Mr. Fire Pants."

"I bought them on the internet. They're the only thing that gets me off these days."

Remi grimaced. "I don't need to know about your fetishes. Just throw whatever you have out here and I'll call it a night."

A moment of quiet had her wondering if he might be following the easy path, which was fine by her. She hadn't intended to get into a fight.

"Screw that! I'm gonna torch you like a bonfire!"

She felt heat emanating out of the room, giving her warning of his approach. She lunged through the gap, slamming the tip of the shock baton into his gut. For a few seconds, she thought he might be knocked unconscious as he shook with his eyes in the back of his head.

Then the baton's plastic casing melted, destroying the wires within. She threw away the weapon and ran for her life, diving when she heard his scream of rage.

The ball of flame hit the edge of the table, flipping it over on her as it exploded. Remi slammed into the wall, which nearly knocked her unconscious, but she fought to her knees and hid behind the table, which was lying on its side.

"You can't torch a bonfire," she yelled from behind the table as she considered the odds of surviving a fall from three stories as her way of escape.

"What?"

He stopped halfway across the room. She could feel his heat reflecting off the wall.

"You said, I'm gonna torch you like a bonfire. A bonfire is already burning, and a torch is considerably smaller. It's like pissing in the ocean."

"I'm still going to burn you alive," said Varn.

Remi eyed the window again. A three-story fall wasn't sounding too bad.

"Yeah, but you should really get your metaphors worked out in advance, Mr. Fire Pants."

A burst of flame hit the wall, sending embers over her. She started to sprint for the window, but he sent another jet of flame over the table, forcing her to retreat behind the solid structure.

"Stop calling me Fire Pants! I'm not wearing any."

"Fine, Mr. Fire Crotch," she muttered, behind the table.

Remi checked her pockets for options, but she hadn't counted on the night turning to a pitched battle with an efreeti.

"You don't happen to have any relatives in the city?" she called over the table.

"What?"

"Any close relations who happen to be a doctor?"

"If I had a doctor relation, I wouldn't be in this mess," said Varn.

"Well, so much for that angle," she muttered to herself.

Remi prepared a blast of earth magic, hoping it would be enough to counter his fire blast and give her a chance to throw herself out the window and grab the waterspout. If she could slide down and jump before he made it to the opening, she might have a chance to get away before he turned her ass to char.

"One, two—"

Remi looked up when she felt the heat. Varn was standing on the burning couch, arms coated in flame.

"Oh no."

Then the apartment door exploded.

Remi wasn't quite sure what was happening until she heard a familiar rage scream. She peeked over the fallen table in time to see a hairy wolf on two legs tackling Varn off the couch. The pair landed against the wall, cracking the plaster.

The smell of burnt hair was horrific. The burning couch produced billowing clouds of smoke. Remi's eyes ached as she coughed, running to the kitchen cabinets where she'd spied a fire extinguisher while the battle raged.

Remi pulled the safety pin as she reached Varn and Damon rolling around on the floor. She pointed the nozzle downward and squeezed the trigger, releasing a cone of white dust across the pair. The blanket of flame retardant immediately put out Varn, which must have been a source of his power, because the werewolf reared back his fist and knocked out the once-flaming supernatural.

With Varn taken care of, Remi turned her attention to the couch and in a matter of a minute put the fire out, leaving them in a smokey apartment. She was coughing and sputtering, searching for a way to clean the air.

"Lystol's Negative Space," said Damon in a rough voice.

The spell was meant to create a negative air pressure for a sealed room in case of pathogens. It took Remi a second to remember, but then she made the gestures, letting faez fill her mind. When the spell completed, the smoke and dust rushed out of the room, along with any small materials not held down until the apartment was clear.

Remi threw herself at the kitchen sink, let the running water clean out her mouth, and splashed some in her face, before she returned to Damon in his werewolf form.

"Merlin's tits, are you okay?"

Patches of hair had been burnt away along his torso and arms where he'd had full contact with Varn. The long muzzle filled with sharp teeth was hard to interpret, but since it was her friend, she approached with her hands up.

"I'm going to cast some burn recovery spells. It's gonna hurt since we don't have any elixirs. Can you manage?"

He nodded.

The spell was more complex than the first. She worked it through her mind before attempting it in the real. The finger gestures were like knitting with an invisible string, and the mental pictures required three-dimensional manipulation. When she was finished, a bluish light attached itself to the burns, sizzling across his flesh as it knit him back together.

Damon leaned his head back and howled. His throaty, pain-filled voice sent shivers through her, making her feel like she was the one being hunted. His muscles rippled with pain and he held his claws above his head, putting gouges in the ceiling.

When it was over, he collapsed to his knees. Remi put her arms around his upper body, cradling him to her midsection.

"I'm sorry."

Damon whimpered softly, but after a few seconds, he rose to his feet. The sound of sirens was approaching.

"We have to go."

"We need the money first."

She rushed into Varn's bedroom, tossing the place for hidden compartments. Damon joined her in werewolf form though he was less effective, tearing up the mattress with his claws when he tried to check beneath it.

When the sirens sounded like they were outside the apartment on the front street, she thought they'd have to give up until she remembered the hot sauces and ran into the kitchen. Quite a few of them had crusty old hot sauce around the lip, but there was a section of clean bottles in the center. A quick inspection proved they were filled with rolled cash. Remi threw them into her backpack before running to the open window.

While she used the drain spout, Damon went down the wall by jamming his talons into the gaps between the bricks. They hit the street and ran a block, throwing themselves around the corner when a fire truck slid into the alleyway.

"That was close."

Damon bent over, holding his gut.

"You okay?"

"Changing."

Remi didn't know what to do, so she stood back and watched him transform. The process was frightening and horrific, but she couldn't look away. His hulking hairy shoulders reduced in size until they were smooth and naked. Talons sucked back into his fingertips, which looked painful by the way he grimaced and silently screamed.

When it was finished, Damon was naked in the snowy alleyway, heaving on his hands and knees. Remi put a weather enchantment on him, but that would only keep the worst of the cold away.

"That looked painful."

He stood up, so she handed him her light jacket while looking away. He wrapped it around his hips. The sleeves were barely long enough to create a makeshift kilt.

"I don't normally change that fast, but injuries can make it happen like that."

Patches of angry pink flesh where he'd been burnt littered his midsection. She ran her fingers across the healed wounds before she remembered he was naked.

"Sorry, habit."

Damon raised an eyebrow as he squeezed his arms around his chest.

"I think we're gonna need to find you clothes this time. You wait here. I'll be right back."

Half a block down, Remi found a clothing store. Breaking in while the lights from the police vehicles outside Varn's apartment reflected on the windows was an interesting experience. She made it back to Damon with a pair of corduroy overalls and a Hundred Halls hoodie.

"Hopefully the fashion police don't pull you over," she said, turning around so he could change. "Sorry, no shoes."

"I think I'll be okay. I reapplied the weather spells when you were gone."

When he was dressed, they headed towards the train station.

"I thought you weren't going to get involved?" she asked him. "Not that I'm complaining. He would have turned me into a shish kabob."

He hung his head. "I'm not proud of myself. Being an enforcer for your shady friend wasn't on my bucket list, but I was sitting with my dad earlier during my break and I realized I couldn't let this opportunity go. What were you doing there? No offense, but you're not exactly an intimidating presence."

"I planned on knocking him out with some of Jeb's magic gas and taking the money before he woke. Didn't work out as planned."

When they reached the station, Remi gave him some money from the hot sauce bottles for train fare.

"Where are you going?"

"To give the money back to Warnock. I figure it's best if he thinks I did this alone, plus I don't think they'll let you into the bar looking like that."

Damon checked himself. "A homeless hipster with bad taste?"

"Isn't that redundant?"

As she turned away, he said, "Remi."

"Huh?"

"Thanks for helping with my dad."

"Thanks for saving my ass when things went sideways."

Before she lost her nerve, Remi ran over and pulled him down, leaving a lingering kiss on his lips. She disappeared into the darkness before she was tempted to return to the hospital.

TWENTY-TWO

The door was locked, but Lily pulled a bobby pin from her tangled mess of rainbow hair and popped it open. Sammie was asleep on his side, snoring softly with his hands clasped under his chin. The furry end of a hoof stuck out the bottom of the thin sheet, kicking as if he were trying to run. His expression broke with fear and his lower lip trembled.

"No! No!" he whisper-shouted.

With the door closed and locked behind her, Lily set down her carryall full of supplies and shook Sammie's shoulder. He recoiled when he awoke until he realized she was standing by the bed.

"Are you okay, my dear?"

He squeezed his eyes closed. "I was back in his basement. He was working on me."

"It was just a dream. A shite one, that, but he's dead."

Sammie pulled himself to sitting and used his knuckles to clean the sleep from his eyes.

"I killed him."

"And he deserved it. Don't ever feel bad about it."

"Have you ever killed anyone?"

Lily lifted her chin. "More than once. And I'd do it again. Some people ain't worth saving and the world can be a shite place."

"It's four in the morning. Is there a problem?"

"I'd like to try something, if you don't mind," she said, putting a hand on his arm.

Sammie checked past her. "I take it this is another one of those illegal things?"

"Aye, but it won't be scary, not like last time anyway. But dangerous yes. I think I might have a way to cure you, but it might kill you too."

"Won't they kick you out if that happens?"

Lily smiled. He was more worried about her than himself. "They would. Put me in jail too. But I'll do it if you're up for the challenge."

"If you think it might cure me."

"You're not afraid of dying?"

He rubbed the hem of the sheet with his forefinger and thumb. "Better to try than continue like this. It's only a matter of time before someone finds out about my blood and I'm back to living in fear." He let out a quivering exhale. "I just want a normal life."

"What I'm going to do won't change what you look like. Whatever beings he combined you with won't go away."

Sammie shrugged. "Hooves are easy to hide and a lot of people like horns."

"That's the spirit."

"What do you have to do?"

Lily grabbed her carryall and removed the medical equipment she'd stolen from the supply closet. She set a dozen fresh bags of blood down next to the phlebotomist kit and two small cleaning devices that looked like plastic boxes with tubes going through them.

"I've been studying your blood and tissue samples," she said. "It's like nothing I've ever seen before. None of the medical journals mention anything like it, which is why the hospital doesn't know what to do with you."

"Good or bad?"

"I don't know what your mage intended, but he was right clever. It was like he was trying to make you Fae without using anything from those realms." She flicked a horn with her fingernail. "Those and your hooves are regular old goat. But your blood, that's different. It's fused with infernal faez."

"Like demonic?"

"Aye, like the Event. But one of the things that gets missed about the invasion is that demons and devils aren't from some misbegotten realm of miscreants. The infernal is one of the earliest realms in existence, back when the rules of creation hadn't quite hardened into the reality we exist in now. Which means creatures from that realm had a lot more freedom to become anything they wanted, which was probably a bit of curse too if you didn't have a sense of self. But that's not important for you. I think your mage found a sex-crazed demon and stripped it of its blood and put it in you. The differences should have killed you, but he made your body resistant to the changes, which is the only reason I think this is gonna work."

"What's that?"

"I need to take your blood out completely and replace it with regular human O-type blood."

"But I'll die."

"Aye. For a little bit. I can put you in a state of stasis while I make sure you're free of the infernal blood and then I'll fill you back up with the good stuff."

"Sounds simple."

Lily furrowed her brow. "It's not."

She would have preferred to have her sisters by her side, but they wouldn't leave the Old Country. Nor did she want to get her friends kicked out. This was her burden.

After setting up the equipment, which included a line that would dump his blood into a hazmat container, Lily applied a trio of enchantments that would help him survive the procedure. His eyes wavered as the sleep spell sent him into oblivion.

Once he was asleep, she set the valve to drain. In an emergency situation using the proper equipment, a body could be emptied in less than a minute using a vacuum pump and layered spells, but she didn't want to stress the body too much and that method required a small team.

As his cheeks grew more emaciated and gray, she had to add new spells to preserve his flesh, putting his body into stasis. Lily imagined this wasn't the first time he'd been modified like this as the original mage that had created him had probably used similar procedures.

As the final pints emptied into the bright red hazmat container, Lily prepared the fresh, unaltered blood for refilling Sammie. She had to act fast. If there was too much time between transitions, he would die, the new blood would become contaminated, or both.

The first signs of trouble came when his body shuddered like a minor earthquake. Lily had her hands full with a blood bag when a low moan issued from his lips.

"You shouldn't be doin' this, Sammie. What's going on?"

"No. Stop."

Lily set the blood bag down and put her hands over the valve. "How are you speaking to me?"

"My work."

"My work? Oh no."

The realization of who was speaking had her cursing under her breath. It wasn't Sammie, but the mage who'd made him. Either the banishing hadn't completely got rid of him, or his life was somehow tied to Sammie's, which made the procedure perilous for the both of them.

A shadow shifted out of Sammie's body, the jagged claws raking Lily's arm as she struggled to counter with a charm. She was juggling so many enchantments and the stasis keeping Sammie alive, which made it difficult to defend herself. Winds rose, whipping around them, sending rainbow hair into her face. A spectral voice shouted in her head.

"He's mine! Mine! For an eternity, he's mine!"

The world raged around Lily. She fought the spectral being, but she hadn't brought her protections from creatures from the Veil and the silver coin was lost from the last procedure.

"Stop it, you mad bugger!"

The shadowy mage drew blood across her arms and face as it poked with its incorporeal flesh. The figure reached its faint arm into her chest, squeezing her heart with wretched fingers. Lily couldn't breathe. She was having a heart attack. Vision wavered. Her knees grew weak.

She wasn't going to last much longer if she didn't set aside Sammie's protections to defend herself, but he would die in the interim. But so would she if she couldn't do anything. She'd have to be quick, if she was going to survive.

Lily dropped her enchantments.

The nearly bloodless body in the bed gasped, arms and legs jackknifing before falling back.

She started to call upon Medb before she remembered she wasn't connected to her anymore, shifting to a Veil counter. Since she hadn't invited the mage into this world, he wasn't as potent as the previous time, but he'd struck at the perfect moment.

The words of dismissal came to her lips easily. Lily chanted the Old

Words. The ones her family had learned from the ancients.

The pressure lessened on her heart. She was winning against the mage, but Sammie was dying. Every second she wasn't protecting him was another second of his body collapsing. If she couldn't get back to him quickly, his existence would be over. Lily put everything into throwing the mage back into the land between the living and the dead.

" Ar ais go dtí an Veil!"

For a moment, she thought him too strong. He hung onto her spirit with sharp claws, making her want to scream.

"I curse you!"

Then his existence popped.

Relief rushed in, but she had no time to enjoy it. Lily replaced the enchantments, rushing through words, knowing that one mistake would be Sammie's death.

His body arched and fell back into the bed when she completed the final word. Blood resumed leaving his body, dribbling into the hazmat container.

When the final drops emptied, she switched the valve to the chain of fresh blood and hung them on the stand so gravity would refill him. Fearing that he'd been unprotected too long, she sped up the liquid with a warmth spell.

It would take longer to fill his body than it had to remove the blood. He looked like a corpse in the bed. She layered spells across him, hoping to reenergize his body.

When half the blood bags were emptied, she worried that he hadn't made it. He looked like a ghoul. His flesh was shades of black and blue from the rapid exit and return of blood.

"Come on, Sammie."

Lily squeezed the bag. She'd cast all the spells she could. Now he just needed to recover.

Or not.

When the seventh bag started entering his veins, she saw a pink color return to his flesh and he seemed to expand like a balloon being filled. Pressing her fingers against his wrist found a weak pulse.

Over the course of the next few minutes, the last pints of blood were put back in his body. He was alive, if unconscious. Lily removed the lines and put an alchemical agent in the hazmat container that would render the blood useless. She didn't want anyone to accidentally get hit by its effects.

By the time she had the equipment completely put away, Sammie's eyes were open. He looked like he'd been through a dozen marathons.

"You okay?"

The words came out as a hoarse whisper. "Did it work?"

"I think so."

His expression broke. "I thought I heard the mage."

"Was only a dream," she said, putting a hand on his arm.

Sammie closed his eyes, tears slipping from the corners. "Am I free?"

"Aye, Sammie. You're free. But don't try to rush anything. You'll need a week or so to recover from that. Was hell on your body. Seven hells."

"I don't know what to say."

"Save your strength. After all, you were dead a little bit ago."

"I have something for you," he said, weakly.

"You don't have to."

"Reach into the mattress. I put a hole in it a while ago."

Lily was too tired to argue. She found the hole, cleverly cut into the threading. After digging her fingers into the stuffing, she found something small and hard. She pulled it out, finding a crimson vial.

"Sammie, I don't need this."

"It's an enchanted vial. I got it from one of the nurses."

"Your blood has no interest to me."

"But it might be useful just the same. Please. I have to give you something in return. Trade it for valuables, I don't care what, but you have to take it."

A bone-rattling exhaustion took hold. Lily collected the warm vial from his hands and stuffed it in her hair.

"I should go rest. I have another shift in a few hours."

Sammie's eyes were closed by the time she left his room. Getting back to the Aura Healers dormitory took all her energy. When she reached her space, the window was open and there was no sign of Remi or Neko. A recovery elixir in the mini-fridge kept her from collapsing. As she finished the thick green potion, a furry head stuck through the open window.

"Neko. You're not supposed to hunt in that form."

She smiled drearily.

Her companion leapt onto the bed. A feline shape with a rat's face and velvet tendrils along the back hips. Neko put his front paws on her leg and licked the wounds on her face from the shadowy mage's claws. The flesh knitted to a light pink.

"I missed you, my love."

Neko purred, pushing away the exhaustion and leaving Lily with warm contentedness. Velvet tendrils caressed Lily's cheek, soothing the ache forming at the back of her head from the heavy faez use.

Before long, Lily was lying with her head on the pillow and a small rat-sized shape curled next to her chest. She put her hand on Neko's back and promptly fell asleep.

TWENTY-THREE

The silvery light of the full moon slipped through the crack in the clouds, cascading over Damon and his friends as they walked the eighth ward. Remi recoiled slightly.

"I've told you a dozen times it doesn't work like that."

She screwed up her mouth. "Not that. But the visions and sleep-walking."

Damon nodded to Lily on the other side. "She gave me a drink to keep it at bay. Wolfsbane, powdered manticore spike, and goose liver oil."

"It'll keep your hair as lustrous as a summer siren," smirked Lily.

He never knew how to take her strange comments, but the radio crackled into life, interrupting his thoughts.

"We have a ten thirty-seven on the ring road near the Herald, any units nearby?"

"Copy, Car Seventeen. Will check it out. Anything to look for?"

"Looks like a black carriage being pulled by skeletal horses."

A sigh. "Thanks. On our way."

When the chatter stopped, Damon looked to Remi, who quickly answered, "Suspicious vehicle."

"How do you know all the codes?"

"Listening to the police chatter was one of the first things my parents had me do during their break-ins. I'd sit in the van and listen to their open channels," said Remi as they walked. She was practicing her five elements, making puffs of air or flame with either hand.

"Are you sure this is going to work?" asked Lily. "We could try a Veil summoning to track the Full Moon Killer."

He caught Remi's wide-eyed stare and brief headshake. "I think we'll try the old-fashioned ways first."

"The Veil is as old as they come," said Lily. "But it's your march."

The next twenty minutes they listened to various codes, which Remi interpreted for them. It wasn't until they neared the Invictus Cryptozoo that anything significant came through the radio.

"Units Five Four Nine, Five Six Nine, and Eighty-Three, we have a ten eighty-eight in the Canal District. South side. Please advise caution."

The three units responded they were on their way. Remi's expression had hardened.

"Yeah. A ten eighty-eight is a supernatural sighting. Could be our guy." She rolled her eyes. "Either one of them. Or both."

Damon waved down a taxi. They threw themselves in back.

"What's the Canal District?" asked Remi.

Damon shrugged his shoulders.

Then the driver said, "Someone thought it'd be a good idea to put a series of canals through the streets like Venice, but then surrounded it by bars and cheap restaurants. It's where all the college kids go when they're visiting the city, and since they're all on break for the holidays, it can be rather nuts."

"I bet that water's gross," said Damon.

"Why?" asked Lily.

"Because, oh, never mind."

The taxi dropped them off at the edge of the district because traffic was thick. The sidewalks were filled with people their age holding plastic cups in the shape of cauldrons or potion bottles that flashed with colorful lights. The noises were overwhelming: firecrackers popping, illusionary banshees screaming overhead, and packed bars announcing their existence with gut-rumbling war horns.

"We'll never find it in this chaos," said Damon.

"We need to get high up so we can see the police lights," said Remi, craning her neck in all directions. "There." She extended her arm towards a balcony on the third floor of a bar called the Horny Devil.

The exterior looked like the face of a devil with the entrance as an open mouth, the upper windows as round eyes, and the balconies as the eyebrows.

The entrance fee was enormous but Damon never went out, so the money he made at the hospital had built up. He took front position, pushing his way through the packed crowd. Occasionally someone would push back until they saw who he was, and once he flexed his claws to give a gentle reminder not to mess with him.

They reached the third floor after a torturous journey, but it was full of a group of well-dressed twentysomethings celebrating as if it were New Year's.

"You're not with the group," said the bouncer outside the balcony.

"How much would it cost to be a member?" asked Remi.

The bouncer crossed his arms. "I don't take bribes."

When Damon stepped forward, the bouncer took one look at him and said, "I can have six guys my size up here in a flash. Don't get cocky."

Lily stepped forward and spoke quietly in the bouncer's ear. She was wearing an emerald green silk dress with fringe along the hems and the material shifted around her lithe form as she stood on her tippy-toes. While she talked, the bouncer's eyes grew ever wider until his face was pale as milk. He cleared his throat.

"I'll talk to them. A moment."

"What did you say?" he asked Lily.

"Nothing important."

He didn't have time to press when they were escorted to the edge of the balcony while the well-dressed twentysomethings glowered at the intrusion.

"We won't be long. Sorry," said Damon, holding up his hands.

"There!" said Remi, extending her arm.

On the other side of the canal and between two rows of apartment buildings, red and blue lights swirled against the bricks.

"I wish there was a faster way down," he said, turning back. Lily put a hand on his shoulder and produced a length of nylon rope from her oversized carryall. He quickly tied it to the balcony and slid down to the street level to cheers from the crowd. Remi and Lily landed moments later and they maneuvered through the busy sidewalks and past the wide canal on which flat boats filled with drunken college students lounged on couches.

The whole time they pushed through the crowd, Damon was certain that the Full Moon Killer would be gone before he arrived. He got impatient and started growling at people to get out of his way.

"Hey," said Remi, grabbing his arm. "You're scaring people. Look at the way they're staring."

Damon checked around them to see alarm on their faces and a few cell phones pointed in his direction. His claws were half extended.

"Sorry. I just want to find out what's going on with me."

The last block took forever. The lights were still flashing on the walls.

When they broke through the crowd, they were stopped by yellow police tape.

"See anything?" he asked.

"I can't tell what's going on," said Remi.

A girl with a Japanese manticore mask on top of her head, holding a glowing pink plastic potion bottle and sporting a dazed look said, "Some dude got cut in half up there. It's crazy. I read about the Full Moon Killer, but I didn't think I'd see his work."

"Did anyone see anything?" asked Damon.

The girl with the mask on her head recoiled. "You undercover or something?"

"What? No."

She shook her head. "You're a little too intense compared to everyone else."

"We have a crime podcast," said Remi, adding a shrug when he furrowed his brow at her.

"Oh, sweet," said the girl. "Anyway, I overheard one of the cops say they think it was a werewolf. Damn therianthropes, can't trust them. We ought to make a law against them. How can we trust someone who hides their true form?"

Damon didn't realize he was growling until Remi pulled him away. The stuffed wolf in his room was one thing, but hearing it from a random person on the street told him how bad things had gotten.

"We should move on. It's not like he's still here."

Damon sighed and looked away. He was staring across the way when he saw a shape shifting across the rooftops of the apartments further into the district.

"Come on," he said, grabbing Remi's hand and leading them down the next street where he saw the shape moving. The crowds, especially on the bridges crossing the canal, were thick and unmoving. Everything smelled like alcohol.

After a few minutes, he thought he'd lost the Killer until Lily spotted him leaping across a gap between buildings. He was headed away from the Canal District. Before long, they were away from the busy streets. Cars passed them on the sidewalk, bright lights momentarily blinding him.

"I think we lost him," said Damon.

A small park with an old-timey carousel at the center shone out of the gloom. A bored attendant was taking tickets for a ride. The slow-moving amusement ride had supernatural creatures like unicorns and dragons rather than the usual four-legged mounts, and meandering music played from hidden speakers. A group of teenagers were camped on a carriage, but otherwise the carousel was empty.

"Ideas?" asked Damon.

Remi had the police radio to her ear. "Nothing here."

"Can we take a ride?" asked Lily, looking like a little kid as she stared at the carousel.

"Why not. It's not like we know where he is."

Damon dug into his pockets for cash as they approached the attendant. Halfway across, the hairs on the back of his neck rose in anticipation and his claws ached like they wanted to come out.

"Stop."

Remi and Lily stared at him strangely.

"He's here."

Remi's head snapped to the side. "He is? Where?"

Damon was about to say that he didn't know when a heavy thump announced the arrival of the Full Moon Killer. The dark shape loomed beneath the canopy of trees while the carousel played its winding dirge.

TWENTY-FOUR

The sword glowed softly in the darkness. Lily reached into her hair, releasing Neko from his nest to land on the cracked concrete. Her companion expanded, growing and rippling, until he was the size of a medium dog. When he finished, a velvet tentacle caressed the back of her leg.

Remi stared at her companion in horror. "Lily?"

"It's Neko. Don't worry."

The figure holding the sword stepped forward. There was something familiar about him even though she was certain she didn't know the Full Moon Killer.

Yet.

Damon hunched forward, a growl emanating from the back of his throat. He was staring at his hands as if he were willing them to elongate.

"Come on," she heard him mutter to himself.

"Forget your claws. Hit him with the elements," said Remi, holding up her hands.

Lily wasn't so sure it was the right move, but she followed Remi's direction, calling up a potent ball of force which she let hover over her outstretched hand.

"Now!"

Three sets of elements—fire, earth, and force—flew at the Full Moon Killer.

The sword flashed.

Elemental magics spun into the darkness, deflected away by the ancient artifact.

"And that was my best one," said Remi with a sigh.

Lily crouched by Neko. "Come, little one, let us see what we can do."

Neko approached the figure in a low crouch while Lily pulled a piece of rusty chain from her carryall, wrapping it around her hands and chanting in a low voice. Her companion mewled while the velvet tendrils undulated. The sword-wielding figure set himself against Neko, and when her companion padded near, he sprang into an attack, the sword swinging unerringly. He moved so quickly there was no time to escape the blow.

But the sword clanged against the concrete, sparks exploding in a mini-geyser.

Neko appeared behind the figure, lunging in to snap at his calves and springing away before he could turn.

Before the Full Moon Killer could do anything else, Lily completed her ritual. Ghostly chains appeared around him, capturing him in a cocoon of incorporeal steel.

"Hit him now!"

Lily launched a new round of spirit magic at the bound figure at the same time as her friends. The glowing masses looked poised to impact him directly, but the Full Moon Killer broke the bonds easily and knocked them away.

"The crows' curse on you," spat Lily.

She reached into her carryall and pulled out a jar of glowing insects. Before releasing the lid, Lily whispered an unlocking spell through the pinprick holes. When she tossed the contents into the air, the luminous insects sped towards the Full Moon Killer. Their size made it impossible for him to defend himself with the sword and he swung randomly, briefly illuminating his bearded face.

While he contended with the latest challenge, Neko leapt in, making snapping attacks at the back of his legs. Remi, in her own furious way, lobbed fire bolts at his head. The combined attacks added up, singeing his dark clothes and causing him to utter cries of pain.

"Why aren't you doing anything?" asked Remi between spells. "We've got him!"

Damon was standing with his hands at his side, forehead hunched with concern. Was he enthralled or confused? Lily ignored his immobility and prepared a new spell, one that would incapacitate the shadowy figure completely, giving Neko a chance to finish him. As she reached deep, drawing on the connection between her and her companion, she heard Damon stirring.

"Wait," he said. "I know him."

TWENTY-FIVE

The sword-wielding figure was encased in eldritch lights, battling the sorceries from his friends. Damon had every intention of transforming into a full werewolf and tackling the Full Moon Killer. More than anything, Damon wanted to know why he was having visions connected to their enemy.

But he couldn't get over the familiarity he felt standing in his presence. The darkness, occasionally banished with fiery spells, gave him brief snatches. The bushy beard hid the contours of the face, but the eyes held secrets Damon felt he should know.

When Neko grabbed the Full Moon Killer's calf and he cried out in pain, the first real time he'd heard him speak, Damon was speared into place with recognition. He couldn't believe it at first. Maybe it was a trick of enchantment, or a deep-seated need for familial connection. After all, their entire clan had been destroyed except for his small family.

"Wait. I know him."

He said the words before he'd fully come to terms with who was standing before him wielding the Shining Sword.

Connor Black.

His father's half-brother. The keeper of the clan's sword. He was supposed to be dead. Not rampaging through the city of sorcery taking heads.

"Help us, Damon," pleaded Remi. "We've got him."

Damon didn't know how it was happening. Or why. The only thing he knew was in that small flash when he saw him clearly, Connor Black didn't seem like himself. Something in his eyes reminded Damon of the people beset by madness from the worms. He was being driven mad.

Lily looked poised to cast another potent spell. The former witch had more tricks in her cloth carryall than he thought possible and her companion was doing Connor real damage.

"Lily, stop!"

She glanced over angrily and continued with her spell.

Damon tackled her.

Rainbow-colored hair got caught in his mouth as he landed on her, harder than he'd intended.

The impact broke her concentration, and the insects that had been harrowing Connor popped like bubbles. He took one look at them and Damon saw his expression clearly. It was one of horror. As if he was coming to terms with what he was doing. Connor sprinted the opposite direction at great speed.

"No! Come back!"

"Get the fook off me or I'm going to stick a wand up your arse."

The Irish accent thickened as Lily slapped and pushed him to get off. He regained his feet and tried to help her, but she knocked his hands away.

"Have you gone bugger mad?"

Remi marched into his space.

"Did he put a spell on you? Shadows below, we had him and you let him go. If anyone else dies, it's on you."

The rebuke stung. He was reeling with his choices, which had happened in the blink of an eye. The way his friends were looking at him had his heart in a blender.

"I couldn't."

"You couldn't? You got us all worked up tracking him down because you've been waking up with his visions in your head, covered in his blood, but now you can't do it?" asked Remi, arm extended in the direction Connor had fled.

"It was Connor Black."

The name brought confusion. The two women glanced to each other.

"My uncle. My dad's half-brother."

Remi sputtered. "But I thought he was dead?"

"I did too."

Their bubbling anger dissipated. Remi glanced around. "We should move. I think that carousel attendant called the cops a little bit ago."

As sirens approached in the distance, they fled the opposite direction that Connor Black had gone. Damon formulated what he was going to tell his friends, but he didn't quite know what he wanted to say. His mind was all screwed up.

Three blocks away, they found an all-night diner. Neko had returned to his rat-shape, but Lily was carrying him. The waitress said nothing about him as they crowded into a corner booth in the back and ordered four plates of a full breakfast and fresh coffees.

As soon as the waitress left, he felt a kick under the table.

"Hey, that hurt."

A second one followed.

"That was from me," said Lily. "What in the green hills of Ireland was that back there?"

"It was Connor Black. I'm sure."

"Then what was that story from your dad? Was he lying?" asked Remi.

"No. I don't know. I don't think so." He gripped his hands into fists. "No. He wasn't lying. Everyone had been killed, there were no eyewitnesses."

"Unless Connor did it," said Remi, lips squeezed into a line. "Come on, Damon. You can't ignore that possibility."

"She's right, you know," said Lily.

A hole formed in his chest where his heart should be. He felt empty inside.

"No, I can't believe that. Not Connor. I grew up idolizing him. He was everyone's favorite member of the clan. He wouldn't have slaughtered everyone, gone into hiding, and then showed up here to kill more people."

"Yet, on the surface, that's what it looks like," said Remi.

"On the surface," repeated Damon angrily.

Four plates of food showed up, pausing their conversation. Lily pulled a piece of bacon from the fourth plate and fed it to Neko, who'd been sleeping in her lap. The white rat's whiskers quivered before it devoured the crispy meat.

"Damon," said Remi, taking a sympathetic tone, "I don't want to presume guilt, but it looks pretty bad. I'm not saying I believe that he killed your family, but the evidence about the killing in the city is not good."

"What about the other guy? The one that showed up at the arcade?"

They shared glances.

"I think it's proof that we don't really understand what's going on," said Remi.

Damon downed his orange juice and stared out the window, trying to ignore the reflection of his friends studying him. Did they think he could go mad too?

"I don't know what's going on, but I know it's all linked. My father's illness, the visions, the appearance of Connor Black, and the full moon. I just don't know *why* they're linked."

Before he realized it, they reached out and captured his hands. He closed his eyes and reveled in the connection.

"We'll help you figure it out."

"Aye," said Lily, nodding intensely. "We're your mates. We won't let you face this alone."

Damon ground his teeth because he couldn't speak. Eventually they released his hands and his stomach grumbled audibly at the smell of the eggs, bacon, and hash browns. The heavy discussion turned to food and the trials of Golden Willow, leaving the question of Connor Black for later.

TWENTY-SIX

A gurney with a facedown Santa sped past Remi. It took her a moment to recognize the blanket covering his backside was sticking up like a tent pole. The smirks on the nurses' faces were all she needed to know about what was going on.

Remi rounded the corner, entering the emergency room, which looked like a madhouse. The old guy who liked to stand on the chairs and yell about the city's demise was in the middle of his spiel, there were at least three pregnant ladies looking nervous, and a group of middle-aged men with fake antlers on their heads were looking morose in the corner.

Remi spotted Dr. Morrison speaking with a trio of nurses near the desk. The doctor's tight braids had slipped around the crown of her head, but she was clearly too busy to worry about fixing them.

"Hey Remi," said Dr. Morrison after sending the nurses to their duties and heading down the hallway.

Remi joined her stride, knowing that to survive in the ER, you had to always be doing at least three things at once. The ropes team hauled a man covered in red and green glowing paint through the door as he laughed hysterically. Watching the broad-shouldered and beautiful Ash easily handle the patient brought a tinge of jealousy. She was like a Viking shield-maiden. No wonder Damon had slept with her last year.

"Remi?"

"Oh, yeah, sorry. Dr. Decker wanted to know if you needed any help."

"That bored in the Supernatural Ward?" asked Dr. Morrison with a smirk.

"No, I think he just thought, since it was the holidays..."

A hand rested on Remi's shoulder. "That was sweet of him, but we're at our normal level of chaos down here. Completely under control. Unless you're desperate for extra work, I'll relieve you of your duties. Go back and up and enjoy the slowness."

At that moment, a door three spots down slammed open and Dr. Paddock followed by a nurse and a pink-faced first year came rushing out. A ball of flame exploded out the opening, licking against the ceiling before sucking back into the room.

Dr. Paddock turned on the student, who looked like he was going to pass out.

"You complete imbecile! You lunatic! You nearly got us killed. Enunciate! Enunciate! Do you think slurring your spells sounds cool?"

Dr. Morrison chuckled.

"Normal level of chaos?"

Dr. Morrison lifted a single shoulder. "I stand by what I said. Go back up. We've got it here. Besides, your class had three times the work last year."

Remi raised an eyebrow as Dr. Paddock pushed the first year back into the patient's room. "Were we this bad?"

"You got better."

When she returned to the Supernatural Ward, Remi heard a whizzing sound and turned in time to see a white disc of energy fly past her head. She ducked, nearly toppling to the ground. The fast-moving object flew around the corner before she could clock what it was.

At the nurses station, she asked, "Did anyone see that?"

Mandy looked up from the plate of cake in her hands. "I heard something." She tilted her head. "I think it went that way."

The left hallway brought her past the NOCAT's room. The door was open, which was unusual, so she stuck her head in, looking for signs of the energy disc. The old woman was sitting straight up, staring at the wall with her eyes wide open.

"Hello?"

The NOCAT didn't react, not that Remi had expected her to. She waved her hand before her face without getting a reaction.

"Was that you? Is that your disc?"

Nothing. No answer.

Remi stared at her for a minute before deciding that the NOCAT was just being her weird self. Before Remi could decide which way to go, she heard a great crash down the hall and ran in that direction.

She arrived to the scene of two young women with broad shoulders and red-and-white striped decorative candy canes in their hands like weapons, smacking the glowing white disc of energy out of the air and laughing. The upper trays on a food cart had already been knocked onto the ground, holiday-themed Jell-O splattered across the wall.

Remi expected anger from the nurses behind the counter, but they were laughing and clapping their hands. Nurse Nina, not known for her humor, shouted at the girls with her hands cupped around her mouth.

"Get it, Nat!"

One of the girls, who had lustrous dark hair bound in a braid, dove across the open air, catching the glowing disc with her bare hands. She wrestled it to the ground. An audible click was followed by the dissipating of light, revealing a solid object in her hands. She shoved it into her small backpack.

"That's how you do it, Talia," said the girl on the ground, which received a stuck out tongue.

The nurses came rushing out from behind the desk, congratulating the girls, which was when Remi realized that she wasn't looking at two random women in the hospital, but Damon's twin sisters, Natasha and Natalia.

"Hey," said Natasha, catching Remi standing by the corner. "You're Damon's girlfriend."

The description sent a spike of confusion through her heart. Remi had feelings for Damon, and they'd had their moments, but she'd never considered describing him as a boyfriend.

The twins came barreling towards Remi. It was like being faced down by a couple of Mack trucks. They weren't as tall as Damon, but had an intense presence as if they might run through a random wall at any moment.

"Hi?"

"Remi, right?" asked Natalia.

Remi felt like she was being picked out at a pet store by the way the twins were staring.

"Yeah. You're Damon's sisters. Does Damon know you're here?"

The twins glanced at each other grinning.

"Not yet," said Natasha. "We thought we'd surprise him, but he's sleeping right now. We have a few days free. We just got to see Dad, but he was tired and is resting now."

Natalia put a hand on her belly. "Where's the best place for food around here? I haven't eaten in an hour."

"An hour, right. Yeah, follow me. I'll take you to the cafeteria."

Remi felt like she was being escorted by giants. The twins waved and said hello to every person they passed, even the unconscious woman on her way to surgery.

When they got to the cafeteria line, the twins piled food on their trays, having to work to keep the half dozen rolls from falling off. Remi paid for their food and took a spot in the corner, then watched as the girls inhaled their food at vacuum speeds.

Remi studied them as they ate, trying to figure out the differences between them. Natasha wore her hair long and had a considerable amount of makeup, while Natalia had short spiked hair with no cosmetics. Their clothes were equally different, with Natasha wearing sporty, but feminine clothes. Her sister was wearing a lacrosse hoodie and jeans. Both of them had nicks and scars on their knuckles, but Natasha surprisingly had red and white painted fingernails.

Natasha hid a belch behind a cupped hand when she was finished, and her sister punched her in the arm hard enough to make Remi flinch.

"That hit the spot. It's so hard to keep up when we're not at home."

"When did you get here?" asked Remi, who'd barely eaten a quarter of her fries and only taken two bites of her cheeseburger.

"This morning," they said at the same time.

"This is your senior year, right? And you won your state championship."

"Yeah," said Natalia brightly. "Coach says we're going to all take a trip together before the end of the year in celebration. I'm hoping Mexico. Beach, baby."

Natasha rolled her eyes. "I want to go hiking, but the beach will probably win out."

"What are you doing after that? Damon talks about you two all the time, but hasn't mentioned that."

The twins looked at each other with slight grimaces. "Because we haven't told him. We're planning on joining the Halls."

"Oh? Which ones?"

Natasha stroked the long braid hanging over her shoulder. "Protectors probably, though I could see myself in Justicars or Explorers too."

"Dramatics all the way," said Natalia.

"Really?" asked Remi, hating the way it came out as a surprise.

"I starred in this year's production of *The Magical Maniac* and sang lead in the school choir," said Natalia, beaming.

Natasha put a hand on her sister's shoulder. "Don't let the short hair fool you. She keeps it that way because it's easier to deal with the wigs."

"I really didn't have much of a high school experience. Probably like Damon."

"Damon? Oh, don't let that pious volunteer crap fool you. He was still involved with everything in high school, including the school play and the Halls club."

"School play? I wouldn't have guessed."

"Only his junior year, but Miss Johnson still talks about how good he was as the villain. It's kind of annoying actually. He's always been good at everything, even if he's not really trying," said Natalia.

With a French fry hovering before her mouth, Remi asked, "I thought your dad had trouble even paying for Damon's entrance fees?"

"Scholarships," said Natasha. "We've got a full ride wherever we want to go."

"Wow, that's impressive."

Natasha leaned forward conspiratorially, eyes wide with excitement. "I heard you spent time in jail for, like, real crimes and stuff before you joined the Halls. What was that like?"

Remi leaned back. "When did he tell you this? Damon's so busy and I've never seen him call you two."

"Oh, he writes us letters every other Sunday. It's his little ritual."

"I feel like I don't even know him." Remi paused. "And I'm not his girlfriend. Not like that anyway. We're too busy."

The look the twins shared had her wondering what he'd said in his letters about her.

"Technically," began Natalia, "he never used the word *girlfriend*, but he never talked about *any* of the girls he dated in high school. Ever. So we figured, you know."

"He dated in high school? I thought he was always at the hospital."

"Oh he was, and dating isn't really the right term. I think they saw him as a prize to be paraded around the school, but after he ignored them, they usually found other things to do with their time."

Natasha crossed her arms. "I would have killed to date half the girls he did. One of them is a model in New York. Another got a minor part on a reality show in LA. He barely looked at them and they came crawling."

Remi was floored by the information. The twins were staring at her, so she asked a question to distract them.

"Love your fingernails. Don't you worry about destroying them if you change? Or get mad?"

Natasha held up her hand. "Oh, these? We don't change like Damon."

"You don't?"

The twins glanced at each other.

"Damon has problems, either changing when he doesn't want to, or not being able to when he needs to. It's because he was in the middle of puberty when the clan got wiped out. It really messed with his control."

"I see."

Natalia put a hand over hers. "Please don't tell him we told you that. He gets pretty sensitive about it. After he messed that kid up in high school, Mom and Dad sent him to therapy with a therianthropic specialist, but he didn't stay long."

"He hasn't been having more problems, has he?" asked Natasha with her head tilted.

Remi hadn't realized she was making a face, but the twins clearly picked up on it.

"Nothing unusual," she lied, not wanting to reveal the visions he'd been having through Connor Black without consulting Damon. For all she knew, the twins weren't even aware of the Full Moon Killer.

"Oh shit," muttered Natasha, looking past Remi.

Damon was marching through the cafeteria on a mission. He started to raise his voice but then lowered it.

"What are you two doing here?"

"We thought you'd be happy to see us," said Natalia.

"Nat, Talia, don't you know there's a killer in the city?"

"Of course, we're not blind, but what are the odds? Besides, we'd mess him up if he dared to show his face," said Natasha, brandishing a fist and a mean mug.

Damon's expression slackened, which only brought suspicion from the twins. Before they could make a jump of logic, Remi said, "He's just worried because we've gotten some of the victims in the hospital."

"Yeah. That's what I'm worried about." Damon sighed heavily. "I'm sorry. Come here, you two."

The twins burst from their chairs and threw themselves into his arms. They weren't that much shorter than Damon and almost as wide. Remi knew nothing about lacrosse except that it was similar to hockey, but she couldn't imagine how frightening it would be to have those two girls after her on the field.

"Have you two eaten? I have a few hours. I could take you by my favorite ramen shop. It's only a few blocks away."

"Hells yeah," said Natalia. "I love ramen."

Natasha pulled Remi to standing. "Come with us. It'll be fun."

"Sorry. I have to go. I'm actually in the middle of my shift. I need to get back to Dr. Decker."

Damon led away his sisters. He checked over his shoulder and mouthed a thank you. Remi watched them leave the cafeteria and hoped the next few days would be quiet.

TWENTY-SEVEN

The voice echoed down the dormitory hallway, bringing anger into Lily's chest and a squeak from Neko in her hair.

"What is she doing here?"

Lily marched in the direction of the half-pixie's voice, skidding to a stop when she saw Damon's sisters talking to Morwen by the lounge. Morwen was wearing a little plastic pink backpack, a plaid skirt, and a white button-down while her hair was flame orange and red.

A flicker of concern flashed through Morwen's eyes as she spotted Lily. The twins spun around.

"Lilith!"

Their good mood stilled Lily's tongue, that and the warning from Dr. Decker, who had made it clear that any further interference would be detrimental to her staying in Aura Healers.

"A good day to you all," said Lily.

"This is our new friend, Morwen," said Natasha.

"I know who she is."

The cold tone brought knitted foreheads from the twins.

"You two used to date or something?"

A curt laugh slipped from Morwen's lips. "She'd sooner date an infernal beast."

"I wouldn't know the difference between the two," said Lily, crossing her arms.

"What happened?" asked Natasha.

"I would say more, but I'm forbidden to, since she's a patient of the hospital."

"Ahh, confidential information," said Natalia, nodding. "She was just telling us about how tough it is being an outsider in the city."

Morwen stared at her feet. Lily was going to tell them it was a lie and she was doing it to con them, but noticed a bruise along the half-pixie's jaw.

"Aye, it might be the city of sorcery, but that doesn't mean everyone wants to row in the same boat," said Lily. "The laws are there, but that doesn't keep people from being arseholes."

Morwen glanced up with surprise glittering in her eyes.

"I'm not blind," said Lily. "But that doesn't excuse an individual's actions."

"Sometimes people have reasons," replied Morwen.

"Aye. Greed. Selfishness."

Natalia hooked her arm around Lily's. "Did you know she has a younger sister?"

"Aye."

"Talwen Clover. Pixies have the cutest names," said Natalia.

"Don't let that fool ya," said Lily.

"Hey!" said Natalia, turning on Morwen. "You should bring your sister to the hospital so we can meet her."

Morwen paled. Her mouth opened and closed, before she finally mustered a response.

"She doesn't really get out much. I don't think that would be possible."

"Come on," said Natalia. "We'd love to meet her. After all, you just spent the last half hour telling us how awesome she was. Why wouldn't you bring her here?"

Morwen swallowed and glanced sheepishly around. "I probably should go. I have to get back."

Before she could leave, the twins gave her huge hugs as if they were old friends. Morwen appeared surprisingly embarrassed, and for once, Lily believed the emotions on the half-pixie's face.

The bruise and the reluctance to bring her sister set Lily's mind whirling, but she didn't get much chance to contemplate when Remi appeared around the corner. She was in her scrubs with a crimson long-sleeve shirt beneath and black hair messily framing her face.

"Did I just hear…?"

"Do you know Morwen?" asked the twins at the same time.

Remi tilted her head at Lily. "Yeah, but—"

"Anyone hungry for a basket of fries? My treat," said Lily.

"Hells yes," said Natalia. "Race you to the cafeteria."

The twins burst into motion, disappearing around the corner before Remi could say anything else.

"What was that about?" asked Remi, falling in beside Lily.

"Do you know the saying, a bog doesn't lie, but it hides?"

"Can't say I have, but I *think* I understand what you're saying."

Lily faced Remi.

"What do you think about Morwen? Am I being too harsh?"

Remi's mouth cocked to the side. "Honestly, I don't know. She has been stealing from the hospital, which I really can't complain about considering my actions last year. I don't know Morwen specifically, but I know that people don't turn to stealing except when there's a lot of other things wrong with their life. Until you know the whole story, I don't think you can really judge Morwen Clover."

Lily didn't realize she was still standing in the middle of the hallway until Remi tugged on her shirt.

"You coming?"

"No, you go on."

Remi headed towards the cafeteria, leaving Lily standing in the same place. A tiny squeak issued from the depths of her hair.

"You think I'm being an arsehole too?"

A second, more forceful squeak followed.

"Fine. But I'm reserving judgement until later. It's not my fault every pixie I've known has been a gigantic pain in my arse."

TWENTY-EIGHT

The machine wheezed as it pumped oxygen into Arthur's nose. Damon watched as his father kept up a fortified smile despite the clear exhaustion evident in his hazel eyes. The twins were busy telling the story of the State finals when Natalia got the game winning goal after Natasha ran over a defender for a 50/50 ball.

"...Nat threw me a BTB dime right in the slot and I pinged it right off the crossbar, into the back of the goalie's legs, then into the goal."

"That's great, girls. I'm so proud of you," said their father.

On the surface his voice sounded strong, but before they'd arrived a nurse had given him a booster shot so he'd have the energy to interact with the twins. His father had made Damon promise that they wouldn't see him weak.

"When will you be coming home?" asked Natalia, leaning on the bed and holding his hand.

"I'm sure it won't be much longer. There are no better healers in the world than Golden Willow. A matter of time, I'm sure," he said with a propped-up smile.

"Sorry, Dad. We've been talking this whole time. Doing anything fun while you're here?" asked Natasha.

"I don't get out much," said Arthur, gesturing towards the equipment.

Natasha's shoulders dipped. "Oh, right." She rolled her eyes. "Stupid question."

"It's okay, I've been watching these afternoon shows, though I really wish they'd run *The Magelings* in order."

"You? *The Magelings*?" asked the twins in unison.

"It's not terrible."

Damon put his hands on their shoulders. "We really should let Dad rest. Nurse Mandy said you should only visit for ten minutes, but it's nearly been forty."

"It's okay, Damon," said his father weakly. "I'm feeling good today."

Natalia checked her phone. "It's okay. We should get to the train to make our flight."

The twins leaned down and kissed their father on the forehead. He squeezed their hands and smiled from his bed.

"I'll walk you out," said Damon when they were finished.

In the hallway, Natasha asked, "He's going to be alright, right?"

"We're not giving up," said Damon.

"That doesn't sound like there's a clear plan," said Natalia, crossing her arms.

Damon carefully calibrated his expression, which was much harder because his younger sisters knew him well.

"I won't rest until he's fixed."

"Good, because I'm sick of having these dreams," said Natasha. "I'm sure Talia is too."

"What dreams?" asked Damon, facing them both.

They shared glances. "Since he's been in the hospital, we've been having these dreams like we're in the city. Running through the streets. We had this one where we cut some hob in half with a sword," said Natalia.

"I assume it has to do with the clan connection. I bet Dad's been watching all the coverage of the Full Moon Killer and then dreaming about it," said Natasha.

"The clan connection?"

The twins shared glances again.

"The link shared by all the members of the clan? I know it's only us left, but don't you ever feel it? Maybe we feel it more because we're twins, but sometimes I can sense what Nat is doing even when we're in separate places."

"Me too," said Natasha, nodding. "Mom said that Zev clan was known for the connection. She doesn't have it, of course, but we've got half the blood, so..."

Natalia tilted her head. "Maybe it's more messed up for you, since everything happened when you were going through the changes."

Damon looked away. He vaguely remembered family talking about the connection when he was younger, but after the clan was wiped out, it was never brought up. Damon remembered the day that it'd happened, he'd had horrible dreams. He couldn't remember them now, but he remembered waking up covered in sweat and blood. He'd somehow bloodied his nose, or at least that's what his mom had told him.

"What's up, big brother?" asked Natasha. "You look like you just saw a ghost."

"Old memories," he said, shaking his head. "Come on. You should get moving. The trains will be packed due to the holidays. Message me when you get to the airport and then when you get home to KC."

"Yes, Damon-Mom," said the twins in unison.

He kissed them both on the cheeks, gave them long hugs, and watched as they jogged across the parking lot, heading towards the nearest station. Despite his fears, he was glad they'd come to visit. He'd forgotten how important family was.

But that connection brought back bad clan memories. He knew, deep down, that part of the reason he'd spent all that time volunteering at KC General was to avoid the thoughts about his extended family getting slaughtered by an unknown entity.

Before it'd happened he'd always asked his dad about news of the clan, exploits of his half-brother Connor Black, and any other information he could squeeze out of his parents. Then afterwards, there was no one to ask about, so he walled that away and tried to forget about it.

But what if that connection could help him now? The link seemed to be strongest near the full moon, which was in a few weeks after the New Year. His father was one hundred percent Zev clan. That might be why he was sick. Whatever was driving Connor Black to kill was eating his father from within. And what if there was a way to use that familial connection to track down Connor before he killed anyone else? Damon headed straight for the hospital library. He had two weeks to figure out a way to use what had felt like a curse as a way to solve his family's problems. And if he couldn't? Then he feared he'd lose his father just as he had the rest of the clan.

TWENTY-NINE

Lily reached for the mass of hair only to find it slicked back, captured into a long braid bound by silver wire. She still wasn't used to it after an hour of enchantments and hair dye. She caught a glimpse of herself in the reflection of the stainless steel lamp base. The black hair clashed with the pale skin and band of freckles across her nose, making her look even younger than she really was.

"I look like a bloody Goth kid with bad taste."

Neko squeaked from the bed covers, making grasping motions with his tiny paws.

"I'm sorry, little one, you can't come. I fear your presence might give me away."

Lily adjusted her cutoff shirt, which showed off the ring in her belly button. The low black jeans threatened to slide down her hips on the way out the door. She passed two nurses who didn't give her a second look.

Lily didn't recognize herself in the mirror, and she was pleased that others saw her in the same way.

The Hollow Nine was bustling when she arrived. With only a day before the new year, people were in a festive mood. The bouncer took a second look at her ID, then shrugged and waved her in when she paid the fee. The tables were packed, so Lily found an open spot at the nearest bar, ordering a cheap whiskey, and turned around so she could watch what was happening.

At the nearest stage, a hob woman with spiked hair and a half dozen rings in her nose and lip gyrated around the pole topless, occasionally dancing near the crowded edge. Her ochre shoulders had been sprinkled with reflective glitter. The hazy eyes and thousand-yard stare told Lily the woman was on drugs of some kind, probably to get through the night of work.

The other stages were similarly occupied. All of them non-humans of some kind or another, though with a few it was hard to tell. Lily imagined they'd been modified by sorcery, or had infusions like Sammie.

A half hour later, the tall, attractive dirty-blond owner of the club strolled through in a black coat over a crimson T-shirt. He wore his arrogance like a badge, which only made Lily want to punch him in the face, or curse him with an impotence hex. He would stop at a table, chat with the guests, and move on to the next.

But Lily wasn't there for him. She looked for the Clover sisters, but neither were visible in the club.

When the owner reached the bar and leaned past the other customers a few spots down to order a drink, Lily walked over and touched his arm. His initial grimace immediately turned to a fake smile upon seeing her.

"Hey, darling. How can I help you?"

He was studying her intensely as if he were trying to figure out how he should know her. The enchantments that she'd layered on herself should have provided some anonymity and add a touch of a beguiling aura.

"You're the owner?" she asked, using a neutral accent that she'd been practicing on her patients.

He held out his hand, smiling wide, which revealed a silver tooth etched with runes. She couldn't tell what kind based on the brief glance, but most likely they were faez detectors to warn him if someone was trying to ensorcell him.

"Felix Marken. At your service. And you are?"

"Genevieve." It was her sister's name. "I was wondering about one of your dancers."

He accepted his drink from the bartender and lifted his chin as he looked down upon her.

"We have all kinds for every taste." He half turned towards the club. "Let me guess, you like the big beefy ones. Magus is in back around the corner in the special room. I promise you his touch is as magical as advertised. Some of the ladies, and a few of the men, that enjoy his show have been back almost every night this week. You won't be disappointed."

Felix winked, which made Lily want to throw up inside. It was the kind of condescending gesture that he probably thought was charming, or endearing.

"I'm interested in a different sort. I have a thing for a certain kind of Fae ladies."

The corners of his eyes creased. "Certain kind?"

Lily inhaled deeply as if she were smelling an intoxicating perfume.

"I have a nose for Fae. The last time I was here I caught a whiff of their presence. Pixies. They're my kink, if you get what I mean. But much to my disappointment, I never saw them take the stage."

His mouth stayed stretched in a smile while his eyes turned hard. He pulled back his jacket as he settled his hand on his hip, revealing a curved blade in a fancy ornate scabbard. The symbols on the outside marked it as a Hathi blade, which were all the rage in the criminal class of the city. A cut from the razor-sharp edge would burn like a white-hot fire, causing immense pain that wouldn't subside for hours. It was like dumping habanero juice into an open wound. The hospital had to occasionally treat people who'd messed with the wrong gangsters, which was how she'd learned about the enchanted weapons.

"They ain't dancers," he said, his pseudo country accent thickening as he stared her down.

"Private sessions only?"

Felix put a heavy hand on her shoulder, gave it a painful squeeze.

"I don't think you're here for a dance. Which means you're probably here on behalf of one of my competitors. I suggest that you take your sweet ass out of my establishment before I ask my bouncers to remove you forcibly."

"I'm not—"

He waggled his finger. "Tsk. Tsk. That's no way to answer me. The proper way is to say, you're right, Mr. Marken, I will remove myself immediately. You see, that's how we move things along without causing a scene. You don't want to be the reason everyone was talking about the screaming lady, do you? You seem like a nice young thing. I'd hate to ruin your day."

Inside, Lily wanted to rage. If Neko had been with her and she'd brought other protections, she might have shown him how big of a witch she was, but that wouldn't have ended well, given the number of his crew in the room.

"I'm leaving now."

Lily spun around and marched towards the door. She felt the heat of his gaze as she left.

"Don't come back," said the bouncer upon exit.

She headed around the corner and leaned over on her knees, frustrated by the result. Before she'd come, she'd thought about involving Remi for her criminal expertise, but hadn't wanted her to get in trouble. That had been a mistake. Lily realized she understood this world less than she'd thought.

She took a step towards the train station before halting on the side-walk. She wouldn't have another free evening for a week and that was already spoken for since it was the full moon.

Lily jogged around the block to come at the strip club from another angle. The back alleyway was lined with expensive cars sporting tinted windows. Business was good for Felix Marken. She spied cameras and two guards standing by a garage door, so she went in search of other entrances.

A rusty ladder led to the second-story roof. She climbed the cold rungs, hating the way they rattled. The flat area was covered in vents and two large HVAC units, humming to keep the club warm. She rubbed her hands together and put a weather enchantment on them.

After a thorough examination of the roof, she realized there was no other entrance she could easily bypass. She found one of the vents, which was a tube sticking out of the tarred roof, and put her ear to it after casting a hearing enhancement spell. Mumbled voices became clearer until she could make out a couple of gangsters talking about their favorite TV shows. Lily moved on to the next tube, but heard nothing. It wasn't until the fifth that she heard Morwen's voice, followed by a lower, angrier one.

"I don't care if she's tired. We've got a shipment due tomorrow. If she can't do it, then the boss is gonna be angry. You're already on his shit list."

"You're killing her," said Morwen. "She can't take much more."

"Not my problem, honey. I'm just here to tell you that the quota has to be met or we're gonna take it out on you."

A door slam was followed by deep sobbing. Lily listened as Morwen comforted her sister. She stayed on the roof until she realized they'd either left the room or were doing something that didn't require talking.

Lily found the ladder and was preparing to leave when a white delivery van pulled down the alleyway. The door opened, but it didn't go inside. Instead, she watched as men loaded the van with cardboard boxes which had a bright purple unicorn on the side. After a few dozen boxes were stacked inside, the vehicle left the alleyway and headed around the corner.

Deep, fist-squeezing anger overtook Lily as she realized not only what was being done to the Clover sisters, but also how she'd treated Morwen. Remi had been right. Most people didn't steal for the reasons you thought. It explained the bruise and Morwen's sister not being allowed to leave the club. Pixies could produce a fine dust which would induce powerful hallucinations, or other interesting effects. Along with the painkillers that Morwen was stealing from Golden Willow, the dust was probably being turned into party drugs based on the logo from the cardboard boxes. Lily didn't know what she was going to do, but leaving the Clover sisters in the clutches of the gang wasn't an option. She wasn't prepared to do anything today, but sometime soon, she was going to come back. No one, not even an annoying trickster from the Fae, should be treated like a slave.

THIRTY

A cold wind whipped through the city, throwing Remi's hair around her face and forcing her to shove her hands deeper into her pockets.

"It's so cold my enchantment isn't working."

Damon had his hood back and was marching forward with an intensity that worried her.

"It's nothing like the winds that come off the North Atlantic," said Lily. "I believe it might be where the term colder than a witch's tit comes from."

Remi raised her eyebrow at her friend, trying to decide if she was messing with her, but Lily was focused forward. They'd been walking around the tenth ward for the last two hours trying to track down Connor Black using the family link. The spell that Lily had put on Damon to help him with the connection had been surprisingly simple, but despite that, he hadn't yet been able to find him.

"He's got to be around here somewhere," said Damon when they passed the corner Wizard's Coffee for the fourth time. "I can feel him somewhere around here, but there aren't any apartments, or places to hide. It's all stupid businesses."

Remi felt something squish beneath her sneaker. She lifted her foot to see a half-eaten chocolate donut with cream oozing out the side. Her sneaker was covered in chocolate and cream.

"Gross."

"I guess they didn't like it," said Lily.

The others waited for her to clean off her shoe with a piece of paper she caught blowing down the street. When she finished, she found a bin nearby and tossed the waste into the opening. Remi was about to continue on until she noticed a smear of chocolate on the concrete where she'd stepped on the donut.

"What if we're looking in the wrong place?"

Damon gestured angrily around him. "It can't be. I can feel him right near here. But I don't understand why we can't find him."

"Right," said Remi. "But what if he's underground?"

Damon ran a hand through his thick black hair. His ice-blue eyes radiated relief.

"I thought I was going mad. I guess we need to look for basement entrances."

"Like that one over there," said Lily.

Remi didn't see it at first. The metal cover had been painted with a textured gray material that made it appear to be concrete. After a brief inspection, Damon found the hook which allowed the doors to be pulled wide, revealing a narrow staircase leading into the darkness.

"You okay?" she asked him when he stayed at the top, staring with reservations on his brow.

"Either we get answers or we have to kill him. Once we go down here, there's no going back."

"We don't have to kill him," said Remi.

The areas around his eyes were etched with intensity. "We do. If he's a danger, and we can't get answers, then we have to. For the good of the city. He's my family's responsibility, and if we find out that he was behind the slaughter of the clan, then he *has* to die."

The weight of that decision was heavy on his shoulders. Remi could easily see that. But what he didn't see was that if he had to kill Connor Black, then he'd never forgive himself, even if it was the right thing to do. She didn't want him to go down, but didn't know how he couldn't.

"We've got your back," said Remi.

Damon stared at his fingers for a moment. No sign of his talons. Could he change if he needed to? Remi hated that they were about to find out.

The metal stairs made no noise on the way down. The entrance looked like it hadn't been used in a long time. In front of the door, the huge pile of old, frozen leaves had been pushed away. An old chain and lock lay impotent, the metal shattered by a single strike.

"Certainly looks like he could be here," said Remi.

"No one does anything until I have a chance to talk to him," said Damon.

Lily touched her enormous halo of rainbow-colored hair. "Want Neko?"

"Not yet. He might get spooked if we bring Neko out."

The metal door creaked when it opened. A narrow passage between pipes led to darkness. Remi thought Damon was going to create light first, but he marched forward. She curled behind Lily, wondering how big an idiot she was for following them into the darkness after a notorious killer. Her parents would have scoffed at her decisions, calling her a fool and a mark, and maybe that's why she kept going despite her reservations.

The winding alley widened as they went down a second set of stairs to an open area that ticked and clinked, old machines shifting in the darkness due to the wintery cold.

"Can you see?" whispered Remi.

A heavy footfall announced the arrival of another person. The noise came from somewhere ahead.

Lily chanted lightly under her breath and a glowing ball of cool light appeared above her outstretched hand, dancing on the tips of her fingers. She gestured, and the mage light surged forward, revealing a larger space than Remi would have guessed. It looked like an old manufacturing space that had been closed down many decades ago.

Remi saw Damon tense before she saw Connor Black herself. The menacing figure stood between two rusting machines, the paint peeled around the solid metal bases. He wore black clothes and his bushy beard turned his eyes into chips of ice deep within the cavernous expanse. The glint of madness, familiar after a year and a half in the hospital, shone from those windows. Connor Black raised the sword, which took on an ethereal glow, and slammed his foot forward, ringing the metal grating.

THIRTY-ONE

Damon had never been so afraid in his life. Not for himself. Not even for his friends. He was afraid for his family, Connor Black included. When the clan had been wiped out, it had destroyed so much. Countless lives cut short. He'd felt guilty that they hadn't been there, even though Damon had just hit puberty at the time. The slaughter had defined his life, made him who he was today, and to find out that his father's half-brother had survived, it turned his head into a tangled mess of emotions.

"Connor, wait, I'm family," said Damon when he stepped forward, his heavy boot ringing against the metal grating.

Connor Black halted, his face etched with confusion. The sword rose a hair.

"It's me. Damon Wolfhard. Arthur's son."

A low growl in the back of Connor's throat was a warning. His uncle had a few inches on him, as well as an ancient sword and the skill to use it. The promise that he'd made his friends outside about killing Connor seemed laughable now.

"I'm not here to hurt you." He thought back to the visions. "I know you're in pain."

The tip of the sword quivered with indecision.

"I don't know why you killed that hob, or the others in the city, but I know you didn't mean to."

"Damon," whispered Remi from the side, but he shook her off.

"Please. I don't know what's going on. Why you're doing this, or who the other person was at the arcade, but I'm here to help. I'm a healer. I work at Golden Willow. Whatever ails you, maybe I can fix. *We* can fix." He gestured to his left and right. "These are my friends. They're healers too. Please, Connor. I'm sure you remember me. I was a scrawny, awkward kid when we met last. You showed me how to howl in human form."

Damon leaned his head back and the sound reverberated out his throat, echoing into the space. Connor stared back without moving, so Damon repeated the howl, letting it carry the feeling of loss and longing that he felt whenever he thought about his family. The mournful tune vibrated his entire body.

At the moment, he thought he couldn't hold it any longer, Connor joined him. The two voices intertwined in the way that only a family of wolves could, calling to each other across vast distances, a reminder of connection that couldn't be broken. When at last they finished, the sword in Connor's fist was no longer raised. The tip lay against the metal grating. Then he turned and headed the other way, disappearing down a passage hidden by the darkness.

"My body is covered in chills," said Remi, staring at the raised hairs on her arm.

Damon followed Connor, the torturous pathway leading to an old office that had been repurposed into living quarters. A camping lamp hanging from a pipe provided illumination. Connor was seated on a bench, staring at the floor while the sword lay on a nearby desk.

"Arthur is alive?"

"Yes," said Damon, nodding.

Connor looked away, lips pinched. "Since I came to the city, it's felt like I could feel him again. When we were younger, we were like twins, hunting, playing, doing everything together."

"What happened?"

Connor closed his eyes and rocked on the edge of the bench. "He hunts me. I thought I was the last."

"Not the last. My sisters, my mom. They're alive too. You're not alone."

His ice-blue eyes, colder than the water at the bottom of the Antarctic, stared back through the hair falling in his face.

"They're in danger. You're in danger."

"Who is he? The guy at the arcade?"

Connor nodded. "A fiendish hunter from the depths of time. Until now, he's never failed a hunt. He has no peer."

"Who?"

"Koschei. The deathless hunter."

An in-breath from Lily told Damon the severity of the news. When he looked to her she responded, "I thought he was a legend."

"Not a legend. Since the day he slaughtered the clan, I've been evading him. No matter where I go, he shows up eventually. I came to the city of sorcery because I thought that the lingering faez and mass of people might confuse the scent, but I was mistaken. He cannot be avoided."

"Is he the one killing people?" asked Damon, still standing on the opposite side of the room.

Connor closed his eyes momentarily. "I wish that were the case. No. That has been me unfortunately. It's the great corruption. It changes me on the full moon."

"The kalkatai," said Damon.

"You know it?"

"Last year, we had to...it doesn't matter. It's affecting you?"

"It affects everything connected to the realm of the summer fae. Since King Nuada pledged himself to the Oak Father, our lives have been entwined with his."

"Is that why Koschei's hunting you?"

Connor shook his head. "His reasons are not visible to me. But whatever his motives, your life is in danger as much as mine. Your father and the twins too, because they have King Nuada's blood."

"Then why are you killing those people?"

Connor squeezed his hands together until the knuckles turned white. "When the full moon comes, I lose myself. I don't know if it's the kalkatai, or Koschei is doing something through my connection to the Fae, but I can't control myself."

"You're hunting people connected to the realm of nightmares," said Lily.

"I am," said Connor. "It pains me. They did nothing wrong, yet I cut them down without remorse in the depths of my madness."

"Why does he hunt our family?" asked Damon.

"I don't know. The first few times we clashed, I thought to pry that information from him, but he would not divulge it. Then I cut him down, thinking that I had destroyed him, only to find him returning months later with no visible signs of his previous wounds. Which were grievous, I might add."

"He keeps his soul in a phylactery," said Lily. "It is said such magics were lost to time, but legends mark him as an ancient being."

"He stinks of the infernal realm, a being molded out of raw creation. Whatever his motives, I cannot escape him." Connor looked up. "Nor you, I'm afraid."

"We'll kill him," said Damon.

"Unlikely," said Connor.

"Are you giving up?" asked Damon angrily.

Connor sat tall. "Can a mountain resist the wind and the rain washing it away?"

Lily stepped forward. "I could give you an elixir. One that would help you with the worst effects of the kalkatai. It might even keep Koschei from detecting you. He's probably using the corruption as a way to find you."

Connor nodded. "I would accept any help you can give in that regard, but for Koschei, it's best if you stay away."

"Stay away? What choice do we have? You said it yourself, I'm in danger because we share the same blood. Koschei is as much my burden as he is yours," said Damon.

"Find his phylactery and he can be beaten," said Lily.

"Why wouldn't he keep it in a remote location far away from the city?" asked Remi.

"It doesn't work like that," said Lily. "He can't get too far from it or he'll be like a puppet without all the strings."

"What can a phylactery be?" asked Remi.

"Anything. Legends are that he keeps it in a duck egg, but that's just rumor and probably encouraged by Koschei himself to confuse his methods." Lily paused. "I'll contact my sisters, see if there's anything in our histories that might help finding it."

"Thank you," said Damon.

Connor grunted under his breath. "Even if you take out his phylactery, he's still a dangerous being. The few times I've managed to hurt him, it was luck and the benefits of the sword. You won't have that same protection if you try and tangle with him."

"I don't want to take him on myself, but to help you," said Damon.

The concern etched in Connor's expression broke. He'd been alone so long he'd clearly forgotten what it was like to have friends.

"Thank you, nephew."

"We should head back if we want to make him an elixir," said Lily.

"Aye," said Connor with a soul-worn weariness. "And if you're right about it, maybe I can lay low for once. Keep my blade dry."

"We're going to get Koschei," said Damon. "Avenge our family and bring you peace."

Connor glanced up. "I'll never know peace again."

They left him sitting on the bed, hands clasped and staring at the floor.

"Are you sure about this?" asked Remi when they were outside.

Damon thought to how his life had been upended by the destruction of the clan.

"I'll never be safe unless we kill Koschei the deathless."

THIRTY-TWO

The weather had broken, bringing warm breezes from the coast. A few scattered clouds dotted the sky above the city of sorcery. Lily watched from the picnic table on the roof, catching the glint of reflections from the glass gondolas soaring across the sky.

Her friends showed up shortly after, both in their scrubs. The sleeve of Remi's shirt was sliced into ribbons while Damon's were fresh as he was heading to his second shift of the day.

"Is this what sunlight is?" asked Remi, squinting at the sky.

"The city seems peaceful from up here," added Damon, wandering to the edge of the roof. "Is this about Koschei? I only have a few minutes before I meet Dr. Hunker for rotations."

"No," said Lily, shaking her head. "My sisters had nothing more that could help us with Koschei, but I ain't done looking. There are other ways of finding the truth. This isn't about our deathless friend or your uncle."

"Is Neko okay?"

Lily smiled. "Aye. Right as rain. I wanted your help, if you're willing. This is about Morwen and Talwen Clover."

"Lily," said Remi, tilting her head. "You know you need to let it go. Decker will kick you out."

"This isn't that," said Lily.

Then she continued to describe the day she went to Hollow Nine to find out more about Morwen and how the head of the gang, Felix Marken, saw through her disguise.

"What are you suggesting?" asked Remi. "It's not like we can go head-to-head with an entire gang. We're in over our heads with Koschei already."

"I know. I know. Tis worse than a lonely magpie. But I'm asking just the same."

Damon lifted his shoulders. "I'd love to strangle that Felix, but Remi's right. They outgun us, and it's not like we can walk into a club and start murdering people. And even if we did, they'd be looking for revenge. We'd only be putting the entire hospital at risk. I'm already jumping at shadows, thinking Koschei is hiding in the patients' rooms whenever I go in."

"If I had a solution, I wouldn't have called you here, I would have gone and done it. But that's what I'm asking."

"The only way this would work is if Felix hands them over and never wants to see them again," said Remi, forehead hunched.

"Yeah, right," said Damon, rolling his eyes. "No way he's giving up his golden goose."

Lily could see that Remi's mind was working on a solution. Her mouth was moving, but no words were coming out. Damon looked like he was going to say something, so she waved him off.

"Unless..."

Remi burst from the table and marched to the edge of the roof. She stilled before spinning around.

"In the world that Felix Marken lives in, might makes right. He's carved himself a little empire with his strip club and drug-making operation. The thing that he fears most is that another gang tries to muscle in—no, not that. It can't be another gang." She paced before the edge. "It has to be someone or something that they're completely outmatched by. Not a gang. A presence. Someone so powerful that even an asshole like Felix Marken can't think about resisting."

"You're not thinking of getting Connor involved?" asked Damon.

"No. They'd put a dozen bullets in his chest before he finished his demands," said Remi.

"Then who in Merlin's name are you thinking of?"

The deranged laugh that came out of Remi's mouth had Lily wondering if she'd made a mistake in involving her friends.

"Do you really want to help the Clover sisters?"

"That's why I asked you here," said Lily.

"I have an idea," said Remi with a heavy sigh. "But it just might get the three of us killed."

THIRTY-THREE

The skin around Remi's eyes ached as if someone had been pinching them all day. She wanted to massage her face, but Damon had warned her that could leave scars if she burst the enraged blood vessels. Vasculitis, a condition that caused inflammation of the blood vessels, was normally cured rather than induced in the hospital, but to fix a problem a healer had to know how it was generated. Her skin, already pale from spending her waking life inside the hospital, looked like tiny crimson worms had taken roost in her face, and her eyes were so bloodshot as to look haunted.

The bouncer recoiled at her appearance, which was the reaction she'd been receiving all the way across the city. Her taxi driver had almost gotten into a half dozen accidents because he'd been so busy staring at her through the rearview mirror.

"Shadow's below, what's wrong with you?" asked the bouncer, putting his hand on the stun baton on his hip. "It'd better not be contagious."

"I'm here to see your master."

The voice that came out of her throat was not her own. More spells, this time to modify her vocal cords, turned her into a three-pack-a-day smoker from the underworld. The rest of her outfit had been borrowed from one of the nurses who spent her weekends cosplaying famous mages from the Halls. The heavy green robes, smudged with fresh leaves and dirt, were dreadfully hot but they made her feel like she could have been the White Worm's underling.

"Lady, it ain't Halloween anymore. Take your freak show somewhere else."

"If you will not allow me to pass then I will be forced to summon my creator. He collects unwilling souls for his menagerie."

Remi surged forward, daring the bouncer to put a hand out to stop her. He let her pass, lips soured by her presence.

The interior of the Hollow Nine was bustling with music and lights. The urge to check the place out was strong, but her persona only had one goal: talking to Felix Marken. She assumed he'd have been warned by radio and she was right as she saw him come out of a back room, headed in her direction. As Remi passed the first stage, the spotted dancer nearly fell off the pole, which only brought more stares from the businessmen in their chairs.

Felix approached with the bravado of a gunfighter. His dirty-blond hair hung in his face and he had his jacket open slightly, revealing the pistol shoved into his waistband.

"I don't know what the hell is going on, but you're scaring my customers. You need to leave before I show you the bottom of my boot."

Remi had never met Felix Marken, but she knew many like him. He was a bully, puffed up on his own self-importance and prepared to do anything to keep atop his little hill. He'd probably started out as a petty thief and eventually realized that he wasn't patient enough for real work, and it was much easier to make others do the work for him. Drugs, stolen goods, exploitation. It didn't matter what it was, as long as he had people under him and the money rolled in.

But what every thug like him feared was someone bigger coming along and taking everything. It happened all the time, which made men like Felix on edge, waiting for the first signs.

"You have my master's property."

They stood in a space between the bar and one of the tables. Felix glanced around and the people nearby moved away quickly, sensing they weren't meant to hear the conversation.

"And what property is that?" asked Felix, tilting his head and placing his hand on the butt of his weapon. He glanced suspiciously at her hand, shoved into the pocket of her robe.

Remi did all she could not to stare at the gun. Damon had tried to talk her into wearing a bulletproof vest beneath her shirt, but she didn't want to risk discovery. Men like Felix sensed anything that wasn't quite right because their lives depended on it.

"The pixies. We've been looking for them for quite some time. One of my hounds picked up their scent and it led me here."

"If you lost 'em then they're mine by rights," said Felix, leaning into a country accent as he glowered. "I rely on them for my business. I'm not giving them up."

Remi gave Felix a flat stare, and based on the reactions of everyone on the way to the club, she was impressed that he didn't immediately recoil. Nothing about her look was fake, which was why she thought it would work. But now that she was standing in his presence, she worried that he was either harder, or more desperate than she first thought.

"I have obligations for the products I provide," said Felix, clearly uncomfortable about her silence. "You can't take them."

Remi continued to say nothing, letting the emotion drain from her face until it was a mask of emptiness. She wanted to check the time on the clock above the bar, but didn't want to look away.

Felix swallowed.

"Who is this master of yours?"

"Do you really need to ask?"

His nostrils flared as he stared back, anger rising to his cheeks.

"How about we take your pale ass and leave it in a ditch over in the twelfth ward. I don't think anyone will miss you, and your so-called master will understand that he made a mistake and now it's time to let his former property go, or lose more of his little weirdos."

Remi pulled her right hand out of the pocket of the robe. She'd kept it hidden the entirety of the trip. As soon as it was revealed, Felix took a step back. Her hand looked like a withered piece of twisted wood with black pus leaking between the cracks.

"You touch me with that and I'm putting a hole through your chest."

"A temporary solution to a thorny problem," said Remi. "It would only delay the inevitable. My master is not patient. He was rather disappointed by events last year."

"Last year?"

Remi squeezed her fist, which cracked the flesh and made more black pus come out. Her skin was on fire, but she kept up a serene expression as she glanced to the clock on the wall, hoping it was correct.

While they'd been talking, Felix's men had come out from the back. Five of his henchmen were arrayed in a semicircle. Nearby customers had fled to other parts of the strip club and the dancers were leaning against their poles, watching the scene with dread and curiosity.

"A flower rots in the darkness," she said cryptically.

Felix checked to see his men were nearby, which was a problem for Remi. Their presence meant he couldn't back down easily. He pulled his pistol out of his waistband and pointed it at her chest.

"I think it's time you spun around and marched out of my club. I don't care who your master is, but if he can't keep his pixies in line, then it's not my fault I've put them to use." He nodded at his men. "Throw her out."

Two of them approached, but halted when the front entrance burst open and the enormous bouncer was hurled through the opening, knocking over a table of bottled beer. Weapons were pulled and customers scrambled to the other half of the club.

When Damon came strolling through the entrance, Remi almost didn't recognize him. He wore a black suit and black tie, which looked sharp on his impressive frame, but what really sold his appearance was that he'd changed to his werewolf form and used an ebony cane. Werewolf Damon approached in a saunter that would have made a pimp proud.

"Now who the fuck are you?" asked Felix. "Is this your master?"

Remi grinned, revealing her blackened teeth. "No."

She was proud of Damon when he came up to Felix, standing in his space and glowering over him. She hadn't quite believed the twins when they'd said he'd acted in the school play, but she understood now. Remi just hoped he didn't play his part too well and get them all killed.

"Fa'lli ach nostrum," said Damon without breaking eye contact. His elongated mouth glistened with sharp teeth.

The Fae words coming out of his lips startled Remi, but thankfully everyone was staring at him and didn't see her reaction.

"What did he say?" Felix asked her.

"Bring them now," she said.

Wheels were turning behind Felix's eyes as he considered everything he'd seen thus far. When she'd come up with this plan, she'd been very clear that under no circumstances should they ever actually say who it was. The imagination was more powerful than any lie. Their best bet of escaping with the pixies and their hides was to never be so direct as to threaten or explain. Real gangsters said as little as possible and let mystery fill in the bits between.

The pulsing of Felix's jaw told Remi that he hadn't quite come around to the validity of the threat. She saw him coming to the conclusion that he had to act now or lose everything.

"Alright, you couple of freaks, let's see how much you enjoy three pounds of lead in your chest."

Felix raised his weapon, which prompted the rest of his goons to do the same. He was halfway through the motion when a woman two stages over started screaming.

The noise startled Felix, who glanced in her direction.

"Somebody shut her the fuck up."

As two men moved to intercept, the woman's limbs erupted with vines and flowers, wrapping around her body, encasing her in plant life. Then as she stumbled away, the leafy materials turned black and rotted away. The woman ran out of the club with material sloughing off her.

"Llagtha yoa emha," said Damon with a toothy grin.

Felix glanced between them, expecting a translation, but Remi just smiled, letting her blackened teeth startle the second row of goons. As she waited for a decision, one of Felix's men ran up and whispered in his ear. He wasn't so quiet, so Remi could hear a description of what had happened at the Fishmarket and then at the Arcane Phylactery charity event. His eyes widened more the longer his henchman spoke. When he was finished, Felix nodded towards the back room. A few minutes later, Morwen and her sister stumbled into the club, clearly confused by events.

"Your service here is finished," said Felix, glowering. "I hope your betrayal is properly punished."

He turned and walked away, gesturing to his men as if he were in control. The Clover sisters stared back at Remi and Damon with utmost concern, but followed them out when they left. A black SUV with tinted windows pulled up the moment they exited the club.

The bouncer had recovered from Damon throwing him through the door and peeked out as they climbed into the back of the vehicle. Remi was last, sitting next to Morwen, who appeared ready to flee and might have except for her sister, who looked pale, her dark brown skin drained of its vitality with huge bags under her eyes.

The driver pulled away.

No one said a word until they went around the block and stopped for a woman covered in rotting vines, yanking the plant material off her body. She climbed into the back and banished the glamour from her face.

"You?" asked Morwen when she realized the woman was Lily. The half-pixie glanced between them shaking her head. "What's going on?"

"My apologies," said Lily. "I'm sorry I was wrong about you and your sister. It wasn't until a few weeks ago that I saw what was really happening and enlisted my friends to free you from him."

The younger Clover doubled over with coughing. The fit lasted until she could sit up.

"Sorry."

"Don't be sorry," said Lily. "We'll get you patched up at Golden Willow."

"Lily," said Remi.

"Aye?"

She held out her desiccated hand. "Can you put this back to what it was before? My face too, but the hand hurts worse."

Lily reached into an inner pocket, producing a vial of bubbling brown liquid. She poured it on the hand, which sizzled as the wood-like covering broke away, crisping into ashes and falling to the floor. Remi cradled her hand against her chest in relief.

"Oh that's better. It was like I'd gotten my hand stuck in the cookie jar and couldn't get it out. That and someone poured acid on it."

A moment later, Damon started transforming back to his human form. The changes looked painful. Remi couldn't help but watch the entire event. When it was over, Damon was leaning back in an oversized suit, rubbing his neck and stretching his jaw.

Remi looked up to see Morwen staring at them with her arm around her sister's shoulders. "I don't understand. Why would you endure this pain and risk your lives for us?"

"Because we're allergic to assholes," said Remi as she stretched out her hand. "It's a really severe condition and knowing Felix Marken even exists was like having a bad case of the mage shakes combined with painful diarrhea. The only solution was to put him in his place."

THIRTY-FOUR

The equipment wheezed air into his father's lungs. Damon watched as he struggled to stay awake. He looked like a bag of bones left to rot in the hospital bed.

"Dad, you don't have to. Sleep if you need it. You need the rest. It's healing."

"No, it's not," came the rough voice.

It didn't sound like his father. Not the hearty, hale werewolf who'd never been sick a day in his life.

"I want you to look out for the twins."

"Of course. I always do."

His father was beset by a wracking fit of coughing. "Not like that. After."

"Dad..."

His father's bloodshot, cavernous eyes were portals into his mental state.

"I can't survive much more like this. After I'm gone, I need you to promise to keep the girls safe. They're reckless and prone to get into trouble."

Damon grasped his father's hand, which felt like a collection of worn pencils.

"We'll figure something out." He let his chin dip to his chest. "I have to tell you something. Connor Black is alive."

"What?"

Arthur broke into a fit of coughing. Damon handed him a glass of water to clear his throat.

"Alive?"

"He escaped the day the clan was slaughtered. There's an ancient assassin tracking him down. He's in the city."

"Who?"

"Koschei."

His father's eyes widened. "A few weeks ago, I woke up to see a man standing in the doorway. He made me afraid. I thought it was the grim reaper coming for my soul."

The idea that Koschei knew where his father was frightened him.

"He must have tracked your scent. Why didn't he kill you?"

"I don't know," his father wheezed.

"I thought he was sent to annihilate our family? But if he didn't try to kill you..."

"Does Connor still have the sword?"

Damon moved closer. "Yes."

"It could be the sword that he wants."

"The sword. Of course. But why?"

"Why does anyone want power, or money?"

Damon rubbed the back of his neck. "I don't think it's as simple as that."

"Do you know why I took the family to Kansas City?"

"You wanted us to have a different life than the clan provided? I don't really know. You've never said."

His father adjusted the tubes wrapped around his nose. "Because there was a disagreement about who should be the Keeper of the Shining Sword. Most of the Elders thought Connor should have that honor, but when they consulted an oracle, it was suggested that I take it and that if I didn't something bad would happen to the clan. This caused Connor and I to have a falling out. He thought I was trying to take it from him, plus he thought I wasn't worthy enough, because I had gone to college and studied to be an accountant rather than the blade."

"You? Keeper?"

Arthur chuckled. "That was the response of most of the clan. To smooth things over, I took us to Kansas City."

Damon slumped into a nearby chair. He saw his father in a different light.

"Son. If this assassin is after the sword, then you have to help Connor kill him. The sword must be kept safe."

"We're trying, but it's not going to be easy."

"I'm sure you'll figure something out," said his father with his eyes teetering on the edge of sleep. "But most of all, keep the twins safe..."

He was snoring two seconds after his eyes closed. Damon checked the machines before leaving his father's room. Whatever was going on, it all seemed to be connected. The sickness that had claimed his father, the slaughter of his clan, the shining sword, and Connor's madness—they were associated with Koschei somehow. Damon didn't know how, none of it made sense medically speaking, but the links were there, and he just had to find the underlying cause and kill the deathless assassin before his father died.

THIRTY-FIVE

Lily was on her way back to the Aura Healers dormitory when she saw Morwen in her orderly whites chatting with Dr. Hunker near the nurse's station. Her former foe was mooning at the doctor as she leaned on the cart she had been pushing.

Until her sister had a chance to heal, Morwen had agreed to work in the hospital and stay in one of the empty dorm rooms. Lily had been surprised that Dr. Decker had not only agreed, but hadn't asked a million questions about the sudden reversal in their relationship, which was almost more annoying. She'd wanted pushback, but he'd just smiled and signed the paperwork.

Lily ran into Remi and Damon around the corner. They were each carrying a stack of tomes from the hospital library.

"Koschei?"

"Anything that might have a reference to a phylactery," said Remi.

"His dad's not doing well. We need to find Koschei soon."

"Even if you kill him, how will that help him?" asked Lily.

Damon's lips were pulled tight. "I don't know, but I think it's all connected. A few days ago, my dad was awake enough to talk. He told me that he'd been considered to be the sword's Keeper, but the Elders overruled the oracle, so he moved our family away from the clan as not to upset things. My dad thinks Koschei is after the sword. The clan just got in the way. It makes sense."

"You can't know that's true," said Lily.

"Koschei visited my dad. Left him be," said Damon, checking over his shoulder. "He only wants the sword."

"That's great, but can we discuss this somewhere I can set these books down?" asked Remi, straining from the load.

"Why is he sick then?" asked Lily. "And why is Connor going mad at the full moon? It's the kalkatai, not the assassin."

"Maybe they're related. The Keeper of the Shining Sword would have the strongest link to the summer realm. If my father was going to be Keeper, then maybe he's too open to the Fae and he's being affected by the corruption. Connor too."

"Really, you two, my arms are shaking," said Remi, red-faced.

"Then if you put a blocker on his faez conduit, you might be able to slow the damage," said Lily.

"Hey guys—"

Damon's eyes widened. "You're right! It won't fix things, but at least it'll slow things down. Give us more time to find Koschei's phylactery."

A squeaky sneaker announced the presence of Morwen. She crept around the corner with a sheepish expression.

"I'm sorry, I was overhearing your conversation about a phylactery. Once she gets better, my sister should be able to help."

"What? How?"

Morwen's eyes rounded. "She has the gift. That's why Felix was using her to make the drugs potent, but she can do other things too."

"Are you sure?" asked Damon. "This could be dangerous."

Morwen nodded. "You risked your lives for us. It's the least we can do."

"Thank you. Once your sister has recovered and all her vitals are back to normal, we'll use her help. Maybe we can track him the full moon after the next. Five weeks should be enough for her to get better." Damon checked over his shoulder. "I should get back to my dad. I think I can try something that will help him resist the kalkatai."

"I'll join you," said Lily. "I know a spell."

"Great," said Damon. "Remi, you take these back to the room. I'll catch up later."

He set his stack into the already straining arms of their friend. A squeal like the air being let out of a balloon escaped her lips the moment before the entire stack of books crashed onto the tiles, forming an unruly pile in the middle of the hallway.

Remi massaged her arms as she gave them an exhausted stare. "I can't hold them anymore."

THIRTY-SIX

The sound of dripping water was familiar in the hospital, but not usually in the alchemical lab, which made Remi want to investigate. The hallway light shone into the darkened room, reflecting off glassware.

"Hello?"

The droplets were hitting something metal at a steady pace. Not the water of condensation. She clicked on the lights and nearly jumped out of her skin when she realized the NOCAT was standing five feet to her left with a bunch of green leafy material sticking out of her mouth.

"Shadows below, you scared the faez out of me," said Remi, holding her hand over her heart and breathing heavily.

The NOCAT stared forward without a trace of movement. Not even a chewing motion.

"How did you get here?" she asked the old woman.

A titration flute had been knocked over, spilling pale liquid onto a stainless steel tray. A sniff revealed it was a cleaning solution, which was lucky, since other materials in the alchemy lab were quite dangerous. Someone had probably left the cleaning solution in the glass to let it work on the gunk stuck in the neck.

Remi pulled the leaves from the NOCAT's mouth. Belladonna. Also known as nightshade.

"You can't eat that," said Remi, knocking the leaves from her mouth and forcing it open, removing the leftover material with a swirling finger.

Using a penlight, she checked the NOCAT's throat. It didn't appear she'd eaten any.

"You'll die that way you know," she said to the NOCAT, gently corralling her arm and leading her out of the lab. Her room was down the hall. She made it back without anyone seeing, which was a disappointment.

The NOCAT blankly followed her directions. Remi got her back into the bed without much trouble.

"I should report that, but I don't know if anyone would care." Remi pulled out her divining rod and placed an analock spell on the tip, which she used to poke and prod the old woman, checking for sores or wounds she'd gotten during her excursion. "I know Dr. Decker says there's nothing we can do for you, but I can't imagine living your life stuck in a bed with no way to help you. It sounds awful. I'd probably try to eat some belladonna to escape too."

As soon as Remi said it, a heavy realization hit her. Maybe the NOCAT *was* trying to escape. Permanently. Which meant she was aware of what was going on somehow, despite appearances. Remi checked the old woman's pupils for dilation. Nothing. The lights were on but nobody was home.

"I have to go, but I haven't forgotten you."

She turned to leave, but thought she saw the NOCAT's head move.

"Hello?" She sighed. "I guess that was my imagination."

Remi closed the door behind her, leaving the NOCAT in the dark. She ran into Dr. Hunker coming the other way. He was reading a chart and glanced up with a smile that put a burst of warmth in her belly.

"You ready?"

"Yeah," she said absently.

His forehead hunched. "Something wrong?"

Remi explained finding the NOCAT eating belladonna in the alchemy lab.

"That is disconcerting. What's your theory?"

"My theory?"

"Yeah, you're a second-year healer. What's your theory?"

She hesitated. "What about rule number one?"

Dr. Hunker smiled. "While I understand what Oren's doing, I also think he can take things too far. Eventually you have to learn to walk on your own. So, theory?"

Remi swallowed. "Based on what little I know, which isn't much, it appeared the patient was trying to end things. But that doesn't make sense because the NOCAT doesn't talk or move, or anything like that, on their own. Except for an occasional spasm, nonsense words, or brief movement, the NOCAT has mostly lain in her room for the last decade. I don't know, Dr. Hunker. What do you think?"

He placed the clipboard under his shoulder. "It sounded like you were working up to a theory. What about that first part? You mentioned an intention from the patient?"

"Yeah. Unless there's another benefit of raw belladonna besides death."

"Why would someone stuck in their bed for the last decade do that?"

Remi snapped her fingers. "Right! Unless she wasn't really comatose, but somehow awake in there, but can't really change things except occasionally. Oh, Merlin, she's stuck asleep, but not asleep, and there's no prince to kiss her."

"Sounds like you're headed in a plausible direction."

"Yeah, but what do I do now?"

"I know we're supposed to do rounds, but this sounds more important. You should head to the library and see if there's anything to learn about her condition."

"I'll do that. Thanks, Dr. Hunk." Her cheeks warmed. "Sorry. Dr. Hunker."

"Don't worry. I'm aware what you all call me," he said with a smirk.

Remi raced off to the hospital library, which was on the opposite side of the building near the chapel. She hadn't been in many libraries, but the one at Golden Willow seemed pound for pound to have the most books per square inch of any she'd ever seen. Granted, most of those were libraries on TV shows when she was home bored waiting for her parents to come back, but she assumed they were either real places, or based on them.

The hospital library aisles were barely wide enough to slide down at an angle, which meant that passing other people required a dance move to get past without touching. Remi first sat down at the computer and put in a number of phrases like "comatose patient commits suicide," "NOCATs who move," or "NOCAT eats nightshade."

With a list half a sheet long, Remi headed into the stacks. She pulled them out one at a time, found the article or study, and read it to see if it was relevant before putting it back. Most of the tomes were unrelated. The key phrases had pulled out tangential titles rather than specific cases involving comatose NOCATs.

The articles she found that had the most correlation were about patients stuck in various forms of stasis that occasionally came to life under specific conditions. She read about an old man who'd accidentally poisoned himself with a powder that ancient sorcerers used to control people and spent the next three months lying in a bed until it wore off and he woke up. There were many other stories just like it. The cause of the stases were a mixture of spells and alchemical agents, but even heavy exposure to lead could cause it.

When her stomach grumbled, she realized she'd been in the library for almost nine hours and would have to get back to her room for a quick nap before the next shift. Reluctantly, she put back the tomes and left with a head full of information about inducing and fixing stasis. She knew most of it had been tried already based on Dr. Decker's history with the NOCAT, but she planned on organizing her notes and talking with him to formulate a new plan.

She didn't realize where she was at until she heard a wavering voice calling out from one of the rooms. It was Arthur Wolfhard. Remi checked the room to find Damon's father with his eyes closed, moaning in a low tone.

"Arthur? Are you okay?"

"No. Not them. Please, save them. Please."

"Save who?" she asked, putting her hand on his arm.

His mouth opened and a pained lament came out.

"Arthur? Save who?"

His bloodshot eyes opened momentarily. He looked like he was stuck in a nightmare.

"The twins."

THIRTY-SEVEN

Damon was applying a necrosis enchantment to a wart around the genitals of a hobgoblin named Jasper Hane when Remi knocked on the open door with an expression of great urgency.

"I'll be a minute." He smiled at Jasper. "Sorry about that. There's never a shortage of emergencies around here. But once I'm finished, the wart should come off on its own in a few days."

Jasper had a mane of black hair that swirled around the crown of his head. Even with his jutting jaw and ritually scarred neck, he was a handsome guy. Based on the shiny and tiny clothes he was wearing when he came in, Damon assumed he sold his body for sex.

"Thanks, doc," said Jasper, fluttering his eyelashes.

"I'm not a doctor, but I appreciate the sentiment." Damon placed his forefinger on the wart, closed his eyes, and focused his faez. A hot-cold sensation traveled from the back of his neck through his arm and into the wart, activating the matrix of runes he'd placed around it. "There, all done. You can wash off the runes any time after an hour. If they start to burn, wash them off sooner, but that shouldn't happen except in rare cases."

Jasper gave him a fist bump and he left the room, collecting Remi away from the open door.

"Is there a fire?"

Remi held her hands out. "First off, he's fine. But I just came from your father's room."

"He's fine, but you look worried."

Damon started moving in the direction of his father's room, but Remi held him back.

"Not Arthur. He was muttering something about the twins. He was worried about them."

Damon sighed heavily. "Yeah. It's been a thing for him. He asked me to look out for them if he died."

"No, I don't think it's that." Her face broke with emotion. "I'm sorry, Damon. That's a tough thing to hear from your dad. We're gonna fix him."

He propped up a smile they both knew was false, but it was better to leave the truth unsaid.

"Really, Remi, it's fine. The twins are back in KC."

"Have you talked to them recently?"

"No, but I know they had their victory trip planned. Probably Cancun or something like that. I'm looking forward to hearing about their adventures."

"I don't know, Damon. This seemed different. It is the full moon tomorrow. Seems like weird stuff keeps happening around that time."

"Mostly me trying to kill you on our dates. Which we were going to try again, right?" He smirked, but Remi barely reacted, so he pulled out his phone. "Will it make you feel better if I call them?"

"I'm probably overreacting, but there's this case I'm researching and, I don't know, what your dad said worried me."

Damon dialed Natasha first because she wouldn't talk as long as her sister. After it went to voice mail, he dialed the other twin. Also voice mail. His gut started to twist, but he knew it was too early to borrow trouble.

"I'll call my mom."

Two rings later, she answered. "Damon? Is everything okay with Arthur?"

"Yeah, yeah. He's fine." Damon winked at Remi, who looked white with fright. "I was just calling to check on the twins. How are they doing? Are they in Cancun or something? On a flight and they can't answer?"

"Cancun? Oh, no. They're not going there. Didn't I tell you?"

"Tell me?"

"It was all planned, but there's a hurricane barreling down on the coast, so they had to make a last-second change. They're actually in Invictus. I'm sorry I didn't tell you, but it's been so crazy. They're going to be going to a Garbage Kings concert at the Glitterdome, and doing a Spire tour. It's not the same as the beach, but they'll have fun."

The color drained from his face, which only made Remi more fraught.

"Damon?"

"Yeah, Mom. Sorry, you know how it is in the hospital. Constant distractions. Thanks for the info. I'll get ahold of them. When did you say they arrived?"

"Last night."

He exhaled. "They arrived last night. Great. I'm sure I'll catch up to them. Take 'em to a show at the Orpheum Theatre or something. You know how they love their musicals. Love you."

"Love you too."

Damon hung up and stared back at Remi.

"They're in the city."

"Yes, but we don't know if they're in danger."

"Damon..."

The phone in his fist buzzed. It was Natalia. He held up the screen so Remi could see.

"See. We're getting all worked up over nothing. They're in the city and they'll be fine." He clicked the green button. "Hey, Nat. Just heard you two are in the city. What do you say to a show at the Orpheum?"

The long silence attuned him to the moment.

"I have your sisters."

The gruff voice sounded like something out of the ancient past with an accent that came out of time. The world dissolved around Damon. He couldn't feel his face.

"I swear I'll tear you limb from limb if you touch either one of them."

"It's not them I want, but I'll kill them if you don't do what I say," said Koschei. "Bring the sword Keeper to the Invictus Zoo, grindylow enclosure, and your sisters might yet live."

The phone went dead.

THIRTY-EIGHT

Deep in her hair, Neko shifted nervously, probably reacting to Damon's pacing and angry muttering beneath his breath. The veins on his forehead were standing tall, but he'd managed to keep himself from transforming. Lily understood his anger. If anyone had threatened her sisters, she would have torn them asunder and sent their body parts to a thousand different realms so their soul could never rest.

"We have to go," said Damon, jaw pulsing.

"We have to wait for the Clovers," said Remi from atop her perch. She was sitting on a desk with her knees beneath her chin.

Morwen and her sister, Talwen, appeared moments later. They'd switched out of their orderly whites and into street clothes.

"Is she going to be okay?" asked Lily, gesturing to the younger pixie.

Talwen's skin was gray and her eyes cavernous. The lack of vitality was apparent in comparison to her sister, whose warm brown skin glowed with supernatural vigor.

"She's got enough in her to find your friend's phylactery. Do you have the item?"

Lily handed over the scrap of cloth that she'd gotten at the arcade. Talwen collected it in her hands, gave the fabric a deep sniff, and closed her eyes. After a long minute, she nodded and opened them.

"I can find it."

Tortured relief shone on Damon's face, but Remi hopped off the desk and pointed at Lily.

"You three are going after the phylactery, we're headed to get Connor and then the zoo. Keep in contact as much as possible."

They left the hospital, climbing into two different taxis. Lily hoped her friends would be okay, but she knew that the night was more likely to end in tragedy than success.

Packed into the backseat, shoulder to shoulder, Morwen said, "We're ready to move."

The driver leaned over his shoulder. "You haven't told me where to go yet."

Talwen said, "South."

"South? That's it? What is this, a scavenger hunt?"

"Something like that," said Morwen. "Don't worry, we'll pay extra for your troubles and you might even get a bonus at the end."

She winked, and the driver blushed. Her pixie magic had softened him. The vehicle lurched into motion, heading west. It took them nearly forty minutes to meander across the city, initially heading south, then veering slightly west until they came to the twelfth ward.

"This is as far as I go, ladies," said the driver, pulling up to the sidewalk and putting it in gear.

"We're almost there," said Morwen, checking with her sister. "Can't you go further?"

"Into the twelfth? Nah. Not worth the trouble. A good chance we get jacked and I lose everything, including the tips you promised. I'd like those now, if you don't mind."

Morwen leaned forward like she was going to charm him, but Lily put a hand on her arm and shook her head. Morwen sighed and produced a stack of bills for the driver. As soon as they were out of the vehicle, he sped away.

"How much further?" asked Lily.

Talwen gave a weak shrug.

Except for a few clusters of apartments or commerce, the twelfth ward was mostly abandoned. It'd been an industrial center in the previous century before the city became a hot bed of tourism. Most of the buildings were in the process of collapsing, and what remained standing was covered in graffiti. It was a home for the little gangs that couldn't make it in the wealthier parts of the city, which made it dangerous to be on foot.

As they crossed deeper into the ward, Lily spotted a brown Buick that passed at a distance twice. It could be coincidence, but she didn't see any reason to let her guard down.

Talwen led them at a languid pace. She looked like she'd finished an ultramarathon and was being asked to go another twenty miles. Lily strolled in the back, next to Morwen, who had her hands deep in her coat pockets, lips soured at their surroundings.

"Where were you before?" asked Lily.

"The city? Or Felix?"

"Both, I guess."

Morwen hung her head. Sighed. "We lived in Azaya with our mother, near a shimmering. It was how she'd met our father."

"He was human?"

"A long-haul trucker who'd somehow driven into the shimmer when he fell asleep between Atlanta and Huntsville. Mom said he must have been touched to be able to travel over without a portal. Maybe he was a dreamer. He spent a month with her before heading back through the shimmer. I don't think either of them knew she was pregnant."

"After a month? How? He shouldn't have been able to leave."

"That's what we thought too, but Mom said it probably had to do with him being a dreamer, or maybe it was because it was the beginning of the kalkatai. The normal rules of Fae were breaking down, even then."

"Is that why you left?"

Morwen nodded. She looked into the distance towards the Spire. "Azaya was an idyllic place on a mountainside with the most beautiful waterfalls in all the summer realm. You could walk the trails and see a dozen of them in an afternoon, but by the time we left, you couldn't find a single one, the pathways were so overgrown by vines and undergrowth."

"Did your mother have theories on the origin of the kalkatai?" asked Lily as she spotted the brown Buick slipping down the street about two blocks away.

"She blamed it on humans. The opening of so many portals has damaged all the realms." Morwen flattened her lips. "That's what she believed."

"She didn't come with you."

"No. I fear what's become of her now."

Lily thought back to the corruption of the Green Man last year. The rot had spread wide. No one was safe in the Wilds. Not even the creatures that lived there.

"Are you okay?" asked Morwen suddenly. "I know who the de Meath family is. You gave up much to come to the Halls."

"The great corruption found its way to this realm. Even Medb wasn't safe. She hasn't lived in the Fae for centuries, but those roots are deeper than the bogs."

Lily's heart ached at the thought of it. She missed her sisters. Missed the forests of Ireland and the Eó Ruis tree, but if she couldn't find a cure, then there'd be nothing to go back to.

A squeak in her hair alerted Lily to danger. She pulled Neko out and set him on the sidewalk. He stayed in his rat form, but could change at a moment's notice.

"The Buick is back."

The brown vehicle rolled down the street like a shark.

"It's not the only one," said Morwen, nodding to the right. A green SUV with purple underlights was headed their direction. Lily spotted a third car coming up from behind.

"Do we run?" she asked.

Talwen glanced back with a clear expression of exhaustion.

"Right. Well, at least this time we've no innocents to worry about if things go pear-shaped."

The SUV pulled up across the street, releasing Felix Marken and three of his goons onto the sidewalk. They brandished pistols openly. If there'd only been one or two, she might have been able to take them, but there were far too many, and too spread out to risk getting shot. Better to wait for a future opportunity.

"Neko, go."

The white rat scurried into the alleyway with an emphatic squeak.

Lily checked ahead and behind but the other two vehicles had released another half dozen of Felix's gang onto the street to block any escape.

Felix strolled up with the swagger of a pirate, his lips curled into a grimace.

"Well, if it isn't my favorite employees. Did ya not think we'd find out about your little ploy? I got eyes and ears all over the city and especially the hospital. How do you think I knew which drugs to ask for? When they told me they spotted you working as an orderly, I almost didn't believe them. Good thing I did. Now I get to take you back and show this rainbow-haired witch that you don't mess with the Hollow Nine."

Felix raised his weapon, pointing it directly at Lily's head.

"Grab the pixies." He jerked his head to the right, staring directly at Lily. She saw the anger deep in his eyes as a snarl rose on his lips. "I haven't decided what I'm going to do to you."

THIRTY-NINE

They were almost to the old underground factory when Damon started to change. Remi realized something was wrong when he was no longer by her side. She checked back to see him bent over on the sidewalk, holding his arms to his chest. An older couple with gray hair slowed, staring at him with wide eyes.

"Food poisoning," she told them. "If you stay a little longer you get to see what he ate."

The couple stiffened and hurried the other way, checking over their shoulder as if they might be followed.

"Damon?"

"I'm fine."

"You don't look fine."

"I was thinking about my sisters and what I would do—"

He arched with the change. Fingernails grew into talons. Remi did the only thing she could think of in that situation. She grabbed him by the neck and planted her lips on his.

There was a brief moment she thought he might rip her throat out as his teeth brushed her lips and he grabbed her by the shoulders, lifting her up. Then as their tongues entwined, he shuddered and relaxed into her. He slowly lowered her to the sidewalk and when she was sure he was no longer leaning into his rage, she pulled away, right as a car passenger whistled.

"That was a cheap trick," he muttered, wiping his mouth with the back of his hand. He stared at the half-formed talons at the end of his fingers.

"It worked. I guess it's true what they say about men and their brains."

"What's that?"

She rolled her eyes. "For a brilliant healer, you sure can be an idiot sometimes." She gestured forward. "Come on, we're here."

The darkness seemed more oppressive than last time even with the floating mage light. As they tramped across the hard metal grating that rang with each step, Remi called out.

"Connor? It's Remi and Damon. We have to talk."

When no answer came, she checked with Damon, who already looked like he was going to break in half. Remi didn't have siblings, but when she was in Utica, she'd had friends that she'd do anything for. And had. That was why she'd been in solitary the last few weeks before release, so she understood a piece of Damon's anger.

"Connor Black?"

She checked her watch. It wasn't technically the full moon, but it was close, which made him more dangerous than under normal circumstances.

They found him in the converted office kneeling on the floor and holding the blade, point down, as if he were praying to an absent god. He was halfway through his change, limbs extended and covered in thick hair, but his face was a mix of wolf and man. The low growl in the back of his throat put doubt in Remi's knees.

"Connor," said Damon. "We need your help. He took my sisters."

When Connor stood, they both took a step back. His eyes were bloodshot and his jaw pulsed with the signs of an internal struggle.

"You should go. I don't know if I can control myself tonight."

He was breathing heavily, teeth glimmering in the mage light.

"Connor. Please. We can't kill Koschei ourselves. We need your help, your sword." Damon held out his fists. "My entire family is going to die if we don't do anything!"

Connor wavered on his feet. When his eyes flashed open, Remi took a step back.

"I don't know if it's wise if I go with you."

Damon closed the distance. He was close enough to have his head taken off if Connor lost control.

"Uncle. Please."

"We can't kill him," said Connor.

"We can. Our friends are going after his phylactery. It's in the city and we know how to find it. More importantly, if we put it in danger, it'll give us a chance to rescue the twins."

Connor closed his eyes as his face contorted. "Natasha and Natalia?"

"Yeah, that's them."

"I remember those little wolflings." Connor opened his eyes, the conflict in his expression lessened. "Come, we should go while I have control."

He grabbed a heavy cloak and threw it over his shoulders, pulled the hood up to cover his face, and slipped the sword beneath his arm. The covering did little to hide the threat that he implied.

When she called the taxi, the driver almost sped off without letting them in until Connor stepped in front and flashed his sword. The ride to the zoo was in silence as the driver kept watching them through the rearview mirror. Remi paid triple the rate.

The Invictus Menagerie and Cryptozoo was closed. The park was dark with few lights illuminating the meandering sidewalks. Damon helped Remi over the ten-foot iron fence while Connor leapt it with ease.

"What about your friends?" asked Connor, glaring into the darkness. Outside his hideaway, he let his seething anger creep to the edge of unleashing it.

Remi checked her phone, keeping a wary eye on Connor. "No news. Last message was five minutes ago. They were about to be dropped off in the twelfth ward. The phylactery is somewhere in the ward."

Damon had been reading the zoo map. He extended his arm. "The grindylow enclosure is on the opposite side. Once we get there, I want you to get inside and free the twins while we keep Koschei distracted. Hopefully Lily and the pixies can find the phylactery soon and we can end him permanently."

"Wouldn't it be better if I helped Connor and you went after your sisters?" she asked as they moved down the sidewalk. "I'm not really a great swimmer."

"Remi, what are you going to do against an immortal assassin?"

She shrugged. "Confuse it with my presence? I've been working on my five elements. Maybe I could singe some hair or give his hair a thorough blow-dry."

"Remi, be serious."

"I am." She sighed. "It's nervousness. I'm not much of a fighter."

"Well, you don't have to be. You just have to free my sisters. Please."

"Of course. You didn't have to ask. The world would be a poorer place without them."

Connor stopped and sniffed the air. "I smell him."

The only thing Remi could smell was her own body odor. She'd never been so terrified in her life and couldn't figure out why she was moving forward instead of fleeing the zoo.

"You know, having friends is very inconvenient."

"What?" asked Damon.

"Never mind."

Remi knew something bad was going to happen when all the lights in the surrounding area, including her mage light, went dark. She threw herself to the ground when she heard the whistling of fast travel, which was the only thing that saved her when a sword came flying over her prone body. She started rolling when Connor leapt at Koschei, sparks erupting from clashing blades. She kept crawling as the fight nearly trampled her, until Damon yanked her away and dropped her onto the grass near a bronze statue of Invictus.

"Get my sisters," he said.

She tried to grab his arm to prevent him from rushing to his death, but he was away in a flash. Damon hit Koschei underneath his arm, throwing him into a wooden direction sign. The urge to stay and watch was strong, but she had to go. Her legs pumped in wild abandon as she sprinted down the paths, but she out of breath by the time she reached the other side of the zoo.

"A little cardio wouldn't hurt you every now and then, would it?" she said, leaning over and heaving. Once she could catch her breath and the stitch in her side had reduced enough to stand again, she surveyed her surroundings.

Remi ran-walked to the grindylow enclosure, which was a cast-iron fence overlooking a pond. At the center of the still water was an island covered in boulders. The twins were tied up atop the rocks, back-to-back with their mouths bound.

The sign outside the enclosure gave ample information about the creatures in the water. She read it quickly, scanning for the important points.

"Grindylows are aquatic, originally from the United Kingdom...

around twenty to thirty kilos...dangerous in numbers...vegetarian but territorial, known to drown children and the occasional adult, but are generally skittish of people. Let's hope that's true. Sharp claws and teeth...can breathe underwater. Great."

She found the gate and worked the locks until she was inside at the edge of the water. The moon was hidden by a bank of clouds, which turned the water as black as night. It was a good fifty feet across to reach the island and she wasn't a good swimmer. She didn't fear the water since she could swim, but it was mostly paddling like crazy to stay on the surface, nothing that would earn her a gold medal or anything.

"Times like this I really wish I'd had a normal childhood."

She'd been through enough suburbs to see the community pools where families enjoyed the water together. She couldn't imagine Archer and Greta in swimwear standing waist-deep like a couple of rubes.

Remi approached the edge, trying to see how deep the water was, but the glossy black surface made it hard to tell. She found a rock and threw it in, shaking her head when it disappeared with a *bloop*. From across the zoo, she heard a roar and saw a minor explosion of sparks as if a power conduit had been cut.

"You don't have much time," she said, stripping off her shoes and shimmying out of her jeans. It was a cold February night. She put a few enchantments on her skin to keep warm, but they were meant for weather, not chilly water.

"Alright, you little bastards," she said, addressing the water. "I need to swim to the island, so you'll have to keep your grubby little claws off me. If you try to drown me, I swear on all the Hundred Halls that I'll turn this pond into a desert. Are we good? Good."

Remi held her arms across her chest as she stood in panties and bra. She dipped a toe into the cold water, grimacing from the shock.

"Let's get this over with."

She waded into the pond.

FORTY

Damon snapped the boards, ripping the sign from the ground and smashing it against Koschei's back, knocking him to his knees while Connor battered him with the sword, but the deathless assassin managed to block each strike. He leapt across the sidewalk, then climbed onto the small restroom building, using the higher ground as a defense.

"You can't win," said Koschei, holding his blade in one hand. "No matter how you try. I've never lost a quarry in all my many centuries of hunting."

Damon approached the building at the same time as Connor, who was growling under his breath.

"We're not giving up," said Damon.

"Your father won't last the month, and your sisters, well, they won't last the night if you don't step away and let me take the sword."

"No," said Damon, immediately. "Why? Who sent you after it?"

Connor shot him an angry glance.

"It doesn't matter. I keep my business with my employers private, but he doesn't care about your family, only the sword."

"If he doesn't care about my family then why did you slaughter them like animals?"

Koschei gestured at Connor. "Because he wouldn't give up the blade."

"It's our family's legacy. I can't give it up," growled Connor. "Come down here so I can cut your head off!"

Koschei looked right at Damon.

"I'm tired of this hunt. It's gone on far too long. Step aside and your father and sisters will be free."

"My father? What are you doing to him? I don't understand."

Koschei pulled a rock from his inner pocket. It glowed with a sickly green light, pulsing like throbbing corrupted wound.

"To drive Connor out of hiding, I used this draemon, which is a stone from King Nuada's hearth in the land of summer. Like everything else in the Fae, it's corrupted. Once I brought it here and intensified its aura, it brought Connor out of his hole. Unfortunately for your father, it felled him in its wake. His bad luck that he chose to come to the city and catch the full brunt of the draemon. So you see, the longer you prolong my hunt, the higher likelihood of his death."

Damon glanced in the direction that Remi had gone.

"Don't you dare," said Connor. "It's our family's duty to defend the Shining Sword. Even if it means our lives. The King of Fae entrusted us with its safekeeping."

Damon realized his mistake when he glanced up to see Koschei staring into the distance towards the grindylow enclosure. The deathless assassin sprinted across the roof and leapt onto the path with Damon and Connor in pursuit. When Koschei soared over a picnic table, Damon caught him on the other side, knocking him off his feet. The two tumbled into the bushes. Damon scrambled away as the sword chopped through the leaves. Backed against the wall, he ducked when the Koschei swung for his head, and the blade contacted with a power conduit, sending sparks in a wide arc.

Before Koschei could catch him, Connor engaged with his weapon. The two clashed in the middle of the sidewalk, blades ringing with impact.

Away from the fight, Damon dared to check his phone, hoping to find a message from Lily and the pixies, but the last note was from Remi asking if they were close to finding it. He looked up in time to see Connor getting thrown across the sidewalk. Damon leapt after Koschei, ripping through his black clothes with long claws. He reached for the hilt, but when his fingers brushed the cold metal, the shock locked his arms and sent him to the ground like a stiff board.

He looked up in time to see Koschei's blade soaring towards his head and rolled away, kicking out at his legs, then rolling back to his feet. Koschei stood between him and Connor, blade at the ready.

"This is your last chance, boy. Help me take his sword and your sisters and father will live. Defy me and you'll count yourself lucky that I only kill you."

The choice was like a vise around his heart. He couldn't imagine his life without his father and the twins. His family was everything. But he couldn't turn on his uncle. It didn't matter why Koschei wanted the sword. The idea that he would help kill his own uncle to save his father and sisters was reprehensible.

"No," Damon growled. "I won't."

Koschei exhaled and stood tall, no longer in a readied crouch.

"I was afraid you'd say that."

The deathless assassin reached into an inner pocket and produced a small vial, which he quickly downed, shuddering immediately from the effects.

"Ahhh, that's better. Now we can truly fight."

Damon extended his arms, showing the full length of his claws. He snapped and snarled. The fear of losing his family brought deep resolve.

He roared and leapt at the same time as Connor. They met at Koschei in the same blink of an eye. Claws extended, Damon planned on ripping out the assassin's innards. He moved at great speed, his anger-fueled leap like a furry missile of extended teeth.

Damon had Koschei dead to rights. He hadn't even brought up his weapon yet. The tip of the blade pointed at the concrete.

Until the last instant.

Koschei blurred with movement.

Damon found himself spinning through the air, crashing through the ur-bear enclosure sign and landing hard against the metal gate, which rattled like dull bells. The impact knocked the air from his lungs, but he struggled to his feet, determined to return to the battle.

Behind him, ur-bears made deep gronking noises from being awoken. The call triggered ethereal howls from the ghost dogs in the next cage over.

Climbing back to the sidewalk, he was presented with a blurred battle of steel. Koschei was battering Connor backwards in a fury, the speed and impact proving to be too much for his uncle.

Damon reached for his phone, finding the screen empty of messages, but even if Lily and the pixies could find the phylactery, he doubted they could kill Koschei. They'd made a terrible mistake.

§

Lily's head caught the doorframe as they shoved her in back, separate from the Clover sisters. Her eyes watered as the pain receded. They'd bound her wrists and ankles with zip ties, stripped her of any trinkets she had on her person, and put a piece of duct tape over her mouth.

Felix Marken climbed into the back of the SUV, sitting beside her. He spoke to his man in back, sitting right behind Lily.

"If she does anything suspicious, put a bullet in her head."

Lily glared at him, wishing her hands were free so she could hex his balls to fall off.

He pulled out a small, thin blade and pressed it against her breastbone.

"This is how this is going to work. I'm behind on my shipments and I don't like being late. My business is extremely important to me. I've done a lot of terrible things to get to this point, so don't think I won't do a few more to protect what's mine. So when we return to the Hollow Nine, you're going to get right to work, along with those disloyal pixies, and complete the shipment. Do you ken?"

She kept staring at him, so he smacked her in the head with the hilt of his knife, bringing stars to her eyes.

"Do you ken?"

Lily nodded slowly.

"Good. Once we get back to our schedule, then we can explore what other kinds of work you can do for me. I thought having a couple of pixies were valuable, but a Hall trained witch? Business is going to be expanding. And don't try to get any smart ideas about escaping, or causing problems. My plan is to keep the three of you in entirely separate places and if any one of you acts up, the other two are going to pay for it."

Felix leaned in her vision, daring her to look away. She kept up the staring contest until he flicked her in the forehead. He leaned back in his seat with the blade resting in his hand.

Lily squeezed her eyes shut in frustration. Everything had gone wrong. She didn't even have Neko. He was somewhere behind them in the twelfth ward, and her friends were battling the deathless assassin, thinking they would find and destroy the phylactery.

It was a worst-case scenario.

Her friends would die, she'd be enslaved with the pixies, and whatever foul plan was being hatched by Koschei's employer would go through. She shuddered to think what kind of mischief would happen if Koschei had the Shining Sword.

Medb help me.

§

The water was so cold it made it hard to breathe. Her muscles tightened, but she kept kicking, hoping the grindylows would find her awkward swimming unworthy of their attentions. She felt like she'd been paddling forever, because the island was still so far away.

Why couldn't I have had a normal childhood?

Remi imagined a different set of parents sitting poolside while she swam confidently up the lane during a competition. They would cheer, of course, no matter how good or bad she did, because that's what parents in the suburbs did. They didn't treat their kids like another arm of their illicit enterprise.

"If I ever see them again, I'm kicking some ass," she said, regretting it instantly as she choked on water. Coughing and sputtering, she halted, swimming in one place even as her arms burned from the effort.

Remi checked behind her to find she was barely a third across. The urge to swim back and try a different way was strong, but the twins were on the island and if she couldn't get them away, Koschei would probably kill them.

As she flattened her body to swim again, something hit her in the left calf. A clawed brush. Nothing broke the skin, but the contact sent her mind reeling. She imagined all the grindylows beneath her, waiting to drag her into the depths.

Remi kicked hard, swimming frantically, hoping her flailing limbs would make it impossible for the grindylows to grab ahold. Defensive swimming. *Sure, the form is terrible, but it's keeping me alive.* She chuckled inside, even as she was frightened to death.

Another claw brushed her leg. Then her hip. She felt them churning beneath her.

Remi wished she could use the five elements, but knew the moment she slowed, they would grab her stilled limbs. She paddled like her life depended on it.

Looking up to make sure she was oriented in the right direction, she spotted a scaly head peeking out of the water. She veered around, swinging her arms heavily to scare the grindylows away.

More heads popped up.

She tried swimming at them, but then there would be three or four of them. Too many to take on in the water.

A hand grabbed her ankle, tugging her downward.

The halted progress only encouraged the watery creatures. More hands brushed her limbs. They were small, barely bigger than a child's, but the collective attacks slowed Remi's already pathetic swimming.

In the churning of her flails, she found herself turned around, swimming tangentially to the island, rather than towards it, but the grindylows seemed to sense her destination and placed themselves in the way.

With arms and legs tiring, she needed a place to rest. She hadn't noticed it from the edge, but she spotted a smaller boulder sticking out of the water, away from the island. The grindylows had left a lane open, so she took it, swimming furiously until she slammed her hand into the rock, breaking a fingernail. She dragged herself onto the shallow surface, barely out of the water, breathing in great heaves, eyes burning.

From the exposed position on her rock, she felt no closer to the island than she had when she first began, and now she was surrounded by a dozen scaly heads. Her fingers were bleeding and her heart was a jackrabbit in her chest.

"Real smooth, Remi. You trapped yourself in a pond full of grindylows with a deathless assassin on the loose."

The wind picked up, blowing cold air across her already chilled body. She checked to the surface to see the grindylows closing around her like a noose.

FORTY-ONE

The SUV rumbled across the ward, heading to the Hollow Nine. Lily knew once she was inside the club that it would be impossible to escape. She wished she still had her connection to Medb. Felix and his gang would be nothing against the powers granted from her former patron.

But she was no longer a witch, but a mage of the Hundred Halls. Not even a straightforward one, but a healer. She'd learned powerful spells in Golden Willow, but they were meant for helping, not hurting. She desperately needed the latter.

And a distraction.

Not just any distraction, but one strong enough to grab the knife in Felix's hand and cut her ties away. Once her hands were loose, she knew half a dozen spells that would make them regret ever grabbing her.

But Neko was blocks behind, the bindings around her wrists were tight enough to make finger gestures impossible, and she couldn't speak through the duct tape over her mouth.

Felix was fiddling with his phone, texting a woman about meeting up later. He was buoyed by his victory and wanted to celebrate.

She brought her hands to her face, which caused a reaction from Felix, but she scratched her jaw. He scowled but returned to the conversation about the night's festivities. Lily kept scratching up her neck until she could reach into her hair, producing the vial she'd been gifted from Sammie.

Felix glanced over, but she hid the object with her hand, bringing them down to her lap, where she worked the stopper loose. Once it was ready to pop out, she turned her head, looking out the window with intensity. Behind her, the goon with the gun followed her gaze, and once he was busy trying to figure out what she was looking at, Lily spun around and shoved the vial of blood into Felix's surprised mouth.

He spat the glass container out instantly, but not before he'd ingested some of the blood. Felix wiped his mouth and glared at her, raising back his arm with the blade.

Then the effect of Sammie's blood hit.

"What's wrong, boss? Are you poisoned?" asked the guy in the back after he smacked Lily in the head with the butt of his weapon. "Pull over! Pull over! She did something to him!"

As the SUV made a stop outside a closed laundromat with iron bars over the doors and windows, Felix was mumbling under his breath and shaking his head. He looked at her with surprise and elation. His eyes were as wide as the moon as he jerked from side to side.

"What's happening to me?"

The door opened and Lily was yanked from the back, hitting the curb hard, but she'd managed to grab the blade from the distracted Felix. She saw the other two vehicles pull over behind the SUV. One henchman pointed a gun at her head while the others climbed in back.

"Felix? Are you in pain?"

He started laughing maniacally. "No, not pain. Oh, Merlin. The devil has me now and it's glorious. Oh, please, call Cynthia, I need her here now."

"Cynthia?"

His cries rose. He was writhing in the back of the SUV, arching his back and clawing at the door.

Lily checked upward to see her captor distracted. She used the space to cut her ties and bent over to remove the duct tape as covertly as possible.

When the thug behind her realized she wasn't lying on the sidewalk quietly, it was too late. Lily reached over as the words of the spell danced across her lips. The moment she grabbed his ankle, a bolt of electricity traveled through her arms and up his leg. He shook intensely from the spell, dropping the gun and tipping over like a stiff board. The spell was a magical defibrillator, meant to be used outside the hospital in emergencies.

Doors flew open on the other two vehicles. She grabbed the guy leaning into the back of the SUV and spun him around. His surprise was met with the slap of a hand across the eyes, which temporarily blinded him. Then she pushed him down the sidewalk, providing a human barrier if any of them tried to fire in her direction.

For the second henchman she applied a nausea spell, pouring heavy faez into it. He went from murderously angry to projectile vomiting and stumbling around like a human food hydrant in the blink of an eye. With Felix screaming from pleasure in back, Lily focused on the other men. An explosion blew out the window as one of them took a shot, so she threw herself behind the door.

Lily yanked Felix out of the back. He was surprisingly pliable, shuddering each time she grabbed him as if each touch was ecstasy. With a blade against Felix's throat, she faced them.

"Oh, please cut me, oh please cut me," he mumbled, grinding his ass into her front.

She ignored his gyrations and focused on his men.

"Try anything and I'll cut his throat."

The four men glanced between each other until one of them fired at the SUV, blowing out the front window.

"Or maybe we kill you both and take over the club. Felix was a shit boss. Right, boys? Lot more money to go around with his greedy ass dead."

Lily cursed under her breath. Her luck to have grabbed a worthless hostage. She thought all was lost until she saw a shimmer in the distance. A block away, but closing fast.

"Maybe we could work together," called Lily. "I'm a powerful witch and I like money. My beef was with Felix here. We could make this a valuable relationship."

The men conferred amongst themselves, but Lily didn't care. It was only meant to delay.

"We discussed it," said the spokesperson. "And we decided we don't work with witches, but we will keep the pixies."

"That's too bad," said Lily.

Four sets of guns rose.

Right as Neko reached the vehicles.

The first guy screamed when Neko's tendrils touched the back of his thighs. He turned and in his confusion fired point-blank at the thug next to him, exploding his face. Two more shots fired wildly as another man went down.

The final henchman had his gun pointed at Neko when Lily reached him. She reached between his legs and turned his testicles to flame, right as Neko leapt for his throat.

As her companion was patrolling the sidewalk, Lily released the pixies from the back of the other two vehicles. Morwen took one look at the carnage, then at Neko's shimmering form, and said, "I'm glad we're friends now."

"Come on," said Lily. "Get in, we have to get back to the twelfth."

She hopped into the front seat as the sounds of sirens neared, drawn by the gunfire. Lily spun the Buick around and pointed it back towards the twelfth.

"Wrong side! Wrong side!" cried Morwen as lights headed towards them on the otherwise empty street.

Lily veered back to the other lane as the passing car honked.

"Sorry, been a bloody long time since I've driven." She checked back to Talwen. "Do you still have the cloth?"

The younger pixie nodded.

"Go left."

Lily turned onto the wrong side of the road again, but corrected quickly. She checked her phone to see no messages from the others, which wasn't a good sign.

"Here!" cried Talwen after a few more turns. Lily slammed the brakes, skidding to a stop outside of an industrial building with boarded-up doors and rusted smokestacks rising above the ward.

"Are you sure?" she asked.

Talwen nodded. "It's here. I can feel it."

Lily wasn't too sure, but she wasn't going to argue with the one with the gift. The front doors were boarded tightly. She could have gotten through, but preferred to find where Koschei made his entrance.

They found it around the corner. A rusted emergency ladder had been pulled down to the ground. Neko could smell his tracks, which confirmed his passage. She led them up to the first landing, where the lock on the window had been snapped. The darkness was thick, so she put a spell on her eyes that would help her see.

Before the enchantment kicked in, she heard Morwen and her sister inhale with surprise. As her vision drew in the interior of the industrial building, she saw an enormous coil at the center of the empty concrete. The scales shifted as the snake, which had to be as big as a small bus, lifted its head, tasting the air with its tongue.

"Where's the phylactery?"

Talwen extended her arm. "That's it."

Lily shook her head. "If there's one thing I hate, as an Irishwoman and a witch, it's bloody snakes."

FORTY-TWO

The assassin was too fast and Damon had no weapon like Connor. It was everything to stay alive. Damon threw himself on top of the pavilion from the gift shop where the battle had been engaged. He landed hard, having had to twist himself as not to get chopped in half.

Before Koschei could follow, Connor attacked him from behind. Their swords rang in the cool night air. The werewolf with a sword versus the all-black assassin.

Damon rubbed his side. He'd probably broken some ribs. Adrenaline was keeping the worst of the pain away, but he knew if he was lucky enough to survive, he'd feel it tomorrow.

When he checked back to the roof, he no longer saw Connor. The assassin was looking out over the zoo, staring in the direction of the grindylow enclosure. He leapt onto the path and disappeared in the direction Remi had gone.

Damon followed, but without Connor and his sword, he felt vulnerable. Had it only been him, Damon would have been dead long ago. He didn't see Koschei when he hit the concrete, which made him nervous that the assassin was leading him into a trap. The ghost dogs were no longer howling and the car noises from the nearest roads grew louder. Damon could hear his heart thundering in his ears and feel the way his ribs ground together at each step. He had small wounds in half a dozen places.

The grindylow enclosure looked unoccupied as he approached. He was expecting Koschei, but the viewing area was empty. Damon ran to the wall to see the twins tied up on the island. He was confused when he didn't see Remi, until he checked away from the twins to find her on a small rock barely out of the water, surrounded by scaly green heads. He climbed onto the wall, preparing to leap into the enclosure when Remi yelled.

"Behind!"

Damon threw himself to the left as a sword sung past his head. He landed awkwardly on his left foot, which sent stabs of pain through his side. Koschei came after him like a whirlwind, forcing Damon to dance away, barely keeping ahead of the sharp blade.

The deathless assassin cornered him against the wall. Damon eyed escape, but Koschei had the reach. There was nothing he could do now.

"Where's Connor?"

"I don't know."

"Wrong answer."

Koschei darted in, blade high for the killing blow. Before Damon could move, a shape blurred into the space between, the clang of metal impacting announcing the arrival of his uncle.

"Go, get your sisters," said Connor over his shoulder.

Damon leapt the wall and ran to the edge of the water. Connor wouldn't be able to hold Koschei long, the assassin was too much for just him. The situation in the pond looked critical for Remi, but if he went after her, he'd get entangled with the grindylows. But if he went after his sisters, then the grindylows might drown Remi.

He hesitated.

He'd spent the last few years managing triage in the hospital, but now that it was people he cared about, he couldn't make the decision. The rules that Dr. Morrison had drilled into him evaporated, leaving him twisted inside.

"Go get them!" cried Remi from the rock as she sent weak blasts of earth magic at the heads of the grindylows, but there were too many of them and her magic was feeble. She wouldn't survive on the rock long.

Damon needed to save Remi first, but he feared he'd lose the opportunity to save his sisters. He cursed under his breath and started wading into the water in Remi's direction.

§

"No! Not me!" Remi screamed between blasts.

She could see the fight between Connor and Koschei was not going well for the werewolf. He was backpedaling, the glowing sword barely keeping up with Koschei's relentless attacks.

As bad as things were for her, she wanted Damon to go after the twins. He'd never be the same if he lost his sisters. He didn't have the time to rescue her with Koschei looming nearby. Once Connor lost, and it was only a matter of time, Koschei would come after them in the enclosure.

A wet clawed hand grabbed her foot. She kicked it off as she spotted Damon swimming in her direction.

He couldn't see how little time they had. She needed him to go to the island. An idea formed in her head which she immediately regretted.

"Are you crazy?" she asked herself, but she knew it was the right solution under the circumstances.

Remi blasted elemental earth at the grasping hands as she turned in a circle, pushing the grindylows away long enough for what she really wanted to do. Once she had the space, she started chanting in a low voice.

§

Damon's powerful strokes pulled him through the water at speed. He wasn't sure what he was going to do once he reached Remi, but he figured he could scare the grindylows off and give her the chance to make it back to the edge while he went for his sisters. He managed to sneak a glance at Remi, who was standing on the rocks, clearly in spell mode. He couldn't hear the words over the slap of his hands against the water, but her demeanor was serious.

The water cascaded over his face as he thrust through the water. He hit the point that would be equidistant from Remi and the twins, but when he checked to the rocks, he saw his friend take a step off her little oasis and plunge into the water directly in the middle of the grindylows. The surface boiled for a moment and then it was still.

"No!"

He choked on water as he swam in her direction for a few strokes, before realizing what she'd done. Remi had taken herself off the board so he had no choice but to go after the twins. He wanted to dive underwater and search for her but he was still so far away and he'd still have to deal with the grindylows.

With tears in his eyes, he stroked towards the island, fueled by his anger and rage. Damon stumbled onto the dirt, wiping the water from his face and hurrying to the twins. A sharp claw cut the ropes, releasing his sisters from their bonds.

Natalia, then Natasha, threw her arms around him. They were wearing their high school lacrosse jerseys and they had bruises on their arms and jaws from when Koschei had captured them.

Once they let go, he checked back to the water to see if he could see Remi, but the surface had turned back to glossy black. She was gone and he'd never be able to repay her.

"We have to get off the island before Koschei kills Connor and comes for us."

"Connor? As in our uncle?"

Damon nodded. "I'll explain if we survive."

He started to head back to where he'd swum across but Natalia grabbed his arm.

"That's not how he brought us over."

Damon didn't understand until Natasha climbed between the rocks to a metal box that he hadn't seen before. Inside was a series of buttons. She pressed a green one and the island shook. Water boiled on the opposite side and Damon watched with horror as a bridge rose from the surface, providing an exit off the island.

"Oh no."

"What's wrong?" asked Natasha.

He couldn't breathe as he looked back to where Remi had gone underwater.

Natalia shook his arm. "We have to go."

Using the back of his arm, he wiped his eyes. Nodded. But before they could step foot on the bridge, a dark shape landed on the opposite side with his sword extended.

"You got what you wanted," said Damon. "Leave us alone."

"He fled like the coward he is," said Koschei. "I can't let you interfere again."

As the deathless assassin stalked across the bridge, Damon crouched and grabbed two large rocks.

"When I attack, you flee across the bridge and go as far and as fast as you can," he whispered to his sisters.

"What about you?"

He growled. "Don't worry about me. Just run when you get the chance."

Frightened but not cowed, his sisters nodded. They hadn't yet changed, but he could see it lurking under the surface of their eyes.

Damon faced Koschei, raised the rocks in his fists, and bellowed like a Viking warrior.

"For Remi!"

He bounded across the island. Mid-leap, he launched the first head-sized rock at Koschei, who tried to bat it out of the air with his sword but it slipped past and slammed him in the shoulder. With the assassin off-kilter, Damon tackled Koschei onto the beach and used the second rock to bash his hand, trying to get him to release his weapon.

The assassin kneed him in the gut and threw him off. Damon felt like a child as he landed against the rocks, barely aware that his side was bleeding. He kicked sand at Koschei when he tried to approach, then leapt backwards, forcing him to follow.

As Koschei tried to reach him, it gave an opening to the twins, who hesitated until he sent them an angry glare and they sprinted across the bridge. The vise around his heart relaxed a turn knowing they would be safe.

But he hadn't been able to save Remi, and that lit his rage into a bonfire.

Damon grabbed another rock and threw himself at the assassin, using the makeshift weapon to deflect the blade. He battered Koschei, using his anger to fuel a relentless assault, until he knocked him down. Damon thought he had him, until Koschei rolled away and found his feet.

"You're stronger than I expected. Stronger than the others of your family I've killed. It's a good thing you're not the one with the sword."

"Fuck you," spat Damon.

Koschei backed across the bridge while Damon followed. The uneven terrain on the island had been in his favor, which was why the assassin was choosing to fight on solid ground. He wanted to check his phone, but he'd left it on the other side before he'd entered the water.

"Ready to die?" asked Koschei when they were on the pathways that led through the zoo.

"You first."

Damon thought he was going to have to fight him alone until Connor came limping up the path with blood dripping from his hairy arms. He looked like he'd been through a shredder. The Shining Sword seemed dull in comparison to earlier.

"Let's finish this," said Connor.

He attacked with the ferocity of a berserker, which gave Damon an opening. He slammed the rock in his fist against Koschei's arm, and to his surprise, he heard a snap. But the broken bone didn't slow the assassin. He hit Connor with the butt of his sword, stunning him and shoving the blade into his shoulder before kicking him into the bushes. Damon was so astonished by the events that he didn't move away as quickly as he'd planned. When Koschei spun around, the tip of the blade sliced across his chest as he threw himself onto the grass.

Damon touched the wound, finding it deep enough to leave him bloody, but no major arteries were damaged. He looked up to see Koschei grunt and bend his broken arm back into place. After a moan and a second snap, the arm looked normal again.

Both he and Connor were severely injured.

Except for dirt and cuts to his black clothes, Koschei looked untouched. The phylactery was protecting him. They could injure him a thousand times and it wouldn't matter.

He only had to kill them once.

Koschei stood over Damon with his sword raised high.

"I'm afraid this little farce is over."

FORTY-THREE

"We have to kill the snake," said Lily as she stared down onto the industrial floor.

The giant snake had brown and black scales that glistened in the darkness like oil on water.

The Clover sisters glanced at each other.

"We're not fighters," said Morwen, clasping her hands apologetically. "Getting you here is the best we can do."

Lily looked to the ashy Talwen. Her normally sandalwood-colored skin was gray and her eyes peered out of deep sockets. She looked ready to fall over.

"Come on, Neko," she said to her companion as she climbed down the ladder to reach the factory floor.

"I'm sorry, Lily," said Morwen, peering over the edge. "I don't know what I can do."

Lily didn't blame Morwen. The enormous snake was well beyond what the Clover sisters had signed up for, which was getting her to the phylactery. They'd never discussed putting their lives at risk.

As soon as her foot touched the floor, the creature lifted its scaly head with its tongue testing the air.

If Lily were still connected to Medb then the fight would be more even. There were a dozen spells she had access to that could injure the serpent from a distance. But those abilities had been cut off the moment she switched her patronage to the Hundred Halls.

"Keep it distracted once I engage," she told Neko.

Her companion stalked forward, shifting forms until it settled on a sleek black panther. Neko slipped away, disappearing into the heavy machinery like a shadow.

Lily summoned her faez, pulling it into her limbs in preparation for a spell. Golden light danced around her hands as she worked the raw magic, focusing it into an ethereal set of chains.

"Nathair a shealbhú!"

The ghostly bonds sped towards the giant snake, wrapping around its arched neck. The serpent writhed to break the chains, which gave her the room to close the distance until she was a dozen feet away.

Before she could cast a second spell, the creature turned its head and locked eyes with Lily. She met its gaze as an act of defiance, but regretted it instantly when she saw swirling stars within the glossy black eyes.

A supernatural calmness came over Lily. She knew she was being stilled by the snake's magic, but couldn't break it. The beast was holding her fast.

The snake rose above her, the ghostly chains slowing, but not halting its movement. It was much stronger than she gave it credit for.

The giant serpent leaned its head back in preparation to strike. She was trapped by its magic.

The moment she thought she was dead, the snake lurched upward, slamming its head against the steel girders, sending cascades of dust.

Neko had hold of the tail with his teeth. He'd ripped through the scales.

The action broke the hypnosis, letting Lily dive to the left as the snake finally struck at the same time it flicked its tail, sending Neko flying into the equipment.

Lily rolled onto her feet, blasting the snake with elemental magics. She twisted earth and water as her sisters had taught her. Green shoots shot up from the concrete, wrapping around the snake. It thrashed, breaking the vines as quickly as she created them, but it gave Neko a chance to return to the fight.

For the next thirty seconds, she kept the snake distracted while Neko struck its other end, ripping off glistening scales with his sharp teeth.

The enormous snake burst the vines and headed away from them. She couldn't let the phylactery escape, so she doubled her effort, focusing on keeping it from fleeing.

But the snake was too strong and the magics she had available when she was a member of the sisterhood weren't the same without Medb.

"No!"

Lily watched as the last vines snapped. Once the snake escaped, they'd never be able to kill it in the labyrinth of the old factories.

She hadn't heard Talwen come up from behind, but then she heard the Fae words and felt the younger Clover sister's touch on her neck.

The infusion of power startled Lily as much as Talwen's falling form. Her sister caught her as she fell to the concrete, but Lily was focused on the snake.

Powered by Talwen's pixie magic, the vines grew exponentially, wrapping around the snake until it was bound within a cocoon of greenery. The creature writhed, trying to break the vines, but there were too many and then it could no longer move.

"Neko. Throat."

Her changeling companion shifted forms again until he had the body of a hyena and the head of a saltwater crocodile. Lily parted the vines around the snake's underbelly and dragged it to the floor so Neko could reach. He climbed onto the plant-mass and snapped his powerful jaws onto the snake's belly.

A horrible hissing sound erupted from the snake as Neko bit through the flesh until he severed the spine and the entire thing went limp. She released the vines, which dissipated into golden fireflies and disappeared.

"It's dead. Is that it?"

Talwen was nearly unconscious in her sister's arms. She shook her head.

"It wasn't the snake," said Morwen, leaning close to her sister's mouth. "It's in the snake."

Lily reached into her carryall, producing a healthy sized knife.

"Where?"

Talwen's arm lifted, indicating the center.

Lily had skinned and prepared her fair share of kills, but never one so large. Blood gushed from the gut as she sliced through its belly, releasing the contents of its stomach. She expected small animals like rats to come pouring out, but the interior was empty except for a single hard-shelled egg the size of two fists. The shell was spotted green.

"A duck egg?"

Lily set it on the ground and used the hilt of her blade to smash the egg. It exploded into white and yellow goo. She thought she was finished until she spotted the needle sitting in the center of the mess.

She lifted it so she could see in the dim light. The needle vibrated with energy.

Lily had never destroyed a phylactery, but she understood the technique. She poured faez into the needle until it glowed with golden light and then she snapped it as if it were a brittle toothpick.

The result was instant.

Black smoke poured out of the needle until it created an enormous cloud in the ceiling of the factory. Lightning crackled amidst the seething mass.

Before Lily could wonder what to do, the black cloud shot out of the factory, leaving her kneeling in the center of a giant dead snake covered in guts and duck egg goo.

"I hope they're going to be okay."

FORTY-FOUR

The razor-sharp sword rose above Damon's head. There was no time to escape and Connor was pulling himself out of the bushes. Koschei's black eyes glistened with delight.

This was the end.

How could it have come to this?

Damon had set out to become a healer, not die in a battle at the zoo.

The sword caught a flash of light upon its descent. Something small, bright, and moving quickly.

Damon didn't understand until the disc slammed into Koschei's shoulder, throwing him off-balance and letting Damon roll to the right to avoid the arc of the blade.

The reason for his escape became clear when the twins ran up the pathway holding wooden rods that looked like makeshift lacrosse sticks ripped from the bottom of a sign.

The glowing disc that had hit Koschei spun away but came rushing back towards the twins. Natalia smacked it out of midair, sending it right back at the deathless assassin's head, forcing him to duck.

"I let you go," growled Koschei at the twins. "You're not going to escape me this time."

Natasha rolled her eyes and glanced to her sister. "We're not letting a gross ol' bag of bones hurt our brother."

"Look at that all black. He thinks he's an assassin but really he's a murdery hobo with bad fashion sense," said Natalia, pulling a second glowing disc from her back pocket.

Damon found his feet away from the pathway, grinning at his sisters' boldness despite the danger. The deathless assassin raised his weapon at the same time the twins lifted their lacrosse sticks.

"Give 'em the claws and teeth?" asked Natalia.

"Absolutely."

They batted their glowing discs at Koschei. He tried to knock them out of the air, but they moved fast and erratically, making him spin off-balance.

Then he marched after the twins.

But the discs slammed into his back, knocking him forward.

"You can't turn your back on them, Bag of Bones," said Natalia.

"That's not how the game works," said Natasha.

Koschei rage screamed and ran forward, but the twins split wide and used their makeshift sticks to take the legs out from under the assassin. He landed hard on the concrete.

Damon had seen his sisters in action on the lacrosse field, so it was no surprise that they were getting under his skin. Nothing was more cutting than the words of a teenage girl with a sharp tongue, so he couldn't help himself when he started laughing.

"Stop it," said Koschei, struggling to bat away the glowing discs that kept assaulting him from different directions. "I'll cut your limbs off one by one."

"Yeah, yeah, yeah, Bag of Bones," said Natalia as she deftly knocked the disc at Koschei's head.

Damon grabbed a decorative bedding brick and launched it at the assassin, hitting him in the thigh. The constant attacks left him spinning around impotently.

In a brief window of respite, Koschei reached into his inner pocket and produced three vials, which he downed quickly in succession. He went from a flailing amateur to a pillar of dangerous muscle. His eyes glowed with power and his jaw pulsed with anger.

"This ends now!"

Damon was about to tell the twins to make a run for it when a great cry escaped Koschei's lips.

His back arched and the sword clattered to the ground as if he were in great pain.

The twins looked to Damon but he could only shrug, not understanding until a black cloud zipped past them and hit the assassin in the chest, burrowing into his flesh. His skin aged rapidly in a few seconds, bunching and wrinkling like it was being put through an invisible taffy machine.

"I will—"

Then Connor Black appeared behind, shoving the blade into the assassin's chest.

"No," whispered Koschei.

Cracks of light climbed up his chest until his entire body glowed.

Then it exploded.

When Damon looked back, a cloud of black dust floated through the air. The ashes of the assassin riding the breeze.

"We won!" whooped the twins, holding their makeshift lacrosse sticks high as Connor fell to his knees cradling the sword, injured, but not downed.

Damon grinned at his sisters.

"I could kill you two for coming back." He shook his head. "But I could also hug you."

When he checked back to the dust that had once been the deathless assassin, he saw it drifting towards the grindylow pond.

The excitement of victory was swallowed by the memory of Remi's sacrifice.

"No."

He ran back to the pond, crossing the bridge in a single bound. On the other side of the island, he spotted her body floating face down. He waded in and dragged her back to the shore.

Damon fell onto the sands, cradling her to his chest as he rocked.

"Dammit, Remi. You weren't supposed to do that. If anyone was supposed to sacrifice themselves it was me."

He closed his eyes and pressed his forehead against her shoulder as he grieved.

The others stood behind him quietly. Damon knew he should be thrilled that only one of them had perished from the night's battle, but he couldn't believe that it was Remi. His heart felt like it was imploding in slow motion.

He held her at arm's length as her head bobbed on a loose neck.

"I can't believe you, of all of us, would have done this. I didn't think you had it in you," he said, laughing and crying at the same time.

From his first interaction when she'd stolen his papers to this. Damon wiped his face with the back of his hand and checked back to see his family watching, but he didn't care. He had something to say, which he couldn't hold back any longer.

"Remi. I'm sorry. But I also want you to know that I was falling for you. Fell for you. I know I shouldn't have. We work together and we're so different, but on the other hand, I've never met anyone from such a messed-up background who was still trying to make themselves better."

He kissed her forehead, finding it surprisingly warm despite the chilly waters. He pushed her head back gently, peering at her face for clues to the reason, when her eyes opened suddenly.

Damon nearly dropped her as he jumped.

Then she vomited pond water all over his lap.

He checked back to his family to make sure they were seeing the same thing—that Remi wasn't a ghost. They looked on with jaws hanging low.

Damon helped Remi cough out the water, patting her back and rocking her until she could finally speak.

"What happened? I thought you were dead."

"The NOCAT," she wheezed.

"The NOCAT?"

"Yeah," said Remi, rubbing her throat. She sounded like a three-pack-a-day smoker, which only made her more attractive. "I think the wandering NOCAT is actually in stasis. But it's breaking down. I've been researching spells in the library, so when I realized you were going to try and save me, I put myself in stasis so the grindylows would leave me alone and you could save your sisters."

"Merlin's tits, Remi. That's insane. You know there's a dozen ways that could have gone wrong."

She shrugged with a lazy-eyed apologetic stare.

"Also," he continued, "nice job with the research. It might not have saved the NOCAT's life, but it saved yours."

As they were sitting on the beach, shivering from the cold near the pond, the clouds parted and the slivery light of the full moon washed over them.

"Hey, Damon," said Remi with a half smile.

"What?"

"I don't think our dates can get any worse than this one."

Damon grinned despite himself. He looked over the pond where the dust from Koschei's body had spread out over the water.

"I don't know, Remi. This one seems pretty great."

FORTY-FIVE

The common area was covered in green and gold crepe paper. A decorative sheet cake with fanciful winged women holding wands was the centerpiece on the table. Lily sat on the love seat watching Morwen and her sister put the finishing touches on the party.

"You know it's customary for those going away to *not* be the ones setting up the party," said Lily.

The color was coming back in Talwen's face. Her lips squeezed into a pursed grin while her eyes sparkled with mirth.

"For everything you've done for us, I wouldn't have it any other way," said Morwen.

While the younger Clover sister wore her dark hair in a simple ponytail, Morwen had shaved her sides and decorated the arcing poof to match the festive colors from the crepe paper. They'd changed out of their orderly uniforms for street clothes, with the older sister looking like she was ready for a second ward rave in a baggy jean jacket covered in crimson sequins.

Remi knocked on the door frame with a single eyebrow arched. "Heard there was a party?"

Morwen skittered over to Remi, grabbing her hands and pulling her into the room.

"Yes! It's a thank you for all you've done for us before we move on."

Remi checked back to Lily, who offered a shrug. "You're leaving?"

"The city of sorcery poses too many dangers and temptations."

Remi gestured towards Morwen's clothes. "One more party before you leave."

Morwen winked. "You got it." She rolled her eyes. "Maybe two or three. We're not leaving until Tal is feeling better."

The younger Clover had taken position on the couch with her knees pulled up to her chest.

"I heard there was a party?" asked Damon, leaning into the door.

"There is!" said Morwen, clapping and running up to Damon to give him a hug. "I'm so glad you were able to kill Koschei."

"All thanks to you and your sister," said Damon, squeezing her to his chest. "There's no way we would have found the phylactery on our own."

"How is your dad?" asked Morwen.

Damon lifted a single shoulder. "Getting better every day. My mom will be here in a few days. I'm hoping he can get up and walk by the time she arrives."

"Are the twins coming?" asked Morwen, looking into the hallway.

"They rejoined their lacrosse team. Today was a tour of the Spire where the Trials of Magic occur, and then tonight they're going to see a play at the Orpheum Theatre."

"I'm glad they're okay."

"Me too," said Damon. "Otherwise my mom would have killed me."

"Have you told her?" asked Remi.

"I'll do that in person once she sees everyone is okay. Right now she's just happy that my dad is getting better, even if she doesn't understand why."

Morwen served everyone cake, including a tiny piece for rat-sized Neko, who was sitting on his own chair, whiskers twitching with delight at the sugary treat. The half-pixie gave extra attention to the rat, which suggested she knew exactly what Neko was but was kind enough not to mention it.

When Remi and Damon were engrossed in conversation with Talwen on the couch, Lily used the distraction to approach Morwen. She'd been wanting to say something since the full moon, but hadn't worked up the nerve, but she knew if she didn't say something now, she'd lose that chance.

"I'm sorry about how I treated you the first part of the year."

"As you should be," said Morwen with a cocked smile which eventually broke. "Sorry. Habit."

The half-pixie sighed and set the fork back on the plate.

"You weren't wrong. I *was* stealing from the hospital."

"Still didn't make it okay how I treated you," said Lily. "I was a right arse, ignoring the signs of what was going on because of my feelings against your kind. Especially since you've been driven from your home by corruption."

Morwen scooped up a hunk of icing with her fingernail and sucked it off with a faraway look.

"I miss my home. The waterfalls, the mountains." She jutted her eyebrows at the surroundings. "This is great and all, but it's not the same."

"Aye. I understand," said Lily, who was still trying to reckon with her past feelings. In her bones, she didn't trust the pixie, but she knew that was just her brain screwing with her.

"That you do," said Morwen, frowning. "Have you figured anything out yet?"

Lily checked back to make sure the others couldn't hear her. "I worry that I've made a mistake coming here. I thought the Halls would have answers for the corruption. Maybe not the big solution, but a way to protect my sisters, my patron from it. But Aura Healers was created to heal individual people, not entire realms."

"You're thinking of leaving," said Morwen flatly.

"It's crossed my mind," said Lily.

Morwen checked back to the others. "They need you. I don't have my sister's gift, but even I can see that. This place needs you too. If my time as an orderly has taught me anything it's that some of the doctors and all of the nurses think you're a shine on the antlers of the Oak Father."

"It's lovely of you to say that, even if it isn't true."

Morwen shook her head vehemently. "I wouldn't lie to you about that."

"But you'd lie to me about other things, pixie?"

Morwen grinned. "I might, witch. I might."

Neko squeaked and held out his little hands for more cake.

"Can I?"

Lily nodded. "He earned it."

"Someday I'd love to hear the story of how you bonded to a changeling from the Fae."

"It's a boring story," said Lily.

"I doubt that." Morwen sighed. "I can see my sister is getting tired. She should probably go rest, but before we go, I needed to tell you something."

"If it's that you've stolen even a single hair from my room, I'll hex you into next week."

Morwen faced her with the seriousness of a funeral. "You know my sister has the gift."

"Aye."

"She said something a few days ago in her sleep. I was just crawling into bed."

"A night in the city," said Lily.

"You know me well. Just like I know my sister. And I know when she's speaking truth."

"Prophecy ain't truth. It can be twisted and misunderstood."

Morwen reached out and grabbed Lily's hands. They were warm.

"I don't remember the exact words, given where I'd been and what I was on, but I heard the warning in her voice. Something or someone is coming for you, Lilith de Meath. I don't know when, or what, but I know my sister is right. Just be careful."

The urge to blow her off was strong, but the intensity in the half-pixie's gaze turned her denials into ash.

"I will, Morwen Clover."

The small party looked to be breaking up. Lily joined the others cleaning up the mess and the decorations. They left the cake out with a note for the rest of their class. Hugs were given all around, even though Lily didn't think it was the last time she'd see the Clover sisters.

FORTY-SIX

Damon was able to get away from rounds with Dr. Decker and make it back to his father's room. The whole family was there when he arrived, including his mother, who was holding tight to his father's hand, staring at him with glistening eyes. The twins were busy telling their parents about the tour of the Spire and how they thought the Trials of Magic would be easy to pass.

"Blood and bone, Damon, you look good in a doctor's scrubs," said his mother, coming up to him and fussing with the hem of his shirt.

"I'm a healer not a doctor," said Damon, leaning down and giving his mother a kiss on the forehead. He could smell the lingering fear on her scent, but it was fading.

"Did you tell them?" he asked the twins.

Flat-lipped, they shook their heads in unison. "No way, Jose."

"Tell me what?" asked his mother.

Damon scratched the back of his neck. "It's complicated and a long story."

Natalia crossed her arms. "It's not *that* complicated. We killed an immortal assassin and got revenge for our clan."

"What?" asked their parents in unison.

His mother checked back to him with a scrunched forehead. "Is this a joke?"

The way she looked at him with accusations in her gaze told him despite everyone's current health, she was going to be cross with him. She was a forgiving werewolf, but it would take time.

"It's not a joke," said a voice from the doorway.

Damon turned to see Connor Black limping into the room, eliciting gasps from his parents.

"Connor?"

His mother ran over and placed her hands around his face.

"Is this really him?"

"It is," said Damon, sharing a nod with his uncle.

There was something haggard and empty in Connor's expression despite the escape from Koschei. After hugging Emily Wolfhard, Connor approached the hospital bed and clasped hands with his half-brother.

"It's good to smell you again," said Arthur.

"You too, now that you're not dying."

Arthur checked between Connor and Damon. "I assume whatever happened had to do with my sudden recovery."

"Your son, the twins, and his friends saved me. Saved you too."

"The twins?" asked his mother.

The twins beamed. "We saved Damon."

Her jaw pulsed with resurgent anger. "Damon?"

Connor put his hand around her shoulders. "It's fine, Emily. They all made it out with barely a scratch. You should be proud."

"I need to know everything. Now."

Connor sighed and over the course of an hour explained everything that had happened since the clan was massacred up to Koschei's death at the zoo.

"It was a corrupted draemon making me sick," said Arthur with understanding.

"Don't worry, brother. It's destroyed now. I found it after the fight and smashed it," said Connor. "Everything's good as gold."

"The hell it is," said Damon's mother, crossing her arms. "Whoever sent this Koschei after you is still out there. Once they learn of the assassin's death, what's going to keep them from sending another? I nearly lost my entire family."

Damon had wondered this part as well, but he'd been too busy with the hospital to think about it.

"You're right, Emily," said Connor, nodding slowly as if he were in great pain. "Which is why I must give up being Keeper. Koschei and whoever sent him wanted the sword."

"Why?" asked his mother.

"I don't know, but it probably has to do with the corruption of the Fae."

Emily glanced back to her husband. "You'd better not be leaving this burden with Arthur. He's barely recovered from his sickness."

"No. I'm not leaving the sword to Arthur even though it probably should have gone to him in the first place."

"I never wanted it, Connor," said Arthur, reaching out.

Connor accepted his hand. "I know, brother. I know. But I was too stubborn at the time. I should have come to Kansas City and visited you."

"Then who gets the sword?" asked Natasha.

Connor turned slowly with mincing steps until he was facing Damon.

"Me?" asked Damon

"Are you mad, Connor? You're putting him in danger again," said his mother.

"I'm not formally handing over the sword. Not as Keeper. Not yet anyway. Not until it's safe to bond with it again."

"I don't understand," said Damon, reeling from the news. Nothing made sense.

"I talked with your friend Lily. She helped me put a warding on the blade. We hid it in the hospital for now, but you can choose another place if you want. That should keep it away from prying eyes, even magical ones."

"What am I supposed to do?" asked Damon.

"Nothing really. But maybe one day it'll be safe to bring out again. Or if things get desperate, you can retrieve it. Bond with it. But once you do, you'll have all the responsibilities that come with it."

Being Keeper of the Sword had never been on his radar. He didn't even know what to say.

"Connor, are you sure? Will he be safe?" asked his mother.

"Positive. His friend is quite the powerful witch. Nothing should penetrate her wards as long as you don't bond with it. Whoever is seeking it will still think I have it."

Damon hadn't seen it at first, but he couldn't help it after two years in the hospital. There was something missing in Connor's vitality, a spark extinguished by the loss of the sword's bond. Damon knew all too well what a dying man looked like.

"You're dying."

Connor's eyes creased. He glanced to the twins.

"I didn't want to say anything."

His mother grabbed Connor's hands. "You can't be serious? There aren't enough of us left. I get to learn you're alive, but you'll die in the same day?"

Damon thought back to everything he'd learned about Koschei and the connection to the Fae King.

"He wants to keep us safe," said Damon.

Connor nodded. "Being Keeper of the Sword matters little if the clan is extinguished. If I try to hide, they'll find you first and use you to get to the sword. I had to give up the bond."

"But it's killing you," said Emily Wolfhard. "That's what's happening, right?"

Damon gave his mother the apologetic nod he'd learned to give when offering bad news.

"Don't grieve for me," said Connor. "Had I let Arthur become Keeper as the oracle said, the clan might be alive."

"You don't know that, Connor," said Arthur. "Prophecies are not truth."

"It's hard to deny it now," said Connor as his shoulders slumped. "Besides, the things I've done in the city should eliminate me as Keeper."

"You weren't yourself," said Damon. "It was Koschei using the draemon."

"It's no excuse. I killed far too many to hold this honored title."

"What will you do now?" asked his mother, dabbing the corner of her eye.

Connor hung his head. "Find a nice place to die out in the wild."

"You can't," said his mother, grabbing his hands.

"It's my right."

He checked out the window.

"I should go before someone recognizes me and sends the cops. I don't want to get you all in trouble."

Connor spent the next ten minutes giving hugs and speaking quietly to each in turn. He came to Damon last, pulling him aside.

"Thank you for finding me and saving me from myself. At least I'll get to die knowing that you're all safe," said Connor.

"I didn't want to be the Keeper."

Connor nodded with his eyes closed. "I know. I know. But there's no one else to take it. For now. Maybe when the twins are older, and things are safe, one of them can be Keeper."

Damon smirked. "I don't think the world's ready for that."

Connor matched his grin. "You might be right."

Damon threw his arms around his uncle and held him tight. After a time, they parted.

"Tell your friends thank you."

Connor slipped out of the room and disappeared down the hallway while Damon felt both empty and relieved. It was all too much. He returned to his family, putting his arms around the twins and relishing the closeness to his family, knowing that nothing was guaranteed.

FORTY-SEVEN

The cafeteria was bustling with visiting families. Remi sat in the corner to get away. The events of the last few weeks had been exhausting and she just wanted to stay in her room and binge *The Magelings*, but the hospital never rested.

Remi pushed the steaming eggs around her plate in absent thought. After weeks of research on the NOCAT, she'd come to a dead end. She was certain that there was something supernatural about her condition, but nothing in her reading had revealed an answer. The only thing good that had come of her time had been learning the stasis spell that had saved her from the grindylows.

A scoop of yellowish eggs on her fork had her staring into the lumps as if they might portend the future. She smirked and let a chuckle out as she thought about Lily telling them how Koschei's soul had been hidden inside a needle that had been placed in a duck egg.

How such a thing was possible was a mystery, but the ancients knew magical tricks that were lost today. The only clues that they existed were myths and legends that hid the truth behind fanciful stories.

She heard excited cooing and looked up to find Dr. Hunker surrounded by a group of middle-aged women. The doctor's shoulder-length black hair glistened in the cafeteria lights. He looked like he was the lead in a television show, not a real doctor, but she'd worked at his side long enough to know he was as talented as he was attractive.

"Are you an efretti?"

Remi chuckled and pushed the eggs away. She wasn't hungry for food, but answers.

No one had figured out the truth about Dr. Hunker and he wasn't being forthcoming. With thirteen free shifts on the line, Remi wanted to win. She could finally get some sleep and catch up on her Aura Healer's readings.

She couldn't decide if he were really an efreeti or not. But she could understand why he wouldn't want anyone to know if he was.

"I should study," she told herself, standing up with the tray, even as she really wanted to return to the library for more research on the NOCAT.

She was halfway back to her room when she had an idea. Remi raced to Dr. Decker's office. He was leaning back in his chair, balancing a coffee cup on his forehead when she rushed in.

The cup toppled off his head, shattering on the floor as he sat up.

"Merlin's tits, Remi. I thought something was wrong," said Dr. Decker, sighing at the shards of pottery.

"I have an idea on how to fix the NOCAT."

He paused halfway after picking up the broken handle and arched an eyebrow in her direction.

"And?"

Remi bit her lower lip. "Can we head to her room and I'll explain?"

Dr. Decker tossed the broken handle into the bin. "Better than cleaning that up."

"I saw Dr. Hunker in the cafeteria a little bit ago."

"Still trying to win the bet?"

"Yes. But he made me think about how in the old days, supernaturals, mages, anyone with magic really, hid their magic because it wasn't safe."

"So you think he's an efretti?"

"I don't know either way, but if he *was*, then he wouldn't want anyone to know. Look at all the mistrust of werewolves in the city right now from the Full Moon Killer."

"Who seems to have moved on, if the papers can be believed," said Dr. Decker.

They reached the NOCAT's room. The old woman was lying in bed, staring at the ceiling. Her dead eyes made no indication that she knew anyone else was nearby.

"You think she's a hidden supernatural?" asked Dr. Decker skeptically. "Why hide yourself in a hospital for a decade or more?"

"I think it's been longer than a decade. As you said, she's been traveling around the hospital system for a long time and no one has any records of her."

Remi captured the old woman's hand and held it up.

"Look any different?"

Dr. Decker shrugged. "Could be the same as it was when I first saw her in Memphis."

"Right," said Remi. "I found records of a woman with a similar condition two decades before and another from the middle of the last century."

Dr. Decker stiffened. "Are you saying she's been in the hospital system for seventy years?"

"Or longer, which means either she tangled with an old supernatural, or..."

"Or?"

Remi almost didn't want to say, because it seemed crazy. "Or she's one herself. Like Dr. Hunker."

"You think she wants to be like this?"

Remi shook her head. "No. But I don't think she wants to commit suicide either."

"The belladonna."

"Right. But who uses plants like belladonna, or speaks in prophecy?"

Dr. Decker checked towards the door. "Witches, hags, and other crones."

"Exactly," said Remi, feeling her chest uncoil. The ideas had been swirling around in her head for weeks, but only now was she allowing herself to completely understand them.

"You think she's a witch?"

"I do. I think either a rival got to her, or she flubbed a spell, or a hex rebounded on her."

"And what's your solution?"

Remi screwed up her face. "There's a hint of truth in myths and legends, right?"

"There can be," said Dr. Decker, screwing up his mouth.

"Would you humor me and give her a kiss?"

A short laugh slipped out his mouth. He looked to the old woman then back to Remi.

"You're serious, aren't you?"

"I'm afraid so." She lifted a single shoulder. "Maybe there were spells that witches used back then that put people asleep until someone kissed them."

Dr. Decker arched both eyebrows. "You really want me to kiss her?"

"Please."

He shook his head. "This feels like one of your cons. I swear if the rest of your class jumps out, or you're taking a hidden picture of me, you'll be doing rectal exams hourly for the remainder of your time in Aura Healers."

Remi said nothing, which eventually brought a sigh from Dr. Decker.

"Only because you've spent a considerable amount of time researching and trying to fix this NOCAT, which, I might add, I explained at the beginning of the year was a waste of effort, but I feel I must reward the effort, however misguided it might be."

Dr. Decker leaned over the old woman's wrinkly face. He pursed his lips and with eyes closed, pressed them against her partially open mouth. When he pulled back, he quickly wiped his lips with the back of his hand.

"I'm going to get fired for that."

Remi stared at the NOCAT, willing her to move or show signs of life. The old woman lay motionless, staring at the ceiling as if it were a parade.

Dr. Decker scratched the back of his neck. "I'm sorry, Remi. I don't think that was the answer."

Remi shook her head. She was certain that it was. There had to be powerful magics at work keeping her both alive and in stasis.

"I thought it—"

The words were halfway out of her lips when the old woman gasped, her back arching as if she'd been hit with a defibrillator.

Dr. Decker spun around and stood by Remi's side as they watched the old woman transform before their eyes. Wrinkles and decrepit skin smoothed away as she grew more youthful by the second. Her hair thickened, turning from a hazy gray to thick, black hair with a fanciful white streak that framed her smooth jaw.

When it was finished, a woman in her mid-thirties was sitting up in bed. She put her hands to her face, feeling around as if she didn't believe them. She was beautiful, but in the way that suggested she knew how to stomp on a heart and ground it into the dirt with her high heels.

Remi backed up when she noted the long fingernails that had grown in that short time. Each one came to a sharp end.

Dr. Decker grabbed Remi's forearm, looking like he wanted to sprint from the room, especially when the woman in the bed smiled, revealing long canines.

"Oh, don't worry dearies," said the woman in the bed in a voice that sounded out of the past. "I would hardly hurt you after you saved me from that waking nightmare."

She sat up and slid her long legs off the bed. Remi heard Dr. Decker's gulp as he was transfixed by her shapely appearance. She could have been a pin-up model in the previous century.

"Who are you?" asked Remi.

The woman checked down the front of her hospital gown. "Blight and bone, I'm happy to see all is back to normal."

She narrowed her gaze.

"I suppose you deserve an explanation for saving me. You were right about your theory."

"You could hear us?" asked Remi.

"I could, which is why I won't pull your heart out and eat it right now despite how hungry I am," said the dark-haired woman, laughing.

She pulled the thick strand of white hair around by her mouth, kissing it before releasing it back.

"I had a rival in my little village. She was someone like me, which was rare for those times, since magic tended to hide itself. I tried to fell her with a hex but it rebounded on me, putting me into a long slumber from which I could not wake."

"How long have you been like that?"

The hag stood up and cracked her neck.

"Longer than I care to think about."

Remi was aware that Dr. Decker was staring with his jaw hanging low. The hag was a frighteningly beautiful woman. She approached him and cupped his jaw with her long fingernails, letting them scrape against his cheek as she drew them away.

"Thank you for the kiss."

She winked at Remi.

"You too."

"What are you going to do now?" asked Remi with a stone in her gut.

The hag smirked. "You're afraid you've released a horror on the world? Don't worry. During my decades in bed, I was listening and paying attention to the changes in this world. It's not the same place I inhabited so long ago. Besides, that backfired curse really put a dent in my hubris."

She stretched her arms.

"Oh, I cannot wait to see this so-called city of sorcery that I've been hearing so much about."

"Do you need any clothes? We have a lost and found where you might find something that fits you," said Remi.

The hag snapped her fingers and in an instant she was wearing jeans and a sequined top, with a heavy purse over her shoulder. She looked like any other wealthy woman on her way to lunch with the girls, except for the glimmer of danger in her brown eyes.

"I'll pick some up later, but this glamour will do for now."

She looked like she was about to leave, but then she grinned.

"I should reward you, Remington Wilde, for what you did. I could tell you some secrets about your future, which is going to be quite interesting, and deadly for sure, but what's the fun in that? Instead, I'll give you something more tangible for the here and now."

Dr. Decker still looked stunned by her appearance and barely stepped out of the way when the woman moved forward. She leaned into Remi's ear and whispered a brief phrase that made her eyebrows wag upward.

"Oh!"

FORTY-EIGHT

The music was too loud, and the beer was flat and tasteless, but Lily was having the time of her life as she watched her friends and instructors gyrating on the dance floor. The space had been created by pushing a few tables out of the way, but the bartender didn't seem to mind since Talwen had whispered in his ear at the beginning of the party.

Morwen returned from the dance floor having slow grinded with Boon despite the fast-paced music. He looked bewildered and sweaty as he leaned against the bar trying to figure out what had happened.

"Up to your old ways, Pixie?"

Morwen threw back a shot and knocked the bright green swoop of hair out of her face, revealing a lopsided grin.

"I wanted to give him a little fodder for his dreams."

Lily frowned over her beer, which brought a sharp spike of laughter.

"Don't worry, I didn't enchant or beguile him. That was straight up womanly work. He'd been hitting on me relentlessly while I was an orderly, and if I was staying a bit longer, I might have taken him up on it. From what I hear, he's talented in all the best ways."

"You stayed longer in the city than expected," said Lily.

Morwen leaned against the bar and fanned her flush chest. "It took Tal longer than expected to recover."

The worry in the half-pixie's eyes flashed back to mirth when Lily checked back with her.

"I'm sure the rave scene had nothing to do with it."

"I will confess that it has made it hard to leave, but my sister is doing better now."

Lily checked back to the other half-pixie, who was dancing the jitterbug with Dr. Hunker and laughing hysterically.

"She looks as fresh as a summer song."

An awkward pause intruded until Morwen gestured towards Remi and Damon. The pair were hooking their arms and spinning around chaotically, bumping into chairs and tables.

"They look unusually drunk," said Morwen.

"It's easy to let go when your shift is being covered tomorrow."

Morwen raised an eyebrow. "She won the bet?"

"Aye."

"And?"

Lily shook her head. "No idea. Neither Remi nor Dr. Hunker would say, except that she figured out the truth."

"You should be careful being friends with her," said Morwen. "She has trickster blood."

"So I've been told." Lily smiled at the half-pixie. "But blood doesn't mean everything."

"Thank you for your help with Felix."

"Twas my pleasure. He had it comin' to him," said Lily.

"It's a shame the world is filled with assholes like him."

Lily clucked her tongue.

"They always lose in the end."

Morwen turned suddenly, wearing a serious expression. "My sister had a vision about you."

"Prophecies are meaningless. I already told you."

Morwen nodded sharply. "I know. But Talwen said she's never had one this strong."

"It doesn't matter—"

"Lilith de Meath. Please. She said what's going to happen in the next few years is going to have grave repercussions for both the Fae and this realm. It's best you know, so you can be prepared."

Lily turned and took Morwen's hands, which were trembling slightly. The half-pixie looked fraught.

"Prophecy is like a dull knife. It'll be more likely to twist out of your hand and land in your foot."

"Are you sure?"

"As rain."

Morwen checked back to the bar. Boon had finished his beer and was staring back at the half-pixie.

"I think I'd better put him out of his misery."

"A last night of debauchery in the city of sorcery."

Morwen leaned over, placing her forehead against Lily's. She looked like she wanted to spill Talwen's prophecy, but eventually smiled wistfully and turned away. Lily watched as she hooked Boon's arm and led him out of the bar, never once looking back.

Lily watched the party from her table, sipping a seltzer water and enjoying the music. A soft squeak emanated from her unruly mess of rainbow hair. Lily turned her head slightly in thought before nodding.

"The longest road out is the shortest one home, Little One."

§ § §

This ends the second book of the Aura Healers Hall series. Stayed tuned for the third book:

BLOOD WITCH CURSE

Special Thanks

From the ashes of failure, new growth can form.

As my newsletter readers know, this series started off as something entirely different. I wrote a book that once I got to the end I realized was neither a Hundred Halls story, nor was good enough to publish. Yet, without it, this series wouldn't exist in the wonderful form that it does. For that I have to thank my best friend and wife of twenty-seven years, Rachel, for her excellent advice as we discusssed what I should do with that failed book on the way to see Phish in Denver for four days. That conversation helped me find clarity of where I'd gone wrong as well as how to start over with fresh eyes.

I must also thank my team who help make each novel as best as it can be: Sasha Almazan & Gene Mollica from GS Covers, Tamara Blain from A Closer Look Editing, the beta reader team (Tina Rak, Andie Alessandra Cáomhanach, Lana Turner, Phyllis Simpson, and Melanie Coupland), as well as my writing group that we affectionately call the Murder Cabin (Andrea Stewart, Anthea Lawson/Sharp, Annie Bellet, Megan O'Keefe, Marina J. Lostetter, Jamie Thornton, and Tina Gower). Additionally, the Vanguard plays defense for little errors that sneak through the cracks, and for this book, I have Leslie King, Debbie Davis, Phyllis Simpson, and Brian Busby to thank!

ABOUT THE AUTHOR

Thomas K. Carpenter resides in Colorado with his wife Rachel. When he's not busy writing his next book, he's hiking, skiing, and getting beat by his wife at cards. He keeps a regular blog at www.thomaskcarpenter.com and you can follow him on twitter @thomaskcarpente. If you want to learn when his next novel will be hitting the shelves and get free stories and occasional other goodies, please sign up for his mailing list by going to: http://tinyurl.com/thomaskcarpenter. Your email address will never be shared and you can unsubscribe at any time.

www.ingramcontent.com/pod-product-compliance
Lightning Source LLC
Chambersburg PA
CBHW030423310726
48979CB00009B/1589/J